P9-DEY-464

# Simple Prayers
## a novel

# Michael Golding

**WARNER BOOKS**

A Time Warner Company

Warner Books, Inc., 1271 Avenue of the Americas, New York, NY 10020

**w** A Time Warner Company

Printed in the United States of America
First Printing: April 1994
10  9  8  7  6  5  4  3  2  1

**Library of Congress Cataloging-in-Publication Data**

Golding, Michael.
    Simple prayers / Michael Golding.
        p.   cm.
    ISBN 0-446-51790-9
    1. Italy — History — 1268–1492 — Fiction.   2. Country life — Italy —
Fiction.   I. Title.
PS3557.03644S56    1994
813'.54 — dc20                                                      93-8876
                                                                              CIP

*Book design by Giorgetta Bell McRee*

*for those who have taught, encouraged, and inspired me —
with gratitude*

Where is the end of them, the fishermen sailing
Into the wind's tail, where the fog cowers?
We cannot think of a time that is oceanless
Or of an ocean not littered with wastage
Or of a future that is not liable
Like the past, to have no destination.

> — T. S. ELIOT
> "The Dry Salvages,"
> *The Four Quartets*

"I have a hundred sheep to go to maket," replied the archpriest, "but I wouldn't want the same thing to happen that occurred today."

"Goodness, no!" said Pirolo. "We won't ever be that unlucky again!"

> — ITALO CALVINO
> "Lose Your Temper, and You Lose Your Bet,"
> *Italian Folktales*

*Note to the Reader*

The Italian words used in this novel are a mixture of standard Italian and Venetian dialect. It is the author's hope that this *misto* works in the novel as it works in life.

# Simple Prayers

# Prologue

*P*iero had barely traveled past the first clutch of pine trees when he came upon the body. The fog was still in and he couldn't see where the island met the water or the water met the sky, but he could see the body. It was lying, facedown, in the inlet that sloped to the water between Siora Bertinelli's hovel and the Rizzardellos' salt shed. It had obviously washed in with the tide, and he knew without even approaching it that it was not the body of anyone from Riva di Pignoli.

He did approach it, however. He stepped off the Calle Alberi Grandi, down into the wet soil, and walked to where it lay like the washed and withered stump of an old tree. Crouching down beside it, he said a brief prayer; then he drew back the arm that covered its face and gave a slight push to the torso so that it rolled back onto its side.

It appeared to have been dead for quite a while. Great knots of seaweed were tangled in its hair, its limbs were swollen heavy with water, and it gave off an odor of urine and dead violets. But what disturbed him most were the strange swellings in its throat and side: purplish black on the outside, pure pitch at the center, they had a hard vitality that sent a chill down Piero's spine.

He didn't know who the body had belonged to. He didn't know where it had come from. He only knew that he had to get rid of it before the rest of the village found out.

# *Chapter* 1

THE ROOM WHERE Albertino sat was not really a room — that is, it had no roof, no door, no *vasi di fiori* hanging from the windows. There was no table, no chair, no desk, no bed — no piece of hand-worked cloth, no favorite churning stool — still, to Albertino it was a room. Set out near the old cemetery, on the tiny island just north of the island where Albertino had been born, its sunken walls rose like a fortress against the waters of the lagoon. There was a north wall and a south wall, an east wall and a west; like everything else in the lagoon, they echoed the points of the fisherman's compass and smelled of the dark, bitter algae that washed in from the sea.

The west wall was largest. Albertino slept with his head

at its foot on a stack of old blankets the Vedova Stampanini had given him: first the chestnut, then the azure, then the crimson; next the emerald, the ocher, the violet, the rust, the gold. The Vedova Stampanini had been careful to instruct him on the names of the colors and to show him the exact order in which they were to be placed, and though he could never remember any of the names, once a month Albertino would shake them out and lay them back precisely as she had indicated. They were worn, and filthy, and in various seasons hosted various pests, but they were Albertino's bed and he was happy with them.

After the west wall came the north wall. Albertino lit his fire there, and hung his boots out, and cooked his meals. The east wall was hardly there at all: at its highest point it came up to about waist level and at its lowest point stood right above Albertino's knees (Albertino considered this part the door). But it was at the south wall, in the protected hollow of what once must have been the hearth, that Albertino kept his boxes. Great somber caskets with intricate clasps, delicate coffers of frosted ivory, wood chests carved over with fabulous three-masted ships. Albertino's boxes were his only vanity; he saved most of the money he made selling fruit and vegetables to go once a year into Venezia to buy a new one. When he left the island, even just to row across the water to fetch fresh dung for the radicchio patch, he carried them to the cemetery and hid them in the bottom of an empty vault he'd discovered behind a shock of cypresses. He kept them oiled and waxed and brushed and varnished, but most of all he kept them empty.

"I don't own anything nice enough to put in them," he explained to his brother, Gianluca, who thought he was *pazzuccio* to spend his money on such extravagant affectations and not even use them. But the truth was Albertino liked his boxes empty. They seemed more honest to him that way.

Spring hadn't come to Riva di Pignoli that year. Rosebuds opened hollow with a sudden crack and a trail of dry smoke. Turnips and cabbages were yanked from the earth like snapped fingers and shrunken heads. The trees stayed bare; the strawberry patch stood firm with tiny pellets of hard, unborn fruit. The weather grew warmer — sultry, in fact — but in the small fields along the island's southern shore, and the gardens that bordered the docks, nothing happened. Nature just didn't respond.

The people tried everything. Midnight incantations and morning prayers. Peppering the land with bits of *bazzatello* and *salsiccia*, hunks of old bread — hoping the soil might recognize, and remember, and thrust up something into life. The other islands were fine: Torcello and Burano to the north, Chioggia to the south, and the great Venezia, which prospered no matter the season or the circumstance. All across the lagoon it was a spring like any other spring, with bright patches of green appearing to balance the surrounding blue. But on Riva di Pignoli the palette never quickened. Brown stayed brown and gray stayed gray, and it might just as well have been midwinter.

Ugolino Ramponi said that it was because Saturn and Jupiter had aligned themselves in a cross-conjunction with Mars. Giuseppe Navo said that it was because he had pulled too many fishes from the sea. But Albertino wasn't fooled. Albertino knew exactly what had caused the troubled earth to hold back its offspring.

"It's that damned Ermenegilda," he said to himself as he lay on his back on his stack of tattered blankets. "She smears herself with so much lilac water and jasmine, and stuffs herself with so many eggplants and artichokes and onions, the damned things just don't want to come up this year."

Ermenegilda was in love with Albertino. The youngest daughter of the only wealthy family on Riva di Pignoli — the only family to have a stone house, the only family to have chickens *and* pigs *and* cows — Ermenegilda would have given her life for Albertino. That her father, Enrico Torta, had chosen to live on Riva di Pignoli in the first place seemed a somewhat perverse joke: Enrico Torta was rich enough to live wherever he liked, and Riva di Pignoli was hardly the sort of place one "chose" to settle in. Besides that, Enrico Torta did his business in Verona and had to travel an absurd distance — a journey of several days — to reach his isolated island home. But most everyone on Riva di Pignoli knew that Enrico Torta would have done his business in Africa if he could have been certain of a good rate of exchange. The farther away he could get from his family, the happier he seemed to be. His wife, Orsina, was a great explosion of a woman, with red-hot eyes and a mouth that poured smoldering lava. Together they had four daughters: Maria Prima, Maria Seconda, Maria Terza, and Ermenegilda (Orsina had wanted to name Ermenegilda "Maria Basta," but Enrico pitied the child and chose "Ermenegilda"; it was only then that the first three girls considered themselves to have been fortunate in their naming). Each daughter was fatter than the former, each uglier, each angrier. Whether their anger came from Orsina's blood, from Enrico's absence, or from the frustration of being wealthy on an island where there was nothing to buy, it was potent enough to make the Ca' Torta a place where even the most courageous Riva di Pignolian was loath to go. Maids and cooks came and went weekly; they could often be seen waving to one another as their boats passed in the lagoon. Women were sent from Padova, Mantova, and Milano to instruct the Torta girls in sewing and weaving; they generally ended up racing from the lavish home with spindles of brightly colored thread ricocheting from their heels. Invitations to dine at the Ca' Torta — which Orsina insisted on sending out, despite her hatred of the villagers — were tossed into the canal, or burned in the hearth, or buried beneath the roses (Siora Scabbri suggested that this was why the spring hadn't come). Only a handful of the people of Riva di Pignoli could read, but everyone knew the kind of hell that was implicit in those carefully calligraphed lines. Orsina made a weekly venture of going about town to draw the latest invitation out of the drinking fountain or the pig shit, and then taking it home to pin to the kitchen wall; it was one of her favorite ways of keeping her anger freshly fueled.

Ermenegilda, infant of the household, was especially malevolent. As a child she liked to go from field to field tying the animals' legs together, until the island was reduced to a bestial symphony of grunts, bleats, and squawks. Later she delighted in pouring rubbish into people's wells and unmooring the boats from the docks so they drifted out to sea. When people saw Ermenegilda coming they shut their shutters. Even the fishermen were afraid of her; they felt she set up a vibration that sent the *salmone* swimming back downstream. But though Ermenegilda was easily the most insufferable of the family, she was also the one for whom there was the greatest hope: Ermenegilda knew how to love — deeply, passionately, without caution or reserve — and in that capacity lay the possibility of her redemption. In Albertino's presence her anger cooled into a kind of glassy-eyed splendor. For a moment of his attention she would sacrifice the most deliciously malicious scheme that boiled in her eighteen-year-old brain and become a great, silent mass of perfumed flesh.

Albertino, on the other hand, couldn't stand the sight of Ermenegilda. Though somewhat odd-looking himself — he had a sort of pasty-nothing face that exhibited the same neutral expression no matter what he was feeling — Albertino was exceedingly sweet of nature. That he chose to spend one afternoon a month with her, however, baffled everyone but Gianluca. Gianluca knew that Ermenegilda gave Albertino boxes. The dazzling silver box with the smooth disks of jade along the rim. The heart-shaped box of red Murano glass with the dancing *pesci gatto* for handles. Albertino could not resist them. So once a month he would walk down the Calle Alberi Grandi with her, and hold her sweaty hand which felt like burst sausage, and sit on the dock at the east of the island while she talked. Ermenegilda spoke sweetly when she was with Albertino. She imagined that she was sylphlike and beautiful, and her wrath dissolved around her like smoke into the damp sea air. If he closed his eyes, Albertino could even bear her stories of crusading knights and their faint, fair maidens. But when the stories ended, and he turned to look at her, he could only wonder himself that a new box could mean so much.

It has to be her, he thought to himself. Who else could scare the blood out of the soil like this?

Albertino rose from his blankets and went to the east wall. He'd lived in his room that wasn't a room for eight years, ever since the great storm that destroyed the hovel that had been left to him and Gianluca when their mother had died. He'd planted the radicchio patch that first year he'd moved in; each spring the purple-and-white heads made him feel hopeful and invigorated. Now, as he looked out over the garden through the morning fog, he saw nothing but an empty expanse of dry, clotted earth.

He climbed over the wall. He walked toward the cemetery. But though it was silent as always, it now seemed to have extended its quiet out to the meadow and across the water and over all of Riva di Pignoli. He walked until he reached the small juniper tree that stood halfway between his room and the cemetery gate. Every year he'd watched it shoot up a little taller, and spread its spiny needles, and drop its tender cones upon the grass. Now there was no grass — and the juniper tree stood naked as December.

"I'd better go talk to Gianluca," said Albertino. "If this goes on much longer, the fruit and vegetable stand won't be a fruit and vegetable stand anymore."

He bent down and picked up a tiny pellet that lay in the cracked soil at his feet.

"On the other hand," he said, crushing the pellet into powder between his thumb and forefinger, "what can Gianluca do that God hasn't already thought of?"

He watched for a moment as the dry breeze blew the crumbled dust toward the gates of the cemetery. Then he walked to his room, climbed over the east wall, and crept back in between the emerald and the ocher to sleep.

❦

PIERO COULD NOT decide what to do about the blackened body. He considered throwing it back into the water, but he was afraid that it would only wash up on some other part of the island — and Piero was convinced that the people of Riva di Pignoli could not handle any more bad omens. An odd wind and the hope of a good catch had blown their fathers' fathers' fathers to this small swelling in the lagoon. And though the fishing had stayed good, and the families had merged into a community, they all knew another good blast up the Adriatic might whisk them right away again. Three generations after the first of their fathers had snared and salted a cod, there was still an air of impermanence to the village and a casual lack of order. Houses made right turns when they hit a canal. Gardens fanned wide at the middle or narrowed down to a point. Roosters and pigs and ducks roamed the island freely, entering and exiting the hovels as they liked; floors and streets were therefore covered with rooster shit, pig shit, and duck shit, which was either washed away with water on the first of each month or covered over with a fine layer of straw and flowers (another reason the villagers missed their spring). Bread not eaten on Monday was saved for Tuesday or Wednesday; bread not eaten on Tuesday or Wednesday was used to serve food on on Thursday or Friday; bread not eaten on Monday, Tuesday, or Wednesday, after having been used to serve food on on Thursday or Friday, was thrown on the floor to feed the roosters, pigs, and ducks on Saturday and Sunday. Baths were taken on Midsummer's Eve and the Nativity of the Virgin. Clothes were changed when they caught fire.

To Piero such things were normal, even though he had been raised in a monastery away on another island. What disturbed him was that things were getting worse. The winters were growing colder and wetter. The livestock was dying because the villagers could no longer afford to spare their grain for feed. Fierce storms were racking the island's shores with greater and greater frequency. And now, in addition to the charred roots and the somber fruit the earth was flinging from its belly, the sea was heaving up dead bodies with horrible midnight swellings in their sides.

Piero heard a rustling behind him and turned with a start, but all he saw was the Guarnieris' sow trotting casually up the Calle Alberi Grandi. When he was certain that it had neither seen nor smelled what he had discovered, he covered the body with twigs and rushes and went to fetch a wheelbarrow; when he returned, however, he found that it was easier simply to drag it. So he pulled it to the edge of the lagoon, hid it beneath the splintered remains of a storm-damaged dock, and then waited until sundown — when he would take it to the field of wild thyme that grew along the north rim of the island, bury it, and then try to find a way to bring the spring.

❦

"MAYBE YOU SHOULD try singing," suggested the Vedova Stampanini.

"Singing?" said Gianluca.

"To the soil. To make things grow. You have an unusual voice, Gianluca."

Gianluca lowered the last of his bread into his *brodetto di pesce* and watched as it absorbed the pale, greasy liquid.

"Albertino wouldn't like it. He hates when I sing. He says it reminds him of when we were little and I used to finish eating before him and I would sing and it would make him feel he had to hurry."

The Vedova removed Gianluca's bowl and took it, along

with her own, to the wooden wash bucket that sat beside the cutting table.

"A little singing would be good for Albertino. The next time he spends the night I'm going to insist on it."

Since Albertino's room had no roof, he spent the cold and the rainy nights with Gianluca in the dark room he rented from the Vedova Stampanini. Gianluca wasn't exactly delighted with this arrangement, as there was hardly a night in the week he didn't bring someone home to share his bed. But Albertino was his brother, and Gianluca had given their mother his sworn promise, when she lay on her deathbed some ten years before, to "take care of Tintino with his heart, his knees, his tongue, his toes, and his liver." Gianluca had no intention of either calling his brother "Tintino" or of honoring his deathbed promise, but when the rains came down in Riva di Pignoli, he allowed him to burrow into a ball on the floor beside his bed on another pile of the Vedova Stampanini's blankets and considered himself generous for the gesture.

"Maybe you could try flirting."

"Flirting?"

"You know — the way you do. Women can't resist it, Gianluca. And don't forget that Nature is a woman."

Gianluca, as the Vedova well knew, was a lover. Tall and handsome, with thick black hair and dark, glistening eyes, he strode down the Calle Alberi Grandi with a look of sated self-satisfaction on his face. One corner of his mouth was always inclined toward the slightest of smiles, one hand was always at his crotch: checking, shifting, squeezing a little life into its roots. Gianluca's penis was commonly referred to as *Il Bastòn*, and everyone on Riva di Pignoli was familiar with its astonishing length. The men had seen it in summer when they went swimming in the cove behind Giuseppe Navo's boat — from the time he was twelve Gianluca had cowed them, from youngest to oldest, into a long, admiring line behind him. The women had seen it by candlelight in the tight quarters of his tiny room; none of them would admit to having been with him, but each communicated an embarrassed warmth when she passed him in the street. Most nights, however, Gianluca brought women from the other islands to his room. It was suggested by more than a few of his former conquests that, more than anything else, he enjoyed the fresh look of awe on their faces as they watched him disrobe.

"I don't think that can bring the spring," said Gianluca.

"You never know," said the Vedova. "With the right inflection, something just might come up."

At eighty-three, the Vedova Stampanini had failed to taste Gianluca's charms herself; but she enjoyed the idea of all this lovemaking going on under her roof so much, she let Gianluca pay his rent in vegetables. Feathery cabbages. Sweet stalks of fennel. Crisp, crunchy carrots. It was common for most villagers to have a small garden of their own, but few could afford more than a little celery and a couple of cauliflower. Gianluca and Albertino fleshed out their meager yields with onions, turnips, parsnips, peas, broccoli, cabbage, eggplant, fennel, carrots, artichokes, and three kinds of *insalata* — not to mention strawberries, apples, pears, and figs on the fruit side of the ledger. The wetter, colder weather made it more and more difficult to work the land, but Gianluca persisted, eliminating asparagus (too reedy) and beets (too red) and keeping two small fields fallow each season to allow for rotation. After a couple of rough seasons things began to improve; the past three years the fruit and vegetable stand they ran at the village market had actually made a profit. But now it was almost May and the parched earth had not spit forth a sign of foliage nor the promise of a thing to come.

"On the other hand," said the Vedova Stampanini, "a woman is entitled to her moods. I gave birth to ten and then buried every one of them. Believe me, Gianluca, it tires you out."

Gianluca listened, but he could not accept the argument. There was another explanation for the spring's delay. There had to be. And he was determined to find out what it was.

The sun had risen just above the horizon when he left the Vedova Stampanini's hovel and took his boat to cross over to the tiny cemetery island; by the time he had docked, and had tied his boat up next to Albertino's, and had walked across to the roofless little room, it was just beginning to lift up high enough to cast its warmth out over the east wall and across Albertino's sleeping body. Gianluca stood there for a moment and thought of how many minutes — hours — days, it seemed — he had spent watching Albertino sleep. But thoughts of time brought thoughts of the reluctant spring, so he moved in closer to the wall and let his broad shadow eclipse the morning rays.

Albertino opened one eye and glared out of it at Gianluca.

"You stepped in front of my dream."

"Get up, little brother. You dream too much."

"It was a nice dream. I was enjoying it very much. You blocked it right out."

"Get up," Gianluca repeated as he stepped over the wall. "The spring is twenty-seven days late. There's no time to be lying in bed having nice dreams."

Albertino rolled over onto his belly.

"Well, what else can I do? I can't work. And if I can't work, I might as well sleep."

"Have you thought about it, Albertino? Have you thought about what it means?"

"I've thought about it, Gianluca."

"Then why don't you seem to understand? If the spring doesn't come, we'll lose everything we've worked for. We can't just lie in bed. We have to do something."

"All right," said Albertino. "What should we do?"

Gianluca began to move about the room like one of Siora Scabbri's chickens. He knew what he was going to say, but he did not relish the thought of Albertino's response.

"I've tried everything I can think of, you realize. And it's all been a waste of time. But this morning I thought of something I hadn't thought of before."

"What's that?"

"Ermenegilda."

Albertino sprang up like the hinge on a mold-board plow. "Ermenegilda!"

"I knew you wouldn't like it. But I think it's our only chance." Gianluca, having reached the south wall, picked up one of Albertino's boxes and began fingering the ribbons that wound through its ornate clasp.

"Put that down, Gianluca," said Albertino. "I told you never to touch my boxes."

Gianluca returned the box to its corner while Albertino slid forward onto his knees. "Gianluca," he said in a whisper, "do you think so, too?"

"Do I think what?"

"Do you think the spring hasn't come because of Ermenegilda?"

"Because of Ermenegilda?"

"Because she's so ugly. Because she's so fat."

Gianluca remained motionless as he contemplated Albertino's words; then he burst into a great gale of laughter. "Don't be a fool," he said. "Ermenegilda is rich, that's all. Enrico Torta is always telling everyone that the Torta money can buy anything. Well, let's put it to the test. Let's see if it can buy us the spring."

Albertino flopped back on his bed. "That's ridiculous."

"We're desperate, Albertino."

"Ermenegilda can't buy us the spring."

"Do you know that?"

"It's the stupidest idea you've ever had."

Gianluca stepped closer to the pile of blankets and crouched down at its side. "Ermenegilda is rich. She'd do anything in the world for you. Tell her you need a spring."

"You've been drinking too much."

"It's our only chance."

"You've been out too long in the sun."

"Albertino . . ."

"No! I won't do it! And don't ask me again!"

Gianluca got down on his knees and leaned right into Albertino's face. "Do you want to spend the rest of your life cleaning *coda di rospo* for Giuseppe Navo?"

Albertino closed his eyes and drew his arms up over his head. Gianluca had to bite his lip a bit to keep from laughing — his little brother's earnest dismay always amused him, but he did not want to offend him when he needed his cooperation.

"Why is it I always have my arms down into the soil clear up to my elbows," said Albertino, "and you've always got a flower between your teeth?"

Gianluca slapped Albertino's thigh and stood; he knew that he had won. "See her today," he said. "There's still time to put down the broccoli before the weather gets too hot."

Gianluca hopped over the east wall and headed back toward the water. There was not a streak upon the fresh blue sky — not a cloud — not a care — not a cabbage, a carrot, a cauliflower. He did not know whether it was foolish or inspired to send Albertino to Ermenegilda. He only knew that Albertino would do it, and that they were running out of schemes.

❧❧

THE CA' TORTA was not only made of stone it was made of *pietra d'Istria*, the same shining marble that was used to face the great churches of Venezia. Enrico Torta had spent a fortune to bring the huge flags of ivory and cream across the cold waters of the Adriatic to Riva di Pignoli. Added to the thick slabs of stone he had sent in from his own country's quarries, including a few choice pieces of Tuscan *pavonazetto*, they made the dwelling sparkle like a diamond in the sun. It took a team of the best Venetian builders over a year and a half to build the house to Enrico's and Orsina's specifications. There were quarrels, conflicts over working conditions, accusations of theft and mismanagement, even a brief fistfight over the placement of an ornamental urn. But the results were worth every denaro spent, every reluctant effort expended. The Ca' Torta was not just a lavish home. It was a palazzo.

Ermenegilda's room, like Albertino's, had a north wall, a south wall, an east wall, a west — but that was where the similarity ended. Where Albertino's room was simple and spare, Ermenegilda's was positively bursting. There were

Persian carpets on the floor, painted frescoes on the ceiling, and embroidered tapestries on the walls. Such lavishness, outside of court, was quite extraordinary. But Ermenegilda liked her comfort, and Enrico Torta had learned that it was easier to see that his baby girl got what she liked than to contend with her wrath when she didn't. Where the three Marias' bedrooms had little furniture besides the bed and the washbasin, Ermenegilda's room had a table, two chairs, a chest of drawers, and a weaving loom. Her bed was canopied with Chinese silks and hung from the ceiling on four sturdy ropes. Her frescoes told the story of Leda and the swan, and her tapestries depicted the four seasons in a series of rural tableaux. If she could not buy them the spring, Ermenegilda might at least lend Albertino and Gianluca her west wall tapestry: it was as lush and verdant as anything their callused hands might draw from the earth.

On the morning in which Gianluca had gone to Albertino and had encouraged him to speak with Ermenegilda, Ermenegilda sat dreaming at her loom. The weaving experiments had long since failed, and she was far from thinking of actually making anything, but the long wooden spindles that lined the frame were the perfect place to stack the ringlike breakfast pastries she feasted on each morning. So she propped herself up on a pair of Turkish pillows, spread her legs wide on either side of the rosewood frame, and lost herself in a *miel-pignole* daze.

Ermenegilda was thinking about her wedding day. It would be out in the Torta garden, and all of Riva di Pignoli would be there. She pictured the long, wide banquet tables piled high with savory delicacies and the path of wild rose petals leading out across the lawn. She pictured her mother, lit up like an altar, and her three sisters, stuffed

and pickled in bolts of imported fabric. She pictured the
fishermen, dressed in stiff tunics and cleansed of the smell
of cod. And she pictured Albertino: quiet, serene, almost
beatific — a man in ecstasy at the thought of his bride. The
only thing missing, the only person absent, was Ermenegilda herself. She pictured only a radiance of light, a bright
field of energy without features or form. A glow in a
wedding veil.

When Romilda Rosetta, Ermenegilda's maid and the
only servant ever to have stayed at the Ca' Torta for longer
than six weeks, rapped on the door and broke her reverie,
Ermenegilda was vexed to find the glow gone to ash
again — to see her enormous legs spread out before her
and feel the great mass of her body squashed between
loom and wall. When the servant told her that "Sior Tonolo" was waiting downstairs to see her, the glow resur-
faced, but it located itself at heart level this time, burning
inside her astonished bosom as she tried to differentiate
between fantasy and reality.

"Sior Tonolo?" she asked, repeating Romilda Rosetta's
announcement half in wonder, half in disbelief. "Albertino
Tonolo?"

Romilda Rosetta had been with Ermenegilda for six
years, since the latter's twelfth birthday. She'd stayed because she hadn't been able to think of anything else to do
and because, being only half the size of Ermenegilda, she
was afraid of what the girl might do to her if she ever tried
to leave. Ermenegilda was a monster to Romilda Rosetta.
No matter how devotedly the diminutive domestic beat
out her tapestries, or clipped her nails in the bath, or
brought her an extra plate of *frittele di manzo* when the rest
of the house had gone to bed, Ermengilda used her to vent
the boiling fury that ran through her Torta blood. When

she was fourteen and Romilda Rosetta forty, she ordered the poor woman to stand on the roof of the Ca' Torta during a hailstorm and imitate a seagull. The following year, on a shopping trip to Venezia, she knocked her down in the Piazza San Marco and left her to be carried home by a stray fishing vessel. She cursed her, mocked her, tormented her, reviled her. Yet no matter how cruelly Ermenegilda behaved, Romilda Rosetta always received her humiliation as so much fire on the path to spiritual purification. The worse the girl treated her, the more convinced she was of her ultimate redemption — and though she cowered at her mistress's commands and occasionally dropped things when Ermenegilda bellowed out her name, inside she felt the peacefulness and serenity of one of God's chosen. It never occurred to her that she enjoyed Ermenegilda's abuse, that without it she would have been nothing more than a very ordinary, extremely short maid. Her ill treatment gave her life meaning; it gave her a sense of martyrdom that thoroughly compensated for her inordinately small stature. It was therefore with great seriousness, when Ermenegilda tried to make certain that it was Albertino and not Gianluca who waited below to see her, that she replied: "It's the little one."

Ermenegilda could not believe her ears. That Albertino would call on her unannounced — on *impulse* — was too much for her to comprehend.

"Well, what are you standing there for?" she shrieked. "Go tell him I'll be right there!"

Downstairs, in the drawing room, Albertino waited uncomfortably on a pink satin sofa embroidered with acorns. He had never been inside the Ca' Torta before; he had met Ermenegilda only at the gate or, at most, the front door. Now he sat on a tufted throne on a golden chamber in a palace of glittering splendor — and he wished he were back with the dirt and straw of his own tiny room. Before he could change his mind, however, Ermenegilda swept in.

"*Bon dì*, Albertino," she chirped gaily.

"*Bon dì*, Ermenegilda," said Albertino, standing as she entered but averting his eyes.

"And how is your little island?"

"Oh, fine, fine. No one's been out since Vincenzo Bassetti was buried, and that was last January."

Ermenegilda issued a high, false laugh, as if Albertino's words were deliciously witty, and began walking slowly around the room in an unnatural circle, as if perhaps her left leg were shorter than her right. She ended up on the tiny sofa in front of which Albertino stood. Albertino had no choice but to sit beside her.

"And your brother, Gianluca? Is he well, too?"

"Oh, yes, Gianluca's fine. Gianluca's very well."

"And your little room?"

"Fine, fine. Everything's just fine."

The conversation kept on in this way for half an hour. But after half an hour a silence descended. Ermenegilda was too intoxicated by Albertino's presence to think of any more questions, and Albertino was too conscious of the closeness of Ermenegilda's body to offer any of his own. But silence led to breathing, and breathing to sweating, and Albertino soon decided that it was safer to explain why he had come than to travel on in the direction they were heading.

"Ermenegilda," he said measuredly, "Gianluca and I were wondering something."

"Yes?"

"Well . . ." He shifted his body slightly. "We were wondering if you could do something to help bring the spring."

Ermenegilda's shoulders twitched involuntarily; she looked at Albertino as if he were a piece of venison someone had already gnawed to the bone. "Excuse me?"

"The spring," he said. "It hasn't come this year, if you haven't noticed. No flowers. No leaves on the trees. And not a sign of a vegetable. I don't know, perhaps you can get vegetables from one of the other islands, but on Riva di Pignoli there won't be any vegetables to be got because there hasn't been a spring. No spring, Ermenegilda. Not a pea, not a bean, not a lentil."

Albertino looked despondent as he explained all this to Ermenegilda; Ermenegilda did not say a word. She merely rose, walked over to the plate of goose-liver tiles Romilda Rosetta had deposited on the side table, and devoured several of them in a single gulp.

"I'd heard something about it," she said flatly.

"Well, Gianluca and I were talking," Albertino continued, "and it suddenly occurred to us that maybe, with all your money, well — maybe you could somehow *buy* us the spring. I know it sounds absurd, but then the spring not coming is sort of absurd. Anyway, I figured it was worth coming here to ask if you thought you could do it."

Ermenegilda had turned back to face Albertino by this time, her hands inert and sticky in front of her. As she watched him sitting there, she imagined him in a dozen guises: fisherman, landlord, pirate; shepherd, eunuch, priest; banker, brigand, bishop, serf, crusader, and hangman. But no matter how he appeared to her — no matter the clothing he wore or the station he represented — she could feel only the tenderest love for him.

"Yes," she said.

Albertino stared at her. "What do you mean, 'yes'?"

"I mean 'yes.' I mean I can do it."

Ermenegilda drew her left hand up to her mouth and licked a bit of goosefat off a fingertip. What mattered was not what he had come for, but that he had come. What mattered was not that he wanted to use her for her money, but that he had chosen to lay his anguish at her waiting feet.

"I can get you the spring, Albertino," she said. "If that's what you truly want."

Albertino could feel his hair grow hot and the tips of his ears begin to tingle. "What do we do?" he asked as he bounded up and hurried to where she stood.

"For now just go home," she said, slipping her arm through his and guiding him toward the door. "Pull the covers up over your head and dream of artichokes and parsley and baby lettuce. Dream of carrots, and cauliflower, and dream of more of them than you ever thought there could be." She led him out of the room, and down the stone stairway, and across the broad gallery that led to the front door. "Then, at midnight, meet me on the dock to your island."

"At midnight?"

"At midnight."

"On the dock to my island?"

"On the dock to your island."

Albertino swallowed hard. "Then what?"

Ermenegilda smiled a broad, honey-dappled smile. "Then," she said, "we make the spring come."

Albertino looked into her ravenous eyes, and though his face registered nothing he knew exactly what she had in mind. What troubled him was that he could not be altogether certain that what she had in mind could not bring the spring. So he turned, placed his hat upon his head, and headed out the front gate.

Ermenegilda watched as he headed off toward the meadow. Then she closed the carved-oak door and climbed the first-, the second-, and the third-floor staircases to reach the chambermaid's quarters, from where she could follow him across the island until he reached his tiny *barca da pesca*. For a moment, as she knelt down before the low, arched window that opened beneath the slanting roof, she was distracted by the sight of another figure dragging what looked like a body toward the lip of the lagoon. But then she spotted Albertino, moving across the dry field like a heartsick badger, and all thoughts dissolved around the sweetness of that image.

A spring. Albertino wanted a spring. And although Ermenegilda knew as much about agriculture as she knew about alchemy, there was someone who just might be able to help her bring it. It was only a hunch — and it traded upon a softness she did not like to admit — but Albertino wanted a spring. And if it meant actually having him in her arms at last, Ermenegilda was going to get him one.

# C h a p t e r
## 2

VALENTINA'S ABUSIVENESS reached its peak when she tried to drown Piarina in the well. The starry child had spent the entire morning cleaning out the hearth, cheeks and forehead turning a murky gray. Yet regardless of her efforts to help, those knobby knees and that phantomlike flyaway hair drove Valentina into a more-than-usual rage. When Piarina slinked out to the well to get the water for the baking, Valentina followed her; as Piarina bent over to scoop it out, Valentina gave a large whack to her little body and the child tumbled over the edge, hitting her head and knocking herself unconscious. When Valentina realized what she'd done — and that she might still need the girl to turn the eel pasties — she called Gesmundo Barbon to fetch her out, cursing the child's clumsiness and the stupidity of having to draw from a well on an island surrounded by water.

It was not a usual mother's affection.

Six months earlier, Valentina had gotten so angry at supper, when Piarina had insisted on squashing open all the peas in her pease pudding, that she'd grabbed the sewing shears and cut off all of Piarina's hair, except for one rebellious clump in the center of her head. She'd painted this clump bright red and in the morning had set Piarina out with the roosters. Then there was the time with the quilting pins. Or the time with the roofing pitch. Valentina knew Piarina was only a child, but there was something in the girl's spirit that created a jangling in her nerves, so that the smallest of her actions led to a series of offhand whacks and casual kicks that made the frail-limbed Piarina sink deeper and deeper into a private world.

Valentina, whose ruddy, robust figure was in direct contrast with Piarina's gamine form, had had her left hand crushed in a rye mill when she was seventeen. She kept a severed hoe handle tied to her left forearm, which she managed to use to remarkable effect, but she used only her flesh on Piarina. Still, on the day of the incident at the well, something snapped. From the time Gesmundo Barbon carried her bent and dripping into the hut and laid her upon the stiff straw bed, Piarina stopped speaking. At first Valentina prodded her, with the tip of her red, right forefinger. When that didn't work she tried calling her names. *Faccia-muto. Sordo Maria. La Maravègia Senza Lingua.* But nothing she either said or did could raise a sound from Piarina. And though she continued to beat the child as regularly as she had before, without at least an occasional yelp something of her pleasure in it was lost.

In time the silence seemed normal. They both began to listen for the rush of the wind through the low thatched roof and the rustling of the rats as they ran across the floor of their filthy one-room hovel. Valentina worked long into the night, making the soap she sold by day. Only a few of the families on Riva di Pignoli actually bought it, as the wax she used smelled of lye, but she was proud to have kept things going with one hand, no husband, and such a sorry runt of a daughter. What difference did it make, in the long run, if the girl could speak? Couldn't she clean the soap knives just as well? Couldn't she do the baking? Valentina ceased to worry about it and in time almost forgot that the child had ever said a word.

Then, one year after the attempted drowning, one year of haunting looks and long, cryptic silences, Piarina spoke again. It was early evening and they were sitting by the pathetic little fire that coughed and sputtered in the crumbling hearth. Valentina coughed, too; she'd been suffering for two weeks with a terrible chest cold and a painful sore throat and could find nothing to ease her discomfort. Piarina listened to the dry rattle as she sat hunched on all fours at Valentina's knees; despite the violence that had shocked her speechless, Piarina loved nothing more than to sit at her mother's knees by the pale flame of the evening fire. Now, without the slightest flourish or the thought that there was anything at all unusual in it, she suddenly said:

"Rhubarb leaves, in honey water, with small pieces of pinecone."

Valentina thought the ghost of her dead mother had

come down through the hearth and into the tiny hut, so used was she by now to her daughter's silence. When she realized that it was Piarina who had spoken, and not the flames, she did not express so much as a single syllable of either gratitude or joy.

"Jesus Savior, Piarina," she said, giving the girl's head a slight knock so that her fine, wispy hair flew up in alarm. "You scared the breath right out of me."

Piarina looked up into her eyes and repeated the phrase. "Rhubarb leaves," she said, "in honey water. With small pieces of pinecone."

Valentina tweaked her ear sharply. "Don't speak non-sense, girl. I'd rather have you mute."

Piarina reached up and placed her hands on the red and swollen throat. "Rhubarb leaves," she said once more. "In honey water. With small pieces of pinecone."

She ducked this time as Valentina's hand flew out to whack her, but she would not give up. Over and over, like a prognosticating parrot, she repeated the strange prescription. Finally, in sheer exasperation, Valentina got up, went to the table, mixed some honey in some water, crushed up a few rhubarb leaves, pounded down a pine-cone to a fine dust, and stirred it all together.

"Like having a retarded animal for a child," she said as she drank down the bitter mixture.

In the morning, however, when her sore throat and cough had completely vanished, Valentina was of a slightly different mind.

"How'd you do that, girl?" she asked the delicate child as she peered down into her sleeping face. But though Piarina woke with a start, she did not make a sound. She simply placed her hands against her mother's now cool throat and smiled her glittery, crooked smile. And no amount of Valentina's encouragements (like dropping chunks from the ice block down her torn and baggy tunic) could raise another word.

Piarina returned to her chores, Valentina to her casual rage. But she was wary of the child now. She stole looks at her when she was bent over strewing calamint in the straw; she sat staring at her for hours after the weary thing had fallen asleep (when Piarina fell asleep she did it literally — she entered into night and dreams with a tumbling intensity that left deep, dark bruises). Something had shifted in Piarina. Something had changed. And Valentina was determined to figure it out.

One morning, about two weeks after she had cured her mother's sore throat, Piarina woke to find Gesmundo Barbon sitting quietly at the foot of her bed. At first she thought she was still asleep: the squashed face and squat body seemed like the traces of some faded nightmare. Her mother's voice, however, stung her quickly into daylight; no dream could ever reproduce the cutting edge that sound had for Piarina.

"All right, Siorina Magica. Go ahead. Let's see you find a cure for Sior Barbon."

Piarina looked at the gross, lumpy man: his skin had gone yellow, and there were broken splotches on his arms, throat, and forehead. Even at her mother's command she could not bear to look at such an unpleasant sight so early in the morning, so she closed her eyes and slid down until her entire body was safely under the covers.

"You come right back out here!" shouted Valentina. "Or you'll have to find a cure for yourself!"

Piarina didn't move. But underneath the covers she closed her eyes, and underneath the covers she concentrated — and eventually her small, thin voice made its way up through the infested blankets like a trickle of steam rising out through a flaw in the kettle.

"Two large turnips, boiled and diced. A pinch of comfrey, a pinch of mugwort. Mix with vinegar. Chill. Apply to hip and neck."

Gesmundo Barbon ran out of the hut before Piarina could resurface, but the next day he sent over six fresh *sogliole* to express his thanks. From then on, whenever the people of Riva di Pignoli felt ill, they called on Piarina. She cured the Vedova Stampanini's rheumatism and the Vedova Scarpa's gout. She removed Fausto Moretti's limp, and she diagnosed Anna Rizzardello's bloated stomach as twins. There was never anything logical about Piarina's cures, they simply worked: physical or mental, terminal or temporal, there was nothing she couldn't fix. She could even tell a bluff.

"Crush five rotten olives in six spoons of lard. Add four pinches of wormwood, two *sarde*, and three beads of coriander. Grind together. Swallow morning and evening."

This was what she prescribed for Brunetto Fucci when he came to prove her a fraud. Brunetto Fucci was the island's apothecary. He never cured anyone of anything, but without a surgeon, or even a barber-surgeon, to tend their ills, the people of Riva di Pignoli had no choice but to go to him. When Piarina's powers came to light, however, Brunetto Fucci's livelihood became endangered. So he feigned a strange malady of the stomach and set out to prove her magic useless. Piarina wasn't concerned. She merely prescribed the worst-tasting thing she could think of and let Brunetto Fucci try to cure a real stomach malady. After a week of acute diarrhea — and no improvement in business — he purchased a new sign for his shop and went into spice selling.

When Piarina began her cures, Valentina stopped beating her. For a while. But the habit was too deeply ingrained; she could hardly look at the glow in the dizzy girl's eyes without wanting to give her a good wallop. So despite the fact that Piarina's cures brought in a little extra money, Valentina soon began her old, familiar violence. Neither of them ever knew when the dark passion would come over her; neither of them could ever guess whether it would be a slap to the back of the head, a jab beneath the rib cage, or a blunt kick in the shins. But to Piarina it was all equal. Soon the witchcraft became just another chore: wash the clothes, weed the garden, cure Maria Luigi's sciatica. Her spirit curled up like a lemon rind in the sun, and her voice, when she used it at all, shrank down to a faint, embryonic whisper.

The situation might have stayed that way if Ermenegilda hadn't become ill. Even with the renown of her cures, the Torta family had stayed away from Piarina's door. If Maria Prima had the grippe, or Maria Seconda an inflamed foot, Orsina would order in a specialist from Padova and pay whatever price was asked to be certain that her daughters got the best treatment in Italia. That the best treatment in Italia was often nothing more than guesswork didn't bother Orsina; the prestige of the physician's degree was what mattered.

The finest physicians, however, could not help Ermenegilda. They tried bloodletting, phlebotomy, cautery, and cupping, but she just continued thrashing in her sleep and sweating through her bedclothes as her skin turned a scaly green. Finally, after several months of pain and at least two dozen physicians, her condition was diagnosed as "untreatable, incurable, and basically hopeless." It was only then, in a dramatic burst of Sicilian despair, that Orsina allowed Romilda Rosetta to take her to see Piarina.

To Piarina it was just another diagnosis. She was surprised at how fat the girl was, and how finely dressed, but otherwise she took little notice of her. She promptly prescribed ten drops of agrimony, two eggs laid precisely at midnight, a few black mustard seeds, and a fistful of fresh earth. These were to be blended together and tied into a poultice, which was then to be tied securely over her buttocks. Piarina went through her usual process — the closed eyes, the palms at her temples, the momentary trance. But something unexpected happened to Ermenegilda. In the midst of her excruciating pain, as she watched the cock-eyed waif press her fluttery eyelids tight and sift through the field of images that flashed across her seven-year-old brain, Ermenegilda fell in love. It was not a sexual love, like the yearning she felt for Albertino Tonolo — a love that set her toes on fire and made her sit in the Torta garden eating lamprey with hot sauce as the sun came up — but it was love all the same. Piarina seemed so odd, so completely unknowing, Ermenegilda's wrathful heart simply melted away.

When the great girl waddled out of the hut, followed by the molelike maid no bigger than Piarina herself, Piarina considered it to have been a cure like any other cure; two days later both she and Valentina knew that their lives had changed forever. Ermenegilda showed up at the door looking fatter and pinker and gayer than she had ever looked in her life, and she brought with her a fleet of Torta servants bearing all manner of gifts: chickens, pigs, and geese; harrows, tubs, and jugs; wardrobes, lanterns, pillows, pitchforks, and lace. But most of all she gave Piarina something the young girl had never known before: the attention and affection of a loving heart. In the late afternoon, while the sun was descending, Ermenegilda would burst into the hut, scoop Piarina up in her arms, and carry her to the western shore to watch the last of the light disappear into the lagoon. When Piarina was sunk in the straw cleaning the tallow knives, Ermenegilda would ease open the door, sneak up behind her, and tickle her until the featherweight child nearly floated away. The two girls rarely did anything, they merely sat together — Ermenegilda on the ground, Piarina curled up gently in her lap. What mattered was contact. What mattered was the warmth of the other's body and the snug feeling of acceptance.

It was therefore to Piarina that Ermenegilda turned when Albertino came to see her about the spring. She wasn't certain the girl's powers could extend that far — and if they could, she couldn't think why she hadn't already used them — but her instincts told her that most likely no one had thought to ask her, and that she was far too unassuming to have suggested it herself. So after Albertino left her on the morning of his strange request, Ermenegilda headed out across the island to find her.

Piarina was sitting in front of the hut plucking a chicken when Ermenegilda arrived. When she saw the familiar shape moving toward her, a great, lustrous smile broke out on her face. As she ran toward the gate, she tripped and fell forward; when she rose, dark clumps of dirt were stuck to her tunic and pressed in her flyaway hair, but the smile remained as wide and as glowing as if she'd been carried to her friend on angels' wings.

When she reached Ermenegilda she reached up and

lightly patted her soft, full cheeks with both hands: her usual form of greeting. Ermenegilda lifted her up, tucked her snugly between arm and hip, and carried her, laughing, to their favorite spot out behind the compost heap. For a long while they just sat there, cradled against each other, Ermenegilda stroking the fine wisps of the fey girl's hair. But Ermenegilda was too full aflame with thoughts of Albertino, so she broke the silence and explained why she'd come.

"He says he needs the spring. He says he needs the carrots to grow, and the dandelions and the blackberries. I don't know if you can do that, but I want you to try. For Albertino. For my funny, silly, stupid little love."

Piarina felt the fingers moving gently across her scalp; their light stroking was like wandering minstrel music to her. She hated to break the contact between them, but something in Ermenegilda's voice made her slither out of her arms and crouch down before her in order to gaze into her eyes — where she saw a love so intense, she could barely balance herself on her heels. She realized that Ermenegilda had spoken of this love before, had even called it "Albertino," but in that moment the force of its meaning struck her for the very first time. Yet much as she wanted to hate Ermenegilda — to drum her out of her heart for daring to harbor this other love — nothing could alter the effects of her affection. She could curse her, beat the ground, dive headfirst into the lagoon and swim to Serbia, but she could never change the fact that the great perfumed girl had held her, and pampered her, and shown her real love. So she lowered her eyes, placed her delicate hands on the barren soil, and nodded.

"Do you mean it?" Ermenegilda asked breathlessly. "Do you mean you can do it?"

Piarina nodded again, and Ermenegilda smothered her with gleeful kisses. Then they sank back into each other's arms and thought about how much toil, and how much pleasure, the coming night would bring.

BY THE TIME Piero returned to the dock, the body had ripened considerably. He had to hold his breath as he dragged it to the north rim, and as the spring hadn't come there was not even the scent of thyme to relieve him when he got there. He had never buried a dead body before, and as he began to dig he discovered that the earth near the north rim was marshy and difficult. The sides of the plot kept sliding toward center, and he worried that with a little wind and a little rain, a hank of hair or a few toes might suddenly stick up above the surface. He could only hope that neither the cats nor the curious would ever find anything to interest them.

As he laid the salty earth in on top of the body, Piero tried to decipher its hidden meaning. It wasn't just a drowning, not with those hellish markings, but where had it come from and why had it washed ashore on Riva di Pignoli? To Piero there was no such thing as accident. Everything had its place and purpose, even if they were not always apparent to him. Had it been a vision, he might have accepted it better. A ghostly phantom of death would have had a clear, if dire, significance. But cold flesh and heavy bones confounded him entirely.

Piero was as accustomed to seeing visions as the rest of the island was accustomed to seeing duck shit, pig shit, and rooster shit. His mother had died bringing him into the world, but as soon as he could speak Piero began holding lengthy conversations with her. Unlike the usual imaginings of a motherless child, Piero's conversations had an eerie reality that made Piero's father extremely uncomfortable; when the young boy sat on the stool by the bed and spoke in gentle tones to the thin straw matting, Umberto Po could smell his poor wife's odor in the room. When these tender visitations were replaced by encounters with the baby Jesus, he bundled the boy up, took him to the monastery island of Boccasante, and left him there to be raised by monks. The brothers of Boccasante were deeply impressed with Piero's religious fervor. They taught him Latin grammar, the rudiments of the vernacular, rhetoric, logic, and mathematics. They imagined a splendid future for him in the arms of a benevolent God.

When he was nine, Piero began seeing dragons. They raged across the ceiling of his tiny slope-roofed cell at the rate of two per week, inspiring more awe in the other members of the monastery than a thousand visions of Christ combined. The brothers of Boccasante were convinced they had a prodigy. When Piero reached puberty, however, all previous apparitions were suddenly replaced by visions of the phallus. He saw them rising in the chapel, and lurking in the gardens, and hovering over the cloisters during matins. To Piero they were a symbol of man's yearning to rise up and out of himself and reunite with God. But here the brothers were less supportive. No matter how much hope the monks had placed in him, nor how much teaching they had invested in his future, once Piero began to shout about "the penis of God" they sent him back to Riva di Pignoli as fast as they could drop oars into water.

By the time Piero returned to the island his father had

died, but the people were so impressed with his spirituality that they welcomed him back with arms open wide. Beppe Guancio was so taken by his intensity, he offered to lend him half his tiny dwelling and to share with him the little he earned cleaning fish for Giuseppe Navo. Beppe Guancio felt Piero should give sermons in the Chiesa di Maria del Mare; he was convinced the glint in Piero's eyes was the light of God. Piero, however, discovered a different focus for his energies: he transformed his corner of Beppe Guancio's hovel into a workshop and began making tiny sculptures out of the fragments of granite and scraps of marble Giuseppe Navo gathered for him on his trips to Venezia. Piero found in sculpting a place to lay his reverent heart. His subjects varied: he sculpted swans and churches and fishermen — with an occasional dragon or phallus thrown in — but even the most conventional of the island's inhabitants had to concede that his work contained a strange, evanescent beauty.

As the years went by, Piero settled into his place in the community. Where Albertino was a patch of moist earth, Piero was a cryptic inscription on a stone tablet. Where Gianluca was a series of lithe and powerful curves, Piero was taut and lean and jagged. As the fortunes of Riva di Pignoli grew more bleak, however, Piero's nature took on a darker tone. When the spring didn't come he knew it was more than just forgetfulness. It was an omen. But like the grizzled, swollen body he was now in the process of burying, he could not interpret its meaning.

Piero worked steadily until there was barely a sign that the ground had ever been disturbed. A faint wind had come up; it brought in the welcome smell of salt off the water. By the time he had finished it was fully dark, and he had to move slowly and carefully to find his way back across the dry fields to the Calle Alberi Grandi. He was exhausted from his labor, and the thought of sleep was enticing, but he'd promised himself that he would find a way to bring the spring, and he was not going to wait until morning.

The only choice was to go to Boccasante. Though the monks had thrown him out, their doors were always open; over the years Piero had visited often and had managed to maintain a strong friendship with a kind-hearted monk named Fra Danilo. It was doubtful that this round-faced soul could do anything to help him, but perhaps he could point him in the direction of someone who could. He returned to his hovel to fetch a cloak and a torch; then he went to where his father's boat lay moored along the western docks and silently guided it toward the shores of the monastery island.

❋

PIERO'S BOAT PASSED close by the dock where Albertino sat waiting for Ermenegilda, but Albertino, who was staring at the water past his dangling feet, did not notice him. At night the lagoon shone black as a fish's entrails; even with a sorcerer's moon hanging high overhead, Albertino could not see a thing beneath its smooth, glittering surface. As he gazed down into the darkness, Albertino felt a faint twinge of longing behind his knees. Why hadn't he been born a fisherman? To live at night, in love with the sea, safe in a world where nothing was fixed but the slim line of the horizon? Sometimes he imagined what it must feel like: that first clean catch of early morning. To spar with the sun. To forget your name. To cast out your spirit on

the strands of a fishing net and carry home the secrets of
the sea. To be always a bit detached, a bit distracted, a bit
alone. Had he been born to it, it might have been the
ideal life for him. Albertino the fisherman. Master of the
crabbed and shallow waters. King of the catch.

But he hadn't been born to it. Even with the smell of
salt in his mother's nostrils and the seaweed that clung to
his cradle, Albertino had been born to the soil. To the hoe,
and the plow, and the poor man's pride of bringing home
the vegetables.

The vegetables. That was why he stood on the dock at
midnight, staring out at the black, black water. His love
for Gianluca, and for the vegetables. For eleven years now
he'd tended the vegetables, like his father, and his father,
and his father before him. As much as he loved anything,
as much as he loved his room that wasn't a room, or
sleeping late, or his magical, gleaming boxes, Albertino
loved the vegetables. So if the spring had decided to go
away this year and had taken with it the turnips and
the onions and the apples and the strawberries, Albertino
would do whatever Ermenegilda wanted him to to make
it come back. Ermenegilda loved him, and he loved the
vegetables — it was a simple equation. So he tried not to
cross his toes inside his boots or bite down upon his back
teeth or think at all about what he was certain was coming.

A few minutes before midnight he heard the snap and
sputter of voices and saw a tiny spot of torchlight appear
on the opposite shore. Shifting his body to face the light,
he watched as it traced a drunken trajectory across the
slender width of water that ran between the two islands
toward where he sat. As the light grew larger he began
to distinguish a tiny boat with two passengers: Romilda
Rosetta, wrapped in a linen shawl, clumsily handling a

pair of wooden oars, and Ermenegilda, swathed in deep, burgundy satin, perched on the seat plank behind her. As they reached the dock, Albertino stood and brushed off his torn, dirty leggings; it occurred to him that perhaps he should have worn his cleaner pair. After steadying the boat and tying it to the post, Romilda Rosetta scurried up the washed-out ladder so that she could give Albertino a hand in helping Ermenegilda up. It was a difficult maneuver — for a moment Albertino envisioned her sprawling into the water, blood red satin spreading out like a sail, fish leaping high into the torchlight to save their lives — but together they managed to hoist her up.

"*Bona sera*, Albertino," she said breathlessly.

"*Bona sera*, Ermenegilda," he responded.

Ermenegilda turned and glared at Romilda Rosetta, prompting the hapless servant to scurry down the ladder as quickly as she had scurried up, and soon the orange torchlight was receding in the distance, a tremulous firefly hurrying off into the night. When they were alone and all was moonlight again, Ermenegilda slipped her fingers through Albertino's and squeezed his hand tightly.

"Are you ready?" she asked.

Albertino nodded. He could feel the inevitable moving toward him like a steady fog, feel it creeping over the lagoon and descending around his shoulders with its damp, cold breath. Ermenegilda began to lead him off the dock and across the little island; when they reached the edge of the radicchio patch, he stopped.

"Where are we going?"

"To your room," she said, pulling him toward the four stone walls that sat across the deadened garden.

Albertino stopped again, this time yanking his hand out from Ermenegilda's hot grasp. In all the time he had known her, in all the time he had walked down the Calle Alberi Grandi with her, and had listened to her stories, and had taken her boxes, he had never let her inside his room. Like the deepest, cleanest place inside his heart, his room was off limits to her. And if he could manage it, he was going to keep it that way.

"You don't want to go to my room," he said.

"But, Albertino — *carissimo* — I do."

"Oh, no, believe me, you don't. It's very damp, what with no roof and all. And the wind can be awful. The rats usually take all the covers."

"The rats?" she said, thinking of her usual safety on the second floor of the Ca'Torta.

"They rarely bite, but it does get rather crowded. I know a much better place we can go."

Ermenegilda slipped her hand back into Albertino's and followed him into the night. She was grateful to avoid the rats, but beyond that she didn't really care where they went. She cared only that Albertino was leading the way, that he was guiding her across the choppy earth of his little island, that the moment she'd dreamed of for so very long was actually at hand. She could barely stand the weight of the dark burgundy satin that clung to her legs as she followed him. She could barely stand the throb in her breast that pounded so loudly she was certain Albertino could hear it.

It never once crossed her mind that Albertino was taking her to the cemetery. When she saw the stone entrance, with its iron gate rusted permanently open and its marble cross perched high overhead, she could think only that she was finally entering paradise. Albertino, for his part, had nowhere else to take her — and he figured that if he had to do what he was about to do, having never done it before, he might as well do it in the company of those who would never be able to talk about it.

The graveyard lay before them like a sleeping village. Since most of the fishermen had died at sea, there were only about a hundred or so graves, but in the intimacy of their arrangement they felt more like a real town than the huts and hovels of the main island. Many of the graves were so close they touched; others seemed to have been positioned so that the occupants could read Tarot or share a glass of hot ale. Sloping palm trees slanted down over the markers, their corrugated trunks providing a post to lean on, their floppy ears creating a canopy to read under. Pine trees stood like sentries on the wall, their pockets overflowing with *pignoli* for the dead. Near to the entrance sat a parcel of stunted rosebushes, their closed heads thrusting forward like blind graveyard beggars. The roses reminded Albertino of the absent spring and gave him the courage to continue on with what he was doing.

They moved through the gates and in past the first markers; then suddenly Ermenegilda's vision of the angelic host gave way to reality.

"Albertino!" she said. "This is the cemetery!"

"It's the best place, Ermenegilda," said Albertino. "You'll feel yourself with God."

Ermenegilda wasn't concerned with God, and she was far too inflamed with passion to suggest going elsewhere. Without a warning she pulled up Albertino's tunic and thrust her hand down into his tights. Albertino let out a yelp that threatened to raise up anyone who had been buried less than seven years — but Ermenegilda managed to raise Albertino up before he could let out another. Holding on tightly to his inflated manhood, she led him along past the florid marble of Silvana Zennaro and the fluted granite of Guido Bo, until they finally reached a plain stone marker set flat into the earth at the edge of the northwest corner, and she lowered them onto the chiseled surface of Cherubina Modesta Colomba Ernesta Franchin.

Albertino was amazed at what the contact of her hand could do to his brain. He watched in bewilderment as his own hands pushed her skirts aside, and reached beneath her buttocks, and guided his captured sex into her body. For the most part he kept his eyes closed; only for an instant did he peer out of the dense fog that filled his brain to see what was truly happening.

Ermenegilda kept her eyes open wide. She wanted to imprint this moment in her mind with every star, every shadow, each strand of hair on the palm tree bark and on Albertino's head. With the coolness of the marker beneath her, and the heat of his body on top of her, she felt caught between two worlds, two different Ermenegildas. The good daughter of Enrico Torta and the lusty wench with her legs spread wide in the graveyard. The naive girl who'd imagined this union as an abstract glory, all puffs of smoke and the scent of lilacs, and the now knowing woman who had never expected so much pain.

If he could have forgotten that she was Ermenegilda — if he could have felt only the soft cream of the inside of her thighs and the tickling warmth of her breath against his throat — if he could have somehow let his heart be his body — let it mingle with the thrills that tightened his calves and the light that expanded his head — he might have thought it was love. But he couldn't. And so, what was excruciating for Ermenegilda was joy to her soul, and what was exquisite for Albertino was anguish to his.

It lasted longer than either of them had expected. When it was finished, and their bodies lay tangled together on top of Cherubina Modesta Colomba Ernesta Franchin, Albertino wondered how the hard marble beneath his knees, and the damp creases of her skirt against his stomach, and the cold sweat running rivers down his back, could all reappear so suddenly. He wondered at how much breathing had been involved, and how much kicking, and at how selflessly Ermenegilda had given herself to the task. But most of all, if this was what it took to bring the spring, he wondered how on earth or in heaven — year in and year out — God could possibly bear the foolishness.

# Chapter 3

THE CHIESA DI MARIA DEL MARE had no transepts, no dome, no pointed rib vaults, no flying buttresses. But to the people of Riva di Pignoli it was everything a place of worship should be. The members of the second generation had decided that it was too much trouble to go to Ponte di Schiavi or Pescatorno for every birth and death and wedding. So they'd gathered their skills and built a simple stone chapel with a plain timber roof and a single, free-standing altar. All told, from the cornerstone to the iron cross-and-banner, it took thirteen years to complete (counting two eighteen-month periods in which no one did anything at all), but Giovanni Sardo managed to mount the cross-and-banner three weeks before he died, at the age of seventy-three,

and the Chiesa di Maria del Mare became Riva di Pignoli's
first landmark.

The walls, which were pale and evenly textured, reflected the sunlight that poured down over the lagoon. The
only ornamentation was the marble archway that framed
the main doorway: here, in two-thirds relief, was the story
of San Nicolo, patron saint of fishermen, virgins, children,
thieves, and practically every home on the island. Inside
the church were ten pews, five on the left side, five on the
right. They faced the altar, which was separated from the
rest of the chapel by a brief step and a low wooden railing.
There wasn't much marble in the Chiesa di Maria del
Mare — Giacomo Navo, Giuseppe's grandfather, had managed to obtain a few choice pieces from a wealthy Venezi-
ana who particularly liked his *baccala* — but what there was
was wisely saved for the altar. The top was a single sheet
of Tuscan *pavonazetto*; the facade consisted of two rose
diamonds, a strip of cobalt blue, and a yellow circle surrounded by six cream-colored cliptei. The altar was so
beautiful it was kept covered with a piece of white cloth;
the people of Riva di Pignoli couldn't bear such ravishment
on a daily basis.

Behind the altar, framed by two bas-relief columns, was
a painting of the Virgin and Child. It was by Massimo
Correlli, the Vedova Stampanini's father, and it was cherished by everyone on the island for its soft tones and its
deep, luminous light. There were only three complaints
hurled at the Correlli Virgin and Child: first, that the
Virgin looked too much like the Vedova Stampanini's
mother; second, that the Child looked too much like the
Vedova Stampanini (even as an infant the Vedova Stampanini had had a delicate look of sensuality that many
found disturbing in a depiction of the baby Jesus); last,

that instead of the traditional golden globe, Massimo Cor-
relli's Child held a flounder in its hands. The Riva di
Pignolian painter could think of no greater symbol of
God's love for man.

Piarina loved many things about the Chiesa di Maria
del Mare. She loved the way it was cool inside when the
summer days were hot. She loved the way the door would
mutter as she closed it behind her, but how the walls would
never, ever utter a sound. But most of all Piarina loved
the candles. Whenever she could she would creep into the
little chapel to sit in the shadows and stare at the flames.
The whole world stilled when Piarina sat before the candles — as long as they were burning, her trampled heart
felt calm. Often she had to restrain herself from putting
her fingers into the flames; she knew the fire would burn
her, but then there was something inside her that longed
to burn.

There were no clergy on Riva di Pignoli — no priests,
no prelates, no clerics, no monks. In moments of great
inspiration someone might give a sermon, but for the most
part worship was between villager and God. Everyone on
Riva di Pignoli had his own way of worshiping. There was
Piero's path of obsessive idolatry and Romilda Rosetta's
path of humiliating servitude. There were the evening
prayers of the island's widows and the dawn conversations
the fishermen held with the images of Santa Maria they
tacked to the prows of their boats. There was no question
of believing or not believing in God. On Riva di Pignoli,
God was a fact.

To Piarina, God was in the candles. If she went to
church and found them low, she would scamper across the
meadow to Beppe Guancio's hovel and tell him they
needed tending. Beppe Guancio had become severely de-

pressed one February late afternoon when he went into the chapel and was not able to distinguish the Christ Child from the flounder; from that moment on he took it upon himself to check the candles every day, before and after his work cleaning fish for Giuseppe Navo and just before he went to bed at night. He took his job quite seriously and needed no reminding, but whenever Piarina rapped at his door he pretended she'd come to him just in time, seeing how much pleasure it gave the child to think she'd saved the light from going out.

When Ermenegilda left Piarina to prepare for her midnight assignation with Albertino, Piarina thought hard about what she had asked of her. She knew that this was not the same as healing Armida Barbon's swollen liver; she knew that for this she was going to need help. So that night, after Valentina had fallen asleep at her side, and Ermenegilda had rowed out to join Albertino on his island, and Piero had gone to seek counsel at Boccasante, Piarina snuck out of her one-room hovel and went to stand before the flames. She didn't think about God as she stood there. She didn't think about anything. She simply let herself be filled with light as she asked for help. Piarina asked the candles for help because of her love for Ermenegilda, who had asked Piarina for help because of her love for Albertino, who had asked Ermenegilda for help because of his love for Gianluca, and for the vegetables. It was a chain of love extending from soil to sky — a chain of hunger and devotion and generosity — and Piarina could feel it tugging at either side of her as she placed her tender soul before the flames.

She almost put her fingers in. Almost. But instead she stood on the tips of her toes, reached up over her head, and grasped the tallest taper. Its hot breath made her hair dance up as she held it out before her, and its smooth body felt hard and clean in her fragile fairy hands. Without blinking she turned around, walked out of the tiny chapel, and set out to cure the land.

❦

IN AN ORDINARY YEAR, the spring would have simply meant a new stack of books to Piero. Fra Danilo was mad for herbs, and each April, in exchange for some crisp catmint or some savory sorrel, he would give Piero a share of the manuscripts that had been donated to the monastery that winter. For twelve years now Piero had traded his fragile bouquets of yarrow and rue for Plato and Aristotle, his tiny sackets of burdock and basil and burnet for St. Thomas Aquinas, Marcus Aurelius, and the two great writers of his day: Dante and Petrarch. Fra Danilo always kept the finest volumes and left the rattiest to Piero, but Piero would read anything and was glad to have them.

This year, without a spring, Piero had nothing to offer Fra Danilo — and he wondered what his friend's reaction would be when he showed up at Boccasante without so much as a dill weed. It was almost midnight when he reached the island; he could hear the distant bells of Torcello and Burano and Mazzorbo as they rang out the hour at slightly different intervals. After docking his boat at the farthest slip — as a sign of respect — he approached the massive doors that stood beneath the stone portico of the entrance. In the blue-black light, the carvings on the walls took on a frightening reality; as Piero's torch cast waves of flame upon the marble he saw two-headed birds break into flight and scraps of Latin dance before his eyes.

Fra Antonio answered his knocking. A slight gnome of a monk, half-blind and three-quarters dead, he considered it his absolute task, as the oldest member of the order, to receive all visitors to the monastery. He recognized Piero more by smell than by sight — slightly woodsy, slightly like something left out in the rain — and nodded slowly as he ushered him inside.

Piero felt as he always felt when he entered Boccasante: that he was glad to no longer be ruled by its laws, and that it would always, in a way, be his home. Many of the monks were already rising for their first prayers; Piero watched as they appeared from the shadows, their faces lit by the candles they held, and then disappeared around corners, through doorways, behind hidden arches. He explained to Fra Antonio that he wished to see Fra Danilo; the elderly monk took him to a small alcove, where he gave him a candle of his own, and then escorted him out to the cloister where Fra Danilo was entertaining a guest.

Piero was not surprised to find Fra Danilo with company, even at such a late hour of the night. Fra Danilo was almost always entertaining someone. The church at Boccasante had been built some ten years before the church of the nearby island of Due Vigne, but after a visit to Due Vigne by a wandering saint named Francesco, that island's fortune had changed dramatically. Religious men came from everywhere to pray at the altar Francesco had prayed at; Due Vigne became the holiest spot in the lagoon. Fra Danilo was certain that with a slightly different wind, Il Santo d'Assisi would have come to Boccasante, so he devoted himself to the cultivation of visitors in the hope that one of them would lend his island the respect and dignity accorded Due Vigne. At first he concentrated solely on other men of the cloth, but over the years he broadened his receiving list to include doctors, theologians, justices, and scholars, having correctly observed that the visionary may as easily hide among the crowd as among the clergy. His fondness for Piero, in fact, was based on this theory: even though Boccasante had thrown him out of their ranks, Fra Danilo felt it was wise to keep the door open just a crack, in case the youth's fantastic visions proved to be of a higher order than his fellow brothers had realized.

Piero entered the cloister, which seemed to float in a magical trance between the light of the candles that stood between the columns and the light of the moon that shined down over the open courtyard. Fra Danilo was sitting on the low wall that ran between the columns, and with him sat a slender, balding gentleman with a great black mustache and tiny eyes that kept widening and closing like those of a moon-dazed frog.

"Piero!" shouted Fra Danilo warmly when he saw him. "I'd almost given up hope of your ever coming!"

"I'm afraid I come empty-handed," said Piero as they embraced. "I'm afraid I have nothing whatsoever to offer you."

"Nothing at all?" said Fra Danilo.

"Not even a sprig of parsley," said Piero.

Fra Danilo leaned close and whispered into Piero's ear, "Is something wrong? It isn't like you to forget the herbs."

Piero inclined his head. "I haven't forgotten," he whispered back. "And something is most definitely wrong. But perhaps it would be better if I spoke with you in private."

"I'll see what I can do. But first let me introduce you to Sior Bon." Fra Danilo took Piero by the shoulder and walked him over to where his guest sat waiting. "May I present Sior Bartolomeo Bon, one of Bologna's finest scholars."

"You flatter me, Fra Danilo," said the scholar with a wan smile.

"Not at all," said the monk. "Your accomplishments are well known, even here in the lagoon. I'd like you to meet Piero Po, a former member of our order."

Piero nodded.

"A pleasure," said Bartolomeo Bon, eyes widening — and closing — as he said it.

"Piero is something of an expert on the legend of San Giorgio," said Fra Danilo. "Not to mention certain other, less orthodox symbols."

"San Giorgio has been worshiped to death," said Bartolomeo Bon. "I prefer San Stefano, or San Sebastiano. Something that can still make you wince."

"But surely you can't deny the power of the image," said Piero, seating himself beside him. "The saint. The dragon. It's man's eternal struggle."

"Oh, I suppose it has a kind of primitive suggestiveness. If you fancy that sort of thing."

"I appreciate any depiction of the conflict between good and evil," said Piero.

"Piero has an extraordinary imagination," said Fra Danilo. "A bit too extraordinary, I'm sorry to say, for some of the brothers of Boccasante."

"Have you read Sior Dante's *Commedia*?" asked Piero.

"I have not," said Bartolomeo Bon. "I do not consider political polemicism to be literature."

"But it's the most remarkable book! You must read it!"

Bartolomeo twisted his legs together and laughed. "I have quite enough to read as it is," he said. "Sior Dante's ideas of heaven and hell seem rather simplistic to me."

"Where I come from simple things are always appreciated the best," said Piero.

"And where," asked Bartolomeo Bon, raising his left eyebrow, "is that?"

"Riva di Pignoli," said Piero.

"I beg your pardon?"

"It's an island just north of here," interjected Fra Danilo. "Small, but very green."

Bartolomeo Bon stared straight ahead for a moment, then shook his head. "Doesn't exist," he said.

"I'm sorry to disagree with you," said Piero, "but it most assuredly does exist. Except for the seven years I spent here at Boccasante, I've lived my entire life there."

"How literal," said Bartolomeo Bon. "I realize that as a few clumps of soil, your little island sits sleeping in the water. But in the sense of mattering — in the sense of leaving any mark on our wretched civilization — it simply doesn't exist."

Piero opened his mouth to argue, but Bartolomeo Bon continued before he could speak.

"The days of the *contadi* are numbered," he said. "These paltry villages with nothing more than a few casks to piss in can't possibly survive the changing times. The feudal system is dead. Living without an education? Dead. The poor fellow who doesn't attach himself to one of the real cities is simply going to find himself feet up in his fields."

"These islands have been around for a long time," said Fra Danilo, trying to soften the scholar's words. "Surely they can survive changing fashions."

"They can't survive," said Bartolomeo Bon, "if they don't exist." He turned to Piero. "This island you speak of. What does it have that will last?"

Piero tried to envision the wobbly landscape of Riva di Pignoli. "It has a palazzo," he said.

"One of those cheap Venetian candy boxes?"

"It has a church."

"Romanesque or Byzantine?"

"Neither. Just a church."

"Can you see it from the water?" asked Bartolomeo Bon. "Does it have a proper campanile?"

"No," said Piero.

"Then how do you know when the day begins? How do you know when it ends? Where is your island's voice? Its breath? Its music?"

Piero had always thought that the day began when it began and that it ended when it was over. But the relentlessness of Bartolomeo Bon's words was making him question whether he could tell the sun from the moon from Siora Bertinelli's pignole pastries. Without speaking, he rose from the cloister wall and walked to the small fountain at the center of the courtyard.

"Is there a piazza on your island?" asked Bartolomeo Bon. "A *campo*? A monument?"

"No," said Piero softly.

"Then how does it even know its own name? If you didn't know your own name, what would it be? Ignazio? Alfonso? Buondelmonte? A town needs to state its name or it isn't a town. An island needs to establish a center, forge its identity in stone, ring out its name on the hour — or it will just be washed away like a few dead seagull feathers."

Piero felt the cool stone of the fountain against the palms of his hands and heard the muffled chanting of the monks inside at prayer. Bartolomeo Bon's words were strong and harsh — but they had a strange effect on Piero.

"Bless you," he murmured to the quiet night. "Bless

you!" he shouted to the startled scholar as he ran to him and embraced him.

"Piero!" cried Fra Danilo. "Have you lost your wits?"

"No, Fra Danilo," said Piero. "I think I've just found them. Sior Bon, I must concede that you are right. In the way that you mean, Riva di Pignoli does not yet exist. But there's still time to do something about it. Thank you. You've helped me tremendously. If you'll excuse me now, I must get back to Riva di Pignoli."

Piero made a slight bow before dashing from the cloister; then he hurried out through the monastery gates and across to the slip where his boat lay waiting. He'd come to Boccasante to find a way to bring the spring back to Riva di Pignoli — but how could he bring the spring to a place that didn't exist? He suddenly understood the message of the dead body — that it was the same as the message of the missing spring. Both were trying to tell the island to wake up. Both were trying to stir it from its dreamlike contentment and convince it to demand its place in the world. Piero knew it was possible. And as he loosened his boat from the dock at Boccasante he knew just what he would have to do to make it happen.

WHEN ALBERTINO WOKE, his heart stopped for three full beats to find itself pressed flat against Ermenegilda's bosom in the thick shadows of the graveyard. Ermenegilda was snoring, the hem of her skirt still up around her shoulders, the look of Maria Ascendente on her face. At first he thought he would have to stay there until morning, but the memory of their midnight lust was too disturbing. Allowing for the chance that he might wake her — and might have to acknowledge the intimacy they had shared — he crawled slowly backward until his forehead met her feet and then quickly lifted himself to a standing position.

Ermenegilda barely moved; only for an instant did Maria threaten to drop from the clouds before an attentive angel swiftly buoyed her back toward God. After pulling up his tights and securing them under his tunic, Albertino lowered Ermenegilda's skirts, folded her hands across her chest, and placed an ashen rose upon her bosom. Perhaps she would wake and think herself the ghost of Cherubina Modesta Colomba Ernesta Franchin.

Albertino headed back toward his room, but his better sense stopped him before he got there. If Ermenegilda woke and remembered who she was, and remembered what they'd done, she was sure to come looking for him. If he went to sleep in his bed, she was sure to heave herself over the east wall and crawl in beside him. Much as he craved sleep — much as he craved the sweet security of his four uneven walls and his eight threadbare blankets — he couldn't bear the thought of her entering his room. So he let himself go in just long enough to fetch the gold blanket, then went down to spend the rest of the night at the dock.

When he reached the floating sanctuary of his beat-up little bark, he lifted up the seat plank, laid the blanket over the ribs, coiled a bit of rope to make a pillow, and settled back in to watch the stars. Albertino knew the stars almost as well as he knew the vegetables; he'd spent his whole life charting their gentle rotation across the sky. The Dolphin and the Hare. The Flying Horse and the Dove of Noah. The stars were friends to Albertino; it was one of the reasons he never felt lonely on his unpeopled little island.

If spring hadn't come, the heavens didn't know it. Albertino could see the Bear, the Lion, and the Crow just as he had each April of his life. The Crab was receding sideways into the east, and on the rim of the west the Virgin was just floating into view. Albertino had been born under the sign of the Virgin. She was a guardian to him, a protectress of sorts. Now, as he thought about his encounter with Ermenegilda, he half expected her to fall out of the heavens and splash into the waters of the lagoon.

How could he have enjoyed it so much?

How could it have been so ineffably, unutterably pleasurable?

He recalled the night, years before, when Gianluca had returned home from his own first experience — abstracted, moonstruck, delirious. That morning, while he was trimming back the broccoli, Maria Patrizia Lunardi, whose father, Cherubino, grew the wheat fields at the east of the island, had sauntered into the garden, slid her hand between his legs, and whispered, "Ten o'clock." Gianluca, who was only fourteen at the time, went instantly rigid and instantly limp; he could hardly keep himself from racing out of the broccoli patch and jumping into the lagoon. At ten o'clock that night he slipped into Maria Patrizia's room; when he floated home at four in the morning he was so lit up with ecstasy that he could not keep from singing. He kept Albertino up until dawn with an explicit description of every position they had employed, using a list of adjectives that began with "paradisical" and then spiraled off into terms he'd created himself. *Spuntinoso. Incardelito. Stronzinfatagura.* Albertino was only eleven, but he never forgot the impression Gianluca had made as his spirit expanded over the joys of Maria Patrizia Lunardi. Now, after so many years of lying on the floor and listening to his brother howl, Albertino finally knew the truth: it was every bit as wonderful as Gianluca had said, and every bit as awful as he had feared.

He tried to push these thoughts from his mind. He tried to concentrate on the stars. But everything in the sky seemed to remind him of his heated encounter. The Centaur. The Wolf. The Water-Snake. Suddenly the heavens themselves seemed to be mingling in a strange, degenerate spectacle: the Lion mating with the Bear, the Crow with the Crab. Albertino covered his eyes, but the images only intensified. So he burrowed down between the blanket and the rope and prayed for sleep to take him from the orgy.

WHEN PIARINA EXITED the church, the streaming taper clutched between both fists, she was already in a trance. Without pausing, she walked straight to the eastern dock and then slowly began to trace a path around the outer edge of the island. Her eyes were wide open, but they saw nothing; only divine protection kept her from tripping over rocks, slipping on sod, banging into trees, and falling into the lagoon. She walked for hours, sketching a faint line of flame around the island. While Albertino and Ermenegilda caught fire in the graveyard. While Piero carried torchlight back from Boccasante. While the hearths of the huts and hovels smoldered down to a handful of glowing embers. The Vedova Stampanini glimpsed her briefly as she set out the scraps for the cats. Gesmundo Barbon saw her float past his *sandolo* as he left for his morning catch. Piarina just kept walking — arms extended, mind extinguished, heart receiving.

By the time the moon had fallen she'd traveled the circuit nine times. Her hands were covered with candle wax, and her dirty tunic was damp from the wet night air. But just as she reached the point where she had begun, on the dock by the eastern shore, at the end of the ninth round, she stopped, closed her eyes, and sneezed. When she sneezed the candle went out, and when the candle went out she knew her task was completed.

She took the tiny plug of wax back to the Chiesa di Maria del Mare, placed it just where she had taken it as a slender taper, and went back home to the narrow bed to lie beside her mother.

❦

ERMENEGILDA WOKE precisely as the first rays of light crept into the graveyard darkness. She was not surprised to find herself sprawled out upon Cherubina Modesta Colomba Ernesta Franchin, and she was not surprised to find Albertino gone — wisps of angel hair still clung to her eyelids, and nothing, either physical or spiritual, could alter the sense of peace she felt inside. Her burgundy satin gown was speckled with crimson blood, but to Ermenegilda it was a symbol of glory.

As she rose to her feet and stumbled past the markers toward the gate, she half expected the skeletons to rise up and applaud her. All laws were suspended, all form and sense and reason turned upside down. She considered going to Albertino's room but decided instead to head straight for the dock; when she got there she stopped cold at the sight of him, twisted up like a puppy and still glowing from their encounter. She might have stayed there forever, content to watch him snore at the bottom of his boat, had she not instructed Romilda Rosetta to return for her at dawn. When the dwarfish servant appeared across the water precisely at half-past six, Ermenegilda cursed her punctuality. But when the elegant little boat arrived, she lifted her skirts and climbed in without so much as a snarl, a snap, or a bellow. She merely lay back against the polished prow, her arms resting sweetly in her lap, and let the confused Romilda Rosetta row her back to the main shore.

Albertino felt a sharp pang in his abdomen when he woke a second time; there was an odd smell that he couldn't quite place and a feeling of jubilance in the air. When he rolled over onto his back he could see that the sun had already traveled a third of its way across the sky; it must have been past ten o'clock. Kicking down the gold blanket, he drew himself to his feet and tried to toss off the traces of his troubled night.

It was lucky he had the posts of the dock to steady him, for what he saw nearly pitched him into the lagoon.

Once again the trim Torta boat was making its way across the slender isthmus of water that ran between the two islands. Once again Romilda Rosetta was at the oars; once again Ermenegilda was the lone passenger. But this time Ermenegilda was standing, and this time she could barely be seen for the sprigs and sprays, the stems and clusters and bunches, of fat, glistening flowers she carried in her arms. Pansies, chrysanthemums, violets, daisies, lillies, lilacs, pinks. Their perfume sent wild ribbons into the air, and their color woke the rabbits.

Spring had finally come to Riva di Pignoli.

And flowers were just the beginning.

# C h a p t e r
## 4

I
T WAS LIKE A GREAT, soundless explosion, the eruption into being of a thought, a dream, a dazzling incantation. In one swift movement the hand of Nature seemed to lower its quill to the surface of the island and etch an unbounded beauty into every inch. Fields that had lain caked and clotted suddenly undulated with life. Trees that had stood frozen and inarticulate suddenly hung down their branches with sweet, dripping fruit. Leaves sprouted like new ideas. Grass appeared like the flurry of cries at the height of a tournament joust.

Everyone on the island had a different story about the moment he first realized what had happened. The Vedova Stampanini had gone into her garden to remove the fishbones the cats always scattered after she gave them their late night feeding. She found, instead, the entire pack of them — Felice, Filippo, Rinaldo, Federigo, Nastagio, Lodovico and Lidia — curled up on a mound of clover that expanded and deepened even as she stood there watching. Siora Bertinelli had been stirring the morning broth when she heard a pelting sound outside. When she opened her door she saw the fig tree in her front yard spewing the fruit from its branches while the startled birds swept down to peck their fill. Ugolino Ramponi had gone to chop some wood for his hearth when he felt a rumbling beneath his boots. Dropping to the ground, he held his arms tightly over his head, certain that the sea was about to suck the entire island up into its gullet; when the trembling stopped, and he opened his eyes, he found himself covered from head to toe with woodbine and narcissus and morning gentian, the smell so intoxicating that he could not stand up for half an hour. Siora Scabbri woke to cries from her henhouse; the sweet violence in the air so shook her fussy brood that she had to take them back to bed with her.

Maria Luigi and Fausto were just sitting down to some garlic and salt cod when the branches of a beechwood tree thrust in through the tiny window above their hearth. Gianluca was in bed with a girl from Pieve di Forna when the room began to shake so wildly, he thought he'd returned to his first ecstasy with Maria Patrizia Lunardi. Orsina and the three Marias were in their chambers preparing themselves for battle when the tapestries leapt from the walls, the torches lit up in their sconces, and the goose-feather pillows exploded into the air as if Judgment Day had come.

Giuseppe Navo and Gesmundo Barbon claimed they saw the entire thing from the lagoon. First there was a blurring, as if the island were moving at a faster speed, sailing through an empty summer, a stale autumn, and a barren, brittle winter before arriving at the richness of an inconceivable spring. There was a silence — which even the fish attended — followed by an explosion of color that shot across the sky: great streaks of grape and celandine, bold patches of wild vermilion, warm rivers of sapphire, indigo, amber, and primrose. It was like a beautiful woman shaking out her skirts to find a fleet of wild birds hidden in the folds. It was like a great wave of laughter rising up from the soil to drench the air with its vitality.

Valentina had gone into the front yard to use the cider press. She and Piarina had a soap delivery scheduled for later that afternoon, and it looked as if it were going to be a long, thirsty morning of sorting and stacking and trimming. As she reached the well she heard a strange ripping noise, followed by the leaves sprouting forth on the branches of the trees. When she saw this she ran back into the hovel, slammed the door, and woke Piarina.

"Jesus Lord," she said in a hushed voice. "You won't believe what's happening out there!"

But Piarina knew. From the moment she'd taken the taper from the Chiesa di Maria del Mare, she'd seen the entire process laid out before her. She only hoped Ermenegilda would be happy — and that she'd done no harm in tampering with Nature's plan.

# Chapter 5

JUST BEYOND THE WALL that surrounded the Torta garden ran a slender canal. Every year, as the weather grew warmer, Ermenegilda would wade in its soothing green water. At the inside corner of the wall stood a great wisteria, which sent its lacy fingers out over her as she bobbed on the surface; on the opposite shore stood a sproutling from that tree whose smaller branches reached back toward the first. For as long as she could remember, as each spring had brought its sudden perfume and its brief flash of violet, Ermenegilda had thought of those trees as herself and Albertino: billowing and timid, yearning toward contact, separated only by a slim boundary of water. She had always believed that when the branches finally met, forming a natural trellis over the clear canal, she and her beloved would be one. Now, however, as she sank into the canal with the first dip of the delayed spring, that union had come and gone — and Ermenegilda wished nothing more than to yank the wisteria out by its roots.

Ermenegilda was angry. It was a burning anger, a concentrated anger, hot and tender like the rosy edges of a fever blister. For after an idyllic few hours in the cozy reaches of Albertino's heart, Albertino had disappeared. For two days Ermenegilda had torn her hair and covered her food with salt and begged the fishermen to drag the lagoon. But then, as simply as he had disappeared, Albertino returned. And when he did he behaved as if their torrid encounter had been nothing more than the sticky midnight imaginings of a girl who'd eaten one too many *miel-pignole* pastries.

To be honest, Albertino felt as confused as Ermenegilda at the drastic fluctuation of his emotions. On that morning when the spring had come — when the landscape had gone mad and Ermenegilda had arrived with all those flowers — he'd felt a sweetness awaken in his heart that was unlike anything he had ever known before.

"It worked," he'd murmured as Ermenegilda placed the flowers in his astonished, opened arms.

"Did you doubt it?" asked Ermenegilda, leading him gently across the radicchio patch to finally enter his room.

For the rest of the day Ermenegilda's voice was a lute song, her cascading hair the sunset waters of a waterfall. They sat on the floor and ate pignoli; they walked around the tiny island holding hands; they lined the east wall with their fragrant sea of flowers. But as nightfall came, the flowers' scent began to fade, and Ermenegilda began to talk about the future.

"I want a house that's even finer than the Ca' Torta. I want my own pastry chef and a personal seamstress, and I want to visit Venezia at least twice a month."

Now Albertino had been intoxicated by the rush of the sudden spring, but he was in no way ready to abandon his room and spend a lifetime with Ermenegilda. A part of him still thrilled at what they'd done in the graveyard, but another part was horrified at the astonishing intimacy of it. So before he could make the fatal mistake of doing it again, he slipped down to the dock and set off in his *barca da pesca*.

He rowed the lagoon for three nights and two days. The dread he felt was like a turnip in his gut, and the only thing he could do to relieve its pressure was to keep rowing. He rowed in circles and zigzags, stopping only for a few brief naps. He rowed past the gleaming spires of Venezia and the sparse scrub of islands no bigger than his boat. He felt the spray on his face as the morning breeze came up, and he followed the seagulls at sunset. He rowed with the fishermen and the cargo boats and the great clumps of seaweed that floated in with the tide. But the longer he rowed, the heavier and harder grew the turnip, until he could feel its stony denseness rotting inside him. Until he could no longer bear the tension between his repulsion at what he'd done on top of Cherubina Modesta Colomba Ernesta Franchin and his aching, feverish desire to do it again.

So he erased it from his mind. On the third night, as his arms could take no more rowing, he simply decided that the whole thing had never happened. And it was with that firmness of conviction that he rowed back to Riva di Pignoli, docked his little boat at his little dock, and wondered who had been so thoughtful as to deck his room with flowers.

Which made Ermenegilda extremely angry. So angry she could barely float in the peaceful waters of the canal. She wanted to yank out the wisteria trees — and the azalea bushes and the gorse hedge and the tulip beds. For a few brief hours, the spring had been a triumph. The shores had shot green and Ermenegilda had been the most beautiful girl in the lagoon. Now every leaf, every breeze, every blossom, was mocking her. And she would not be content until their laughter was fully silenced.

❧

WHEN ALBERTINO rowed off into the lagoon, he forgot about the miracle of the resurgent spring. When he returned, however, on that third morning after the bay trees had appeared and the pomegranates had turned their delicate, whimsical pink, he was even more stunned by the richness and beauty of the landscape than he had been when he'd felt its first awakening vibrations. As he walked through the fields on his way toward market, he considered that there must have been a thousand different shades of green, each with its own power to soothe and cool and comfort. The butterflies alone were enough to amaze him: he'd never seen such transparency in their wings or such weightless ecstasy in their flight. Yet even as he marveled at these splendors, it never once occurred to him that the market would in any way be different from what it had always been before.

The Riva di Pignoli market was a rather lazy affair.
People came and went at a casual pace, buying a few
carrots Monday, some eggs Wednesday, a nice fish Friday.
There was never any hurry and never any wait; everyone
knew that what they didn't buy today would always be
there tomorrow. There were certain days on which certain
stalls flourished — Siora Bertinelli's pastries did well between Christmas and Epiphany, Ugolino Ramponi could
never stock enough pigeons at Easter, and Fridays were
always good for Giuseppe Navo and Gesmundo Barbon —
but most of the time the market was merely a slow parade
of lookers and feelers, with more people coming to spin
the island gossip than to actually buy anything. The stalls
were set up in two short rows that faced each other: eggs,
pastries, pork, and gowns on the north side of the field,
fruit and vegetables, fish, game, and fowl on the south
side. The stands were a combination of splintered casks
and sawed-off tree stumps, laid over with torn-up planks
from the storm-beaten docks. Spread out over the stalls to
protect them from the sun were canopies made from the
sails of Giuseppe Navo's boats and a few of Maria Luigi's
less elaborate gowns. Spread out under the buyers' feet
was a mixture of rotting fruit, matted chicken feathers, pig
shit stuck to stale pastry, and fish heads grinning up at the
morning sun.

Albertino depended upon the market's simple and bor-
ing nature in the same way he depended upon the Swan
to rise in the summer sky. So when he finally reached the
stalls, in the field between the Guarnieris' smoke shed and
Siora Scabbri's henhouse, he was thoroughly unprepared
for what he found.

Siora Bertinelli was wrapping up her pastries before
they'd cooled. Maria Luigi was dancing with her gowns.

The Guarnieris were slicing up soft pink mountains of ham; the fish stalls were brimming with catfish and sardines, with moon-surfaced crabs and dark black pools of *seppie*. But nowhere was the rapture more evident than at his very own fruit and vegetable stand. In one stunning stroke, the spring had delivered produce that usually took until June or August or October to ripen — every shape and variety and of the most glorious quality that anyone, from the Vedova Stampanini down, had ever seen. Radiant radishes with hot flushed cheeks and long pointed witches' chins. Great knobby fennel with beefy thighs and veins the color of hope. Bruise-tinted eggplants, bound forests of broccoli; iridescent apples and dark, moody pears. They flooded out of baskets. They flowed over the sides of crates. They rose into lavish pyramids in the salty air.

At the center of it all, moving like a highly varnished top, was Gianluca. Gianluca was not inclined toward tearing his hair, and he hardly ever put salt on his food, but he had been almost as upset as Ermenegilda at Albertino's disappearance. For close to a month they had waited for the slightest glimmer of the spring; then, when it finally burst upon them, full blown and practically dripping, Albertino suddenly vanished. Knowing his younger brother's diligence and his fierce dedication to the crops, Gianluca could only think that perhaps he really had drowned in the lagoon. So when he saw Albertino's blunt little body moving determinedly toward the stall, the only thing Gianluca could think to do to thank God for sparing him a watery death was to send an enormous eggplant flying straight toward his head.

"Welcome home, Albertino!" he shouted out after the eggplant. "And if you say one word about where you've been — one word — I'll stuff every piece of produce on this stand down your stupid throat. Now get over here and start helping!"

Albertino was not very happy at being greeted by a flying eggplant — which only just managed to miss him as he ducked beneath its flight — but he recognized the danger in Gianluca's tone. So without so much as the clearing of his throat, he scurried in behind the strawberries and set to work.

The day continued on as it had begun. By late morning Siora Scabbri and Siora Bertinelli were out of eggs and pastries, but they kept people at their stalls by singing fishing songs they'd learned from their fathers. By early afternoon Maria Luigi had given up dancing with her gowns and had turned the task over to her father-in-law, Fausto; though sixty-six years old, he could do a tarantella that no one on the island could match. Sometime toward late afternoon there was a fight at the fish stalls: Brunetto Fucci accused Gesmundo Barbon of placing seaweed on the scales, whereupon the bearded fisherman tried to strangle the dour apothecary with an eel. And through it all were the constant cries of *"Atenziòn!"* and *"Diese per do denari!"* as Armando Guarnieri moved his broken-handled broom through the muck.

It was into this maelstrom of activity that Piero brought his excitement about the future of Riva di Pignoli. After he had left Boccasante, Piero had gone home to his corner of Beppe Guancio's hovel and had begun working with his chisel on a small piece of granite. He did not know what he was after; he knew only that he had somehow to focus the energy of what he had just discovered in the cloister. Eventually he fell into a deep sleep, only to be awakened the next morning by the most remarkable news.

"Piero!" cried Beppe Guancio. "Wake up! The spring has finally come!"

Piero leapt to his feet and ran out into the quickening landscape. But instead of filling him with joy, it only confused him. If the spring had come, perhaps Bartolomeo Bon's warning was without cause. Perhaps Piero's plan to revitalize the island was unnecessary. For the next two days he sat in the field of wild thyme where he'd buried the swollen body and wondered whether everything Bartolomeo Bon had said had been foolish and exaggerated. While Albertino was out rowing the lagoon, Piero sat contemplating the island's very existence. But, finally, the memory of those dark swellings convinced him that even if danger had passed them by this time, it would not leave so easily the next. So late in the afternoon on the same day Albertino returned from rowing the lagoon, he went to the market to share his new vision with the people of Riva di Pignoli.

"Piero!" shouted Siora Bertinelli as he approached the line of stalls. "You look as if you've just had lunch with the Devil!"

"Not lunch, Siora Bertinelli," said Piero. "Just a few sips of *vin santo*."

"I wouldn't waste *vin santo* on the Devil," said Ugolino Ramponi. "Ordinary *bianco* would do."

"All wine is *vin santo* to Piero," said Siora Scabbri. "It's in the way he holds the cup."

"He looks to me as if he's just got out of bed," said Siora Guarnieri, wiping her stubby hands against her aproned belly. "Piero! Since when is it like the blessed of God to sleep until late afternoon?"

"Is it afternoon?" said Piero. "I thought it was still morning."

"Piero!" said Maria Luigi. "It's almost time for supper!"

"How do you know, Maria Luigi? How can you tell one hour from the next?"

"You could try looking at the sun," offered Gianluca. "Here on Riva di Pignoli there's generally a sun up in the sky."

"And how do you know we're on Riva di Pignoli? How do you know it's not San Cortino or Borgomagnolo or Terra del Pozzo di Luna?"

"He's been drinking *vin santo* all right," said Ugolino Ramponi. "And the Devil did the pouring."

" 'Can ye drink of the cup that I drink of?' " asked Piero. " 'And be baptized with the baptism that I am baptized with?' "

"This is a market, Piero," shouted Gianluca. "The church is on the other side of the island."

"Are you sure, Gianluca? How can you tell where anything is on Riva di Pignoli?"

Beppe Guancio laid his fish knife beside a bank of *coda di rospo*. He'd kept silent while Piero had asked these strange questions, but now he went over to him and placed his hand upon his shoulder. "Piero," he said, "what's wrong?"

Piero leaned his hand against the frame of the fish stall and looked out over the market like a prophet over a vast, unlistening crowd. "You're all delighted that the spring has come," he said. "Life couldn't be better. But has it occurred to any of you why the spring was so late in the first place?"

There was a rapid exchange of looks and a rustling of goods, but no one had an answer to Piero's question.

"Why?" asked Siora Scabbri.

"It couldn't find us!" said Piero. "If you row six leagues out from any point along the Riva di Pignoli shore, you can't see the top of either the Ca' Torta or the Chiesa di

Maria del Mare. You can't see anything — because there isn't anything to see! Outside of Riva di Pignoli, Riva di Pignoli doesn't exist! Even the birds that fly overhead refuse to shit on us."

"That," said Fausto Moretti, "is not entirely true."

"If the spring was twenty-seven days late," said Piero, "it was trying to tell us something. It was an omen."

"What was it saying, Piero?" asked Albertino.

" 'Exist!' " cried Piero. "It was telling us to confirm the fact that we exist!"

"And how," asked Ugolino Ramponi, "do we do that?"

Piero stood very still as he looked out over the faces of the crowd. Then he reached his hand into the basin of shellfish and drew out a great pink lobster. With a quick jerk of his body he threw it high into the market air — above the faded canopies of the flowering stalls — above the aureate glow of the setting sun — until it reached its zenith, far over the island's rooftops, and then fell with a giant smack into Beppe Guancio's waiting hands.

"*Numero uno*," he said. "We build a *campanil* for the Chiesa di Maria del Mare."

"A *campanil*?" said Siora Bertellini. "What do we need with bells ringing all day long?"

"*Numero do*. We build a *campo* at the foot of the *campanil*."

"A *campo*!" said Maria Luigi. "What's the matter, Piero — San Marco isn't good enough for you?"

"*Numero tre*. We build a monument at the center of the *campo*, at the foot of the *campanil*, to symbolize Riva di Pignoli forever."

"With you as sculptor, Piero?" said Siora Guarnieri.

"We don't need any more dragons, Piero!" said Gesmundo Barbon.

"Who's worried about dragons?" said Siora Scabbri. "I'm worried about what else Piero might erect!"

The market exploded in laughter.

"And who's supposed to pay for all this?" asked Ugolino Ramponi.

"It won't cost twenty denari if we gather the materials ourselves," said Piero. "And if we each work a little."

The people of the market grew quiet as they began to consider Piero's proposal. On the heels of the delirious spring almost anything seemed possible; the color of the fields and the sweet honey in the air seemed to disintegrate their reason. Piero watched their faces as they tried to picture what he had described: Siora Scabbri chewing vigorously on the inside of her cheek; Ugolino Ramponi screwing his nose up as if he smelled something bad; Beppe Guancio staring dumb-faced and dreamy at the muck that splattered his feet. Yet the face that stayed in Piero's mind — the face that edged him forward and fueled his objective — was the washed-out face of the body he'd buried in the field of wild thyme.

"It's too difficult, Piero," said Gesmundo Barbon. "We've got enough to do to keep up with the work we already have."

"With a spring like this," said Gianluca, "it's all we can do to harvest the vegetables."

Piero moved in toward the center of the crowd.

"Then why not build it to say *grazie*?" he said. "If God has been so good to you, in the face of so much trouble, why not extend His house and grant His island a place for its people to congregate?"

The villagers were quiet again; Piero could feel them considering what he had just said.

"I could get the stones for the *campanil*," said Giuseppe Navo.

"I could get the beams," said Paolo Guarnieri. "My cousin Francesca's husband works at the Arsenale. That's how I got the wood to build the smoke shed."

"I could help you build it," offered Albertino.

"You're not even back half a day and already you're giving your time away?" said Gianluca.

"It's for the island," said Albertino. "It's to see that we get a summer, and an autumn, and a winter. You can't be too careful, Gianluca."

Gianluca thought about this for a moment — looking first at Albertino, then at Piero, and finally at the dazzling sea of vegetables that spread out around him. "All right," he said. "All right. I'll help, too. If you'll just shut up and let us get back to work!"

Piero assented, and the market gradually wound its way back to the bright rejoicing he'd interrupted a few minutes earlier. Now, however, the rejoicing contained an element it had not contained before: for the first time in their lives, the people of Riva di Pignoli were thinking about how Riva di Pignoli looked to the rest of the world. And spring or no spring, such thinking was bound to change things.

❧

ERMENEGILDA TOOK HER ANGER, wrapped it neatly in bolts of the best imported silk, and presented it to Piarina.

"Take it back," she said. "The fruit, the fields, the grass, the trees, the vegetables. *Especially* the vegetables."

Piarina felt grateful to be mute — for had she had ten

thousand words at her disposal, she would not have known what to say. When Ermenegilda had asked for the spring, she had covered herself in candle wax to bring it. But she had no means to take it away again. Piarina could cure, but she could not condemn. She could bring health, and growth, but she could not take away the life she'd given the land.

When she realized Ermenegilda was in earnest, Piarina went and picked a flower from the cluster of wild iris that grew along the path to her hovel and carried it back to where she stood. Look, her eyes seemed to say. Look how beautiful it is. How fragile, and full of joy. How could I ever damage even a single petal?

Ermenegilda looked at the flower, and its spread-open petals made her think of herself in the graveyard. She could not bear such a painful reminder of how her love had been rejected — so she broke off its head, crushed it hard in her fist, and hurled it upon the ground. Then she went to the pear tree and tore a pear from its branches. After forcing it apart with her fingers, she proceeded to squash it to pulp against the side of the hovel. Next she went to the herb garden. Valentina had planted only basil and thyme, but Ermenegilda ripped them both out cleanly by the roots and threw them into the well.

When she was done, she looked at Piarina to offer her a final chance. But Piarina could only hang her head and try to hold back her tears. So Ermenegilda snatched up her anger, tucked it under her arm, and stormed back off to the Ca' Torta.

After she'd gone, Piarina stared at the crushed iris head that lay at her bare feet. She traced her finger through the squashed pear pulp that dripped down the side of the hovel. She fetched a ladle and scooped out the leaves of the herbs that were thrown in the well. Then she took a basket, placed all the items inside, and sat at the edge of the compost heap, rocking them gently in her abandoned arms.

# Chapter 6

THE VIGOROUS, sleek-muscled spring kept on without hesitation; the people of Riva di Pignoli soon relaxed into an acceptance of plenty and a deep sense of well-being. The joy they felt for the landscape spilled over into the plans for the *campanil* — work could not actually begin until the stones and the rigging and the lumber were gathered, but preparations soon swept across the island. A schedule was devised that would allow each member of the village one morning and one afternoon a week to help with the labor: the young and strong, like Gianluca, could do the hoisting and the heavy lifting; the more frail, like the Vedova Stampanini, could help mend the ropes or pick twigs out of the mortar. It would certainly not rise overnight, but Piero believed that if they started by Pentecost, they could finish by the Naming of the Virgin, leaving enough time to complete the *campo* and monument by Christmas.

Piero's attention became so focused upon the creation of the new town center, all other concerns fell away. He fixed himself upon the stump of an old pine tree not far from the doors of the church and virtually willed the new structure into existence. He ate there and slept there, wholly convinced that if he imagined each detail of the final result, it could not help but come into being. So intent, so obsessive, so fixed within his aim was he, he might have remained there until the last stone was laid had it not been for the sudden appearance of Miriam — like a flash of summer lightning — on Midsummer's Eve.

No one actually saw her arrive. No strange ships stopped along the island's tattered shore, no mythic birds swooped down to drop her from their talons. But nearly everyone took note of her arrival. In the first place they were all in the bath, Midsummer's Eve being one of the two nights a year they allowed themselves this privilege. In the second place they had never seen such an absolute stranger give off such an absolute sense she'd been among them all their lives. Nearly everyone stood dripping at the window of his hut as she moved up the Calle Alberi Grandi in the loose white dress that, had it not cut so freely across her voluptuous figure, might easily have been her bridal gown. Nearly everyone stared dazzled at the honey-and-apricot tresses that fell over the slender shoulders, the full, sensuous mouth that was parted in childlike wonder, and the lucid, topaz eyes that seemed focused on some inner destination. Nearly everyone tried to guess what she carried in the small burlap bundle she clasped to her breast: Ugolino Ramponi claimed it was filled with gold florins;

the Vedova Stampanini said it contained a hand-sown deerskin coverlet; Beppe Guancio insisted it held a wooden cask, which in turn held a velvet sack, which in turn held the Holy Infant's baby teeth. They watched as she reached the first cluster of pine trees that made the road curve about in a half-moon, stopped, removed her slipper, and shook out a bright blue stone. They watched as she crossed the field in front of Maria Luigi's hovel, picked some flowers from Maria Luigi's windows, knocked on the door, handed the flowers to Fausto, and asked if she might live with him. Fausto was stunned — he thought a brace of summer thrush had fluttered into his doorway — but without a word he ushered her in, escorted her to the small alcove where Maria Luigi's cottons and muslins lay folded and draped, and told her to make herself a place among the needlework. When Maria Luigi came in, Fausto took her to the alcove, where Miriam lay sleeping on a bolt of Turkish linen. Maria Luigi simply covered her with an embroidered shawl and then went into the kitchen to take her bath, convinced that her humble goodness had finally merited the visitation of an angel.

The following morning, when Piero caught sight of that angel as she approached the Chiesa di Maria del Mare, his first thought was of an image from a Chinese picture book Fra Danilo had once given him. On facing pages, in brilliant blues and flashing reds and golds, were a wild-eyed tiger chasing a beautiful princess and a beautiful princess taming a wild-eyed tiger. Piero was struck by the sense that at one and the same moment this delicate creature was all four figures: tiger stalking, tiger tamed, princess chased, princess governing. When she disappeared for a moment behind the cluster of pine trees, he felt as if he'd tumbled from a trance. When she cleared the trees and approached the barren stump where he sat musing, he knew that the trance was what had possessed him while she was absent, and that her smile was the first real waking he had ever known.

"Excuse me," she said in a clear voice. "I would like to know if I might use the *chiesa*."

"The Chiesa di Maria del Mare is always open," said Piero. "God welcomes you whenever you wish to enter."

"Thank you," she said, lifting her eyes to his briefly before turning to leave.

"Where have you come from?" said Piero, stopping her.

"A village called Abrodando. In the mountains."

"It sounds far."

"It is far."

"What brings you to Riva di Pignoli?"

Miriam paused. "It's a beautiful island," she said. "Perhaps I craved the silence."

"I see."

"Or the water."

"Of course."

She smiled the faintest of smiles, her face remaining relaxed but something behind it softening. "Or perhaps I just like pignoli," she said.

"Pignoli," said Piero. "Well, we certainly have lots of pignoli."

She looked at him again with a look he could not decipher; an extraordinary radiance seemed to flicker behind her eyes. Then she drew her arms across her bosom and glanced over toward the tiny chapel. "I would like to pray now," she said. "If you will excuse me."

"Of course," said Piero.

She turned and walked through the feathery grass toward the Chiesa di Maria del Mare. Piero sat and closed his own eyes then — half-certain that she did not really exist, that she was only another of his smoky, mystic visions. But when he opened them and looked across the field to see her pale hand reach up to the door — and her firm legs move across the threshold — and her full hips sway beneath her gown — he knew that she was undeniably real.

In that moment Piero understood that dragons and phalluses — and maybe even God — were suddenly, hopelessly, behind him.

PIARINA STILL BELIEVED in God. But when Ermenegilda stopped coming to see her, after she refused to take away the spring, she began to wonder if the flickering candles could sustain her. Life without Ermenegilda was awful; the absence of the great girl's affection was like a bite taken out of her heart. But Piarina's sorrow did not reach its apex over Ermenegilda. For when Ermenegilda stopped coming to see her — and stopped bringing otter-fur capes and roasted finches and wide-necked vessels overflowing with shimmering coins — Valentina began beating her again. It was not the first time she had resumed her casual violence after a protracted period of grace. But this time Piarina's reaction was different. This time Piarina knew what it meant to be held in someone's arms, and warbled faded lullabies, and stroked like a newborn lamb. So although she showed no outward reaction when Valentina once again began cuffing and slamming and whacking her, inside she began to imagine ways to murder her.

At first these thoughts came only in dreams. Piarina

would wake in the night from having poisoned Valentina's pudding or having knocked her unconscious with the skillet while she laced her boots. Soon she began to fear going to sleep at night; when darkness fell she would lay sharp stones on her side of the bed or stick her toes into cold porridge. Anything to avoid the ghastly acts she might perform once her mind let go of wakefulness. But sooner or later she would always succumb — bent over the broth pot or crouched down beside the salting box — and another dream would sketch its sticky plan across her brain. Pushing Valentina into the fire as she stirred the bean paste. Chopping her into pieces with the pickax as she scattered the morning straw.

Eventually the dreams stopped waiting for sleep. Valentina would leave her to evaporate the lime water, being sure to punctuate her orders with a jab or a swift kick — "And *don't* let the flame get too close to the water — " Whack! "Last time the lime smelled as bad as the lye."

— and Piarina would imagine herself reaching for the tallow knife and plunging it into Valentina's heart. Piarina was horrified at what she envisioned; she tried to squeeze her bitter fancies back behind the veil of consciousness; but more and more they began spilling out into her day. And although she knew quite well the difference between fantasy and reality, deep in her heart she began to fear that one would begin to merge with the other and that something awful would happen.

So she went to the Chiesa di Maria del Mare and spoke to the candles. She offered to stop eating. She offered to give up her magical powers to heal, to do whatever it took to make the black imaginings go away. But the candles merely trembled in the cold stone shadows. And Piarina's murderous visions continued to come.

[ornament]

MIRIAM WAS CONCERNED with issues of a far less deadly
nature. At the moment, she could not decide whether satin
or lace would be better to kneel upon. Satin had the
smoothness of God's grace and brought a sweet gladness
to her meditations. Lace, however, tended to leave a faint
imprint on one's knees, which reminded one of the body,
which Miriam found reassuring. She knew that God loved
her body as well as her soul; she craved the lace not to
punish that body, but to keep it softly present in her
prayers.

Soon after she had settled into the small alcove in Maria
Luigi's hovel, Miriam began to fashion a simple shrine in
the corner, between the bolts of linen and the bundles of
lace. Maria Luigi had given her permission to place a small
statue of the Virgin — one of the objects contained in her
bundle — on a piece of watered silk that Fausto had found
on a trip to Vicenza, surrounded by a circle of flat stones
and a plain ceramic bowl filled half-full with water. The
Chiesa di Maria del Mare had proven harmonious to her
sensibility, but Miriam needed a place to pray that was
hers alone. Now, as she knelt down before the makeshift
altar (she chose lace for her knees), she tried to make
sense of the emotion and excitement that had filled her
first days on Riva di Pignoli.

Before the first week was out, Miriam had managed to
affect the lives of nearly everyone on the island. She
showed Maria Luigi a new way to stitch seams that used
half the thread but was twice as strong. She taught Siora
Bertinelli how to make a special bread that yielded six
times the volume of its ingredients. She showed Giuseppe
Navo a quicker knot to use for tying up his boat, she
taught Albertino how to prevent maggots from invading

the onion patch, she gave Fausto a tip on how to keep his beard from turning yellow in the sun. In return, Siora Scabbri gave her work in her henhouse, the Vedova Stampanini coached her slightly ladino tongue in the basics of the Riva di Pignolian dialect, and the villagers soon began calling her by special names: Siora Guarnieri called her *La Colomba*, convinced that she would fly off one evening as inexplicably as she had flown in. Brunetto Fucci called her *La Santificata*, and had to restrain himself from bowing when she entered his shop (in the end he could only manage to half resist the impulse, stopping himself at a slight tilting of the head and a caving in at the shoulders, which Miriam interpreted as a nervous tick). Siora Scabbri called her *La Furba*, because of her ability to coax her old clucks into laying twice their normal yield. Even Ugolino Ramponi, who had hardly a kind thought for anyone, could not resist laying an occasional goat at her door.

Miriam had always had a strong effect on people. Her parents had been noted for their uncommon generosity: everyone in her tiny mountain village knew they could get a glass of ale or an extra bit of *pan dolce* at their door. In time, however, people began to abuse this generosity. Early in the morning, while Miriam and her parents were still asleep, villagers would come in through the unlatched door and seat themselves at the wide trestle table that stood beside the hearth. When Miriam's parents woke and found them waiting there, they would hasten to the dying fire to fix a little broth with bacon or some cabbage and onions. Soon people began coming as Miriam and her parents lay down at night — dogs and cats would wander in — visitors from neighboring villages would stretch out to sleep on the rough wooden benches that sat by the wall. Miriam watched as her parents grew haggard, as her home became a wayfarer's inn. Until one morning she climbed up over the rumpled bodies, stood squarely between the beans and the brewet, and said in a powerful voice, "Go home!"

Everyone, including the cats, seemed grateful.

Miriam tried not to question her ability to solve problems, to take action, to give aid. She tried to accept that appetites flared when she passed at mealtime, that tempers cooled when she neared a dispute. Yet within herself Miriam had always felt a strange longing. She'd placed it upon her mother and father, she'd placed it upon an old gray ass her village had named San Tomaso, she'd placed it upon a long succession of slender boys and laughing, beautiful men. But nothing she'd placed it upon seemed remotely to quench it, so she simply went on with it burning inside her like a handful of hot peppercorns. Once she removed it from parents, and asses, and men, it became a fire that illuminated her, a searing flame that knelt her down in the blue light of dusk, or the long, flat shadows that extend before sunrise, in the belief that she needed nothing, and no one, at all.

Miriam was aware that it was the light of this longing that dazzled the people of Riva di Pignoli. Yet she also saw that for all their love and easy acceptance of her, they could not help but wonder why she'd come to them. Why on the final day of a spring-that-went-beyond-spring? Why when they were just about to build a *campanil*, and a *campo*, and a monument?

"Miriam! *Pranzo!*"

The sweet odor of mint and onions, and the sound of Maria Luigi's voice, penetrated Miriam's reverie.

"*Grazie*, Maria Luigi!" she called. "I'll be there in a moment!"

"I've made a pigeon stew and some *pan da pistor*. I hope you have a good appetite."

As she listened to Maria Luigi's cheerful tone, it suddenly struck Miriam that she had come to the woman's home uninvited — just as the people had come to her door when she was a child, the people she, and only she, had had the courage to send away. Yet as she stood, and lifted the square of satin from the floor, and folded it, and placed it beside the statue of the Virgin, she knew that there was a reason for her to be there. The only problem was to try to explain it to the people of Riva di Pignoli. She might have told them that she'd left her mountain village to make a pilgrimage — that she'd envisioned herself arriving barefoot and radiant at the gates of the eternal city — but she could not have explained how she'd managed to wind up on a curving path that led through a clutch of pine trees on an island she vaguely suspected did not even exist.

It would have interested the people of Riva di Pignoli to know that Miriam was going to have a baby. But since she'd only just arrived, and was really still a stranger, and since everyone was so preoccupied with the coming of spring and the construction of the new village center, Miriam decided not to mention it.

Why start unnecessary rumors?

Why speak of something that would become evident soon enough?

IF THE VEDOVA STAMPANINI had known that Miriam was going to have a baby, she would have made her a hearty

*ـopa di verzurra*, a fragrant *poloʃtrone roʃto*, and a feather-light *croʃta di mele*. As she did not know, and merely wanted to make her something because she liked her, she decided on a nice, crisp *pan duro* with aromatic herbs. Of all the many people who made their hearts and homes freely open to Miriam upon her arrival on Riva di Pignoli, the Vedova Stampanini was the one who treated her most like family. Three times a week the old woman helped her to soften her consonants, and lengthen her vowels, and adopt the more standard phrases of the Riva di Pignoli slang. For Miriam this was a privilege, for after losing ten children, but not the capacity to laugh, the Vedova came closest of anyone on the island to the sort of understanding Miriam yearned for. For the Vedova, however, it was something more. The young girl's presence was like the opening of an extra window in her small, dark hovel; when she came for her lessons the Vedova noticed spoons in the straw and knots in the rafters she hadn't seen in twenty years.

A *pan duro*, therefore, would be excellent: brittle, teased with oil, slightly bubbly, slightly burnt. But if she was going to make a *pan duro*, why not make two? A little salt and flour, some olive oil, some herbs, where was the extra work in an extra portion? The Vedova knew Miriam wouldn't care if she made a second one — and more important, she knew Giuseppe Navo would be delighted.

The Vedova Stampanini and Giuseppe Navo were lovers — though they had never once, in fifty-seven years, made love. It had begun in the earliest days of the Vedova's marriage: one night, over a plate of sardines and a white-bean stew, the then young fisherman (who was eleven years the Vedova's junior) gave her a look across the table that caused her to pour so much coriander onto her plate, she had to run to the well and douse herself with water.

Giuseppe Navo soon became a regular guest at her dinner table; her husband and children would listen to his stories of the sea while she returned the heat of his glances with saffroned beef and gingered capons and hot-and-cold cinnamon jellies. It became common to make "one for Giuseppe Navo" whenever she made one of anything. A meal would scarcely be a meal without his well-heaped plate.

The practice continued throughout the Vedova's marriage, through all the many years of birthing and burying her many children. When he couldn't come to table a plate was always left, in the garden, by the cold press, for Giuseppe Navo. And when twenty-one years had gone by, and all the Vedova's children, and even the Vedova's husband, had died, a strange thing happened: Giuseppe Navo came to the Vedova's door one night flushed with desire for her, shot her the feverish look that had passed through more than two decades perfectly intact — and the Vedova handed him a crayfish pastry and a bowl of milk cabbage. And Giuseppe Navo was content. For after over eight thousand meals of searing looks met by spicy delights, neither the Vedova nor the fisherman wished to tamper with the recipe. For the next thirty-six years they continued to meet — and to eat — with the same thrill of secrecy that had given them so much pleasure when there was still someone there to keep secret from.

Which was why the Vedova smiled as she placed the salt, the flour, and the oil on the table that had borne the weight of all those glances, and paid extra attention as she measured out the herbs. Rosemary, oregano, basil, sage; all she lacked was a bit of thyme. The Vedova knew that neither Miriam nor Giuseppe Navo would notice if the *pan duro* lacked thyme, but why do a thing, she asked, and not do it well? So she put on her straw hat, took up an old straw basket, and set out toward the field of wild thyme that grew along the north rim of the island.

The bright June sun was hotter than she'd expected. It made her small, drawn body tighten up like a fist and her brain run loose like a stallion. She traveled up the Calle Alberi Grandi past Maria Luigi's hovel — past the Chiesa di Maria del Mare and the Ca' Torta — past the Rizzardellos' salt shed and the fields that backed Gianluca's and Albertino's vegetable garden — until she finally reached the field of wild thyme. It was richly abundant, a tribute to the new spring. But she'd gathered no more than a few bright sprigs of it when she noticed something strange near her feet. She thought she was imagining it, she thought the sun had affected her vision, but there, jutting up from the soil, were the blackened, withered fingers of a human hand.

Without pausing she turned, walked back to her hut, and carefully prepared a pair of gleaming *pan di casa*, with thin strips of onions, slender rivers of prosciutto, and bright, heaping handfuls of olives — green, green, green as a wild spring day.

❧

ALBERTINO WOULD HAVE LIKED to contribute more than just one morning and one afternoon a week to the construction of the *campanil*, but the startling bounty of the late-but-luscious spring seemed only to intensify with the increase of summer. Albertino could work from the first rays of dawn to the last glow of twilight and there would still be tender berries hidden in the soft growth and perfect pea pods left on the vine to languish. Yet hard as the labor was — much as it required delicate timing and absolute, unwavering attention — to Albertino it was as natural and joyful as lying in the evening at the edge of the lagoon and counting the stars in Orion.

Albertino loved harvesting. The joy of finally drawing the fruit from the earth. The sense that the soil was actually handing it up to you. He considered himself a vegetable midwife, birthing fine young cabbages, cradling infant cauliflower, guiding fresh-born radicchio heads into the waiting world.

Today Albertino was harvesting carrots, and carrots were complicated. If the soil was too sticky, the roots would fork. If there was too much sunlight, the crowns would turn green. Not to mention the dangers of slugs and snails, cutworms and wireworms, motley dwarf virus and violet root rot. Yet Albertino's carrots were sleek and hardy, with nice fat tops and finely tapered tips. He shook them as he slipped them from the soil, to remove any large clumps of dirt, and then separated them into two groups: those that were headed to next day's market, which were tossed gently into a grass-lined barrel, and those that were to be saved for winter, which were cropped of their foliage and placed between layers of sand in a shallow box. When the sun was at its hottest he crept over to the eggplant patch to have his lunch and rest. The curve of an eggplant could please Albertino for hours; he could lose himself completely in the specks of gold that broke through the blackened purple and the glossy surface that seemed so taut yet yielded to his touch. Today, however, the eggplants made him think of Ermenegilda. So he ate his lunch as quickly as he could and hurried back to work.

Toward midafternoon, as the sun gradually began to relinquish its insistent supremacy in the pale blue sky, he saw Gianluca approaching the carrot patch with an unusual vigor in his gait.

"*Ciao*, little brother."

"*Ciao*, Gianluca."

"I've brought you a pair of *coda di rospo*."

"Thanks."

"Gesmundo Barbon said to grill them with a little sage. They're too nice to fry."

Albertino was surprised at his brother's carefree manner; considering the heat and the amount of work there was to be done, it seemed slightly ludicrous to him.

"How's the work today?"

"Fine, Gianluca."

"And the carrots?"

"The carrots are fine." Albertino raised a soil-flecked specimen to demonstrate. "Would you like to try digging up a few to see for yourself?"

"If you'd like that. It's a blazing day. I'm sure you could use a rest."

Albertino paused midcarrot and looked up. "Are you all right?"

"I'm much better than all right," said Gianluca. "I'm well, Albertino. Really, truly well."

"Because if you're serious," said Albertino, "we could trade jobs for a while. I'll work the market, you work the fields."

Gianluca thought about this for a moment and then shook his head. "It wouldn't work."

"Why not?"

"You're too good-natured. When I'm not there you give away as much as you sell. It's bad for business."

"You're lying, Gianluca. That's not why you won't do it."

Gianluca drew his forearm up to his mouth and smoothed the silky hairs along his wrist with his lower lip; then a strange new light broke over his face. "She might come to market while I'm gone. I can't take the chance. Even now I might be missing her."

Where Miriam's presence on Riva di Pignoli had turned Piero's spirituality into carnality, it had had precisely the opposite effect on Gianluca. From the first morning she had appeared at the market — her flowing hair tied back in one of Maria Luigi's silk ribbons, her clear, luminous eyes dancing briskly between the romano and the radishes — he'd felt a rising in his breast that was even greater than the usual rising at his groin. Not that he was oblivious of Miriam's body: Gianluca would have to have been dead not to notice the white throat as it curved beneath the loosened collar of her gown or the slightly tapered belly as she stood, suspended, before the strawberries. But where such charms had before been sufficient in themselves, they now seemed a stunning veil over something deeper — some quality beneath her flesh that produced an entirely new response beneath his.

"May I help you?" he'd asked, burning behind a pyramid of onions.

"Yes," said Miriam. "I would like to buy some fruit."

"Why?" he'd said, closing his eyes.

"Excuse me?"

"Why?" he'd repeated, opening them again to bask in her light. "You will only make them feel embarrassed to be seen beside the sweet *grape* of your eyes . . . the ripe *prugne* of your cheeks . . . the rich *ciliegie* of your lips . . ."

Miriam had turned and left without so much as an *albicocca* — so Gianluca had begun to court her. This was not an ordinary experience for him; he was used merely to swaggering up to whomever he happened to desire, leaning his strong, solid body against the frame of her door or the gate of her salting shed, and letting the honey pour down from his smiling eyes. Miriam, however, was different: from the moment he saw her, he could see no one else. So he had dedicated himself to a gentle, persistent wooing of her soul. Each morning, before he went to market, he would stand outside Maria Luigi's hovel and sing ballads in which Miriam chased the summer rains or stirred the winter breezes to blow. Each evening he would lay at Maria Luigi's door a pumpkin or a cantaloupe into which he'd carved, with a stickpin, a finely detailed scene of Miriam conversing with angels or dancing in a field of flowing wheat. The day now possessed two tasks and two tasks alone: selling the vegetables and winning Miriam.

"I've never seen you like this," said Albertino as he watched his brother's eyes gloss over. "It's very bizarre."

"It's love, little brother. Reverent and holy love."

"Reverent and holy?"

"I swear to you. I feel as if God has come and clapped me on the back and said, 'Take heart, Gianluca. It's not too late.' "

"Too late for what?"

"For God, for Christ's sake! For heaven and angels and holy ghosts. The whole ordeal."

Albertino looked hard into his brother's eyes and saw the shimmer of halos and the white tips of furiously flapping wings.

"What about *Il Bastòn*?"

"He's not quite convinced. But I'm working on him. He hasn't tried to thwart me so far."

"And what about Piero Po?"

Gianluca fingered *Il Bastòn* lightly and spat upon the

ground. "Piero Po is an imitation insect with an obsession for what he lacks. I can't take such a bug seriously, and I'm sure she feels the same way."

"That doesn't sound very Christian, Gianluca."

"Some attitudes take longer to develop than others, little brother."

"Tell that to *Il Bastòn*," said Albertino, pointing to his brother's as-ever distended crotch.

*"Basta!"* said Gianluca, giving a playful swipe to Albertino's head. "I said I'm working on it."

He tossed the pair of *coda di rospo* upon the basket of carrots; then he sauntered back toward market, whistling pale inversions of the liturgical chants he remembered from childhood mass. Albertino returned to the carrots, finishing out the rows he'd marked for that day before giving a look to what needed to be done tomorrow. Then he crossed the fields to the western docks and began rowing back to his island.

As he moved across the water, his body felt wonderfully well used from the day's long labor. Gianluca's visit stood out as a patch of oddity in an otherwise average afternoon, but Albertino chose to concentrate on the nice pair of *coda di rospo* he'd brought him for supper and the small basket of apricots he'd gathered himself to enjoy afterward. When he reached his island he docked swiftly, eager to hurry home and light the fire to cook the fish. But before he got even halfway to his room he completely lost his appetite.

It was not the first time it had happened. Two weeks earlier he'd found a basket of butchered artichokes by the east wall when he'd gone to empty his night bucket. Three weeks before that he'd come home to a slimy carpet of pulverized plums. But what he saw now made both those incidents seem like child's play.

Every last head of the radicchio patch had been brutally hacked off. Then one by one they'd been placed in a long, leafy arrow pointing accusingly toward the graveyard.

# Chapter 7

A T THE HEIGHT of summer, Riva di Pignoli
reeked of *cefalo, ombrina, ghiozzo, corvina, sogliole, rombo, acchiuge, sardina,* and *seppie.* Even
with the continued bounty of the miraculous
spring, the market energy slowed to a lazy peacock's strut
and an invisible shroud of lethargy fell over the island.
Fausto Moretti could be found, almost daily, standing
perfectly motionless on the Calle Alberi Grandi. The three
Marias tied poultices of lavender about their heads and
stayed in bed until after sundown. Valentina took to standing with her head in the well, unaware that with Piarina's
new state of mind she was placing herself in grave danger.

Yet despite the heat and the bitter stench, work on the
*campanil* kept on at a steady pace. There were no masons

on Riva di Pignoli — no carpenters, no cutters, no mortar makers, no blacksmiths — but the villagers applied themselves to the various tasks of construction with a determined zeal. By mid-August the walls had risen above Piero's head and scaffolding had to be built to continue higher. A light wooden frame was erected outside the walls to complement the heavier one, which had been raised to support the bells, inside. Siora Bertinelli converted her second pastry oven into a kiln, and she and Siora Scabbri took turns roasting limestone into quicklime and placing it in a pit lined with clay to make a mortar that would, it was hoped, resist both time and beetles.

As the labor became more complicated and the structure began to take on a real shape, Piero asked the villagers to decide upon one afternoon a week in which they might all work together as a team; it no longer seemed likely they'd finish by the Naming of the Virgin, but he was hoping for at least the Feast of Michaelmas. Thursday afternoons were selected — and it was then that Miriam's subtle authority came into play. She seemed to hang on the fringe — sprinkling lime on the ropes, sharpening the axes with a whetstone — but in truth she was the central force that got the *campanil* built. When the workers began to tire from climbing the frame with the heavy stones strapped to their backs, she devised a special pulley that could accommodate the multiknotted ropes and cut their labor in half. When the workers began to tire from heaving down on the weighted ropes, she casually observed that one of the empty *baccala* barrels would make an excellent windlass, and their work was halved again. She showed Siora Bertinelli how to tilt the mortar bucket so the mortar would not dry in the sun. She showed Paolo Guarnieri how to bend his knees when he lifted the lumber so his back would not go out. And her mere presence inspired Gianluca and Piero to scramble and hammer and hoist until the sweat poured off their bodies.

"How does it look?" Gianluca would shout as he placed the heaviest of stones at the highest of heights.

*"Atenziòn!"* Piero would cry as he waved his arms to give instructions from the center of the field.

When Gianluca began his elaborate schemes to win Miriam, Piero had no choice but to try to court her as well. But where Gianluca's previous attempts at wooing had involved at least a grin and a shifting of the hips, Piero's had been virtually nonexistent. So now that he felt this strange fever in the backs of his legs and this spinning in his solar plexus, the only thing he could think to do was to follow her. Out through the waist-high grass that led to Siora Scabbri's henhouse, up the Calle Alberi Grandi to watch the evening sunset, he traveled behind her like a rat on an invisible leash. And gradually, as his footsteps behind her footsteps became a faint, familiar echo, he found himself having visions again.

They started with snakes. Tiny, slithery snakes with opalescent eyes, which gradually gave way to bloated, seething, monstrous snakes whose faceted skins reflected Piero's face in endless distortion. They emerged, in coiling numbers, from the base of the stump where he slept. They spread across the grassy expanse that footed the Chiesa di Maria del Mare. They wove themselves, like a chain of poison, into an intricate, ever-writhing ring — out of the center of which rose Miriam.

Miriam, in a cloud of light. Miriam, daubed with honey, dusted with dry snow, naked, breasts shining, arms floating, eyes glistening.

Piero watched as his own naked form moved in toward

the light. But then he stopped. For before he could reach her, the serpentine circle began to transform itself into a twisting band of horned beasts, hell-sprites covered with tangled hair, three-faced demons with flaming bellies — and dragons. Piero had not seen such dragons since his days at Boccasante: malevolent creatures with steam-soaked wings, great polished devils with lightning-and-onyx eyes. They bristled in a foul *balotondo*, they mocked the pale simplicity of his and Miriam's nakedness. And they kept him from her. With their scabbed, scaly backs they raised a fortress between their bodies, with their hot, ashen breath they cast a screen between their souls.

Piero could not help but think of the swollen, blackened body; it circled in his mind the way the beasts and dragons circled in his dream. He could not shake the memory of its bloated limbs, the smell of its putrifying flesh. And though he did not know how his visions were related to the corpse, he knew that there would be no easy path to Miriam.

❦

WITH THE EXCEPTION of Orsina's self-interested donation of stone for the central monument, the Torta women contributed virtually nothing to the construction of the town center.

"I will not stand in the mud with a bunch of filthy peasants to help build some holy sand castle," announced Orsina when Piero came to ask for her and her daughters' help.

But even if Orsina and the three Marias had agreed to raise the uneven structure with their own eight hands,

there was a crisis within the walls of the Ca' Torta that
would have kept them from the task.

"It's awful!" cried Maria Prima. "It's like sleeping with
your head inside a pig oven."

"It's digusting!" cried Maria Seconda. "My room smells
like a cesspool!"

"You've got to stop her, Mama!" cried Maria Terza.
"She's going to burn the whole house down!"

For as if the smell of fish at the height of summer were
not punishment enough, Ermenegilda had begun burning
produce in her bedroom. Each day she would venture out
of the Ca' Torta at mezzogiorno with a great straw basket
slung over her shoulder and would not return until it
was filled to the brim with turnips and mulberries and
dandelions and fennel and watercress and maudlinwort
and daisies. Anything that grew — anything that blos-
somed, either wild to the wind or carefully cultivated —
was fair game to Ermenegilda.

When she got it home she would dump it all in the
center of a small pyre she'd built at the foot of her bed and
then set it on fire with one of the long wooden matches
she'd had Romilda Rosetta steal from the kitchen. The
flames were never very great, but the smell was horrific —
it stank like the end of the world, like a hog in heat, like
a river of dung peppered over with last week's vomit. To
Ermenegilda, however, it was merely the faded perfume
of a love affair come undone.

For the first few weeks, Orsina tried to ignore it. Her
room was farthest away from Ermenegilda's, and to be
honest, she was somewhat frightened of her youngest
daughter. But now that the fumes were in danger of as-
phyxiating the entire household and the complaints of the
three Marias were becoming intolerable, she soaked a linen

handkerchief in some marigold and rose water and went to have a talk with her.

"Ermenegil-da!" she called from outside the door. "Your mother wants to speak with you."

Inside the room, Ermenegilda sat transfixed before the flames that rose from the stinking pyre. The air was dense and heavy with smoke; Ermenegilda used it as a fog to buffer sensation. Her heart pined for Piarina, and it was better to feel nothing than to feel what she felt for Albertino, better to shroud herself in vapors and blot out her pain as firmly as he had blotted out his memory. What wrong had she done beyond laying her heart at his feet? What crime had she committed besides hopelessly, helplessly loving him?

Orsina rapped loudly upon the door and called her name again; Ermenegilda did not answer, so she pushed the door open and entered the fuming chamber.

"Ermenegilda!" cried Orsina. "I order you to stop roasting vegetables this instant!"

"It's mostly herbs and flowers, Mama," said Ermenegilda. "And a few moldy pears. He won't let me near the vegetables anymore."

Ermenegilda kept her eyes on the pyre as Orsina made a thin veil of the handkerchief she carried and came to sit on the edge of the bed just opposite where Ermenegilda sat.

"Ermenegilda," said Orsina in a lighter voice. "Come to your senses. You can't go on like this."

"Why not?"

"Because you're tormenting yourself. Such a smell should only come from the inside of hell."

"I like the smell," said Ermenegilda.

"You like the smell."

"It makes me feel safe."

Orsina recoiled. "But it's the middle of August! The entire house is roasting!"

"It's good for the skin, Mama. You won't have to go to Padova for your fancy treatments."

"I'm warning you, Ermenegilda. Your sisters are going to kill you if you don't stop this."

"They don't understand," said Ermenegilda. "They have no idea what I'm feeling."

"Well, I understand," said Orsina. "Believe me, Ermenegilda, I understand." Fanning the smoke with one hand and holding the handkerchief tight to her face with the other, Orsina moved even closer to Ermenegilda, until she sat beside her before the pyre. "When I was seventeen, your father used to come to my house on horseback and fling wild violets in through the window. People called him 'the Cavaliere of the Wild Violets.' I thought my family was rich? Well, instead of asking for a dowry your father offered my parents three times their year's earnings for my hand in marriage. The first time we made love your father held back his own pleasure until he had satisfied mine no less than fourteen times. And do you know what? I still wish I'd listened to my own mama's advice to take the boat to Corsica and hide out at my uncle Ergolello's until your father had found some other girl to make his slippery blood boil. I know you're infatuated with this vegetable farmer. And who knows, perhaps he has some hidden charm I just don't see. We all know about his brother. But he's not good enough for you, Ermenegilda. He's short, he's poor, and — most of all — he's from Riva di Pignoli!"

"But Mama," said Ermenegilda, *"we're* from Riva di Pignoli!"

Orsina bolted to her feet. "*Not* by choice! Now I demand you stop loving him this instant!"

Ermenegilda turned her gaze, for the first time, from the dancing plumes of smoke to her mother's bedeviled eyes. "But I don't love him, Mama," she said. "I hate him."

"It's the same thing, Ermenegilda! You'll soon find out it's the very same thing!"

Ermenegilda rose slowly and spoke in a quiet, even tone. "I hate him like a slug you scoop up out of the mud and you squeeze inside your fist until you can't tell what's the slug and what's the mud. I hate him like those little gnats that come up out of the canal in October and bite you on the insides of your thighs. I hate him like bream pasties, and canker sores, and the bloody time of the month. I hate him, Mama. I hate him. I hate him."

"Fine!" shouted Orsina. "Hate him! Just stop creating this infernal stench inside your bedroom!"

"*No.*"

"Ermenegilda — if you don't do what I tell you, I'm going to lock you in here, with no meals, until you wish you'd never seen a scorched turnip!"

Ermenegilda planted her feet into the carpet and expanded to her fullest, most imperious stature. "And if you do, I'll climb out the window and light a stench you can't even imagine in every room of this godforsaken hell manor!"

The two of them stood nose to nose, a pair of primitive warriors armed only with the fire inside their breasts. Orsina's fire, however, had been raging for a long, long time and could not hold its own against the youthful blaze that burned inside Ermenegilda. So she threw her handkerchief in the young girl's face and marched violently out of the room.

Ermenegilda caught the handkerchief as it slapped across her smoke-stained cheek and twisted it into a tight ball. For a moment she thought of Piarina — of the sweet child's smile and the loving caresses that might have soothed her in her suffering. But Ermenegilda's pride was too great to allow her to go to her, and beg her forgiveness, and lay down in sorrow beside her. She could only spin around quickly and fling the handkerchief into the flames. She could only try to come up with a better way to wreak revenge on Albertino.

AT THAT MOMENT, precisely three leagues into the water off the southwest shore of the island, Piarina and Valentina were on their way to the neighboring island of Terra del Pozzo di Luna; Gesmundo Barbon had lent them a small fishing vessel because Valentina had heard, through a series of rumors, that Terra del Pozzo di Luna was in short supply of soap. Valentina was rowing — one oar clutched tightly in her fist, the other strapped securely to her stubby forearm, her large, strong body pitched forward with the exertion of her efforts. Piarina sat behind her on the short plank at the aft of the little rig, surrounded in all directions by an immaculate sea of soap. Soda soap and lime soap, fish-oil and goat-fat soap, it rose about her in stack after stack of dullish gray- and faded bone-colored cakes. Valentina was in an unusually cheerful mood, singing gaily and talking to the seagulls that swooped and cawed above them. Piarina was silent — the bob of the boat against the wake of the waves luring her closer and closer to danger.

"I'm telling you, Piarina girl, they're going to buy the

whole lot. Every last cake of it. Why Cunizza Scabbri said they haven't washed out a pair of hose since the Celebration of San Marco!"

Piarina closed her eyes; the boat was rolling with greater and greater intensity, and the smell of lye was too much for her. In a dreamy haze she saw herself reach for one of the cakes and bring it cracking down upon Valentina's skull, over and over again, until the woman lay sprawled upon the endless stacks, their washed-out surfaces spattered with specks of blood.

"If they buy it all," continued Valentina, "we could set up a regular trade. A full shipment, every other month. We could eat like we did when your overgrown friend used to come round!"

Piarina pulled her knees up and clasped her hands over her eyes, but the mention of Ermenegilda sent her teetering over the edge again. She could feel the weight of the oar in her hands as she yanked it from Valentina's grip, gave it a broad, sweeping swing, and sent the woman flying into the water.

"Who knows?" Valentina chattered. "Maybe we'll move there for good! I'd give anything to leave that foul little hut and have a real home, with a pair of windows and a washtub!"

Piarina couldn't stand it. Trapped inside the tiny boat, between the sea of soap and the sound of her mother's voice, she simply could not escape her mind's dark plans for murder. She considered throwing the cakes into the lagoon, she considered drilling a hole in the hull so they both might drown, but nothing could save her from her terrifying thoughts of destruction. So while Valentina was babbling on about all the dresses she would buy with all the money she would make from all the soap that she would sell, Piarina stepped up onto the highest stack and jumped overboard.

Valentina felt the boat shift and heard the sudden splash, but she could not believe her eyes when she saw Piarina swimming briskly back to shore.

"Piarina, you idiot! You come back here! How do you expect me to handle all this soap myself? You come back here, I tell you!"

But Piarina kept swimming. She knew that when Valentina eventually returned home — having sold no more than a handful of her smelly cakes of soap — she was sure to give her an especially vigorous thrashing. But at least for the next few hours the young girl's troubled mind could think of butterflies, and light rain, and a host of other pleasures that were lately stained over with murder.

OUT OF PIERO'S hideous vision of dragons and snakes emerged the tender seeds of a fantastic notion. With work on the *campanil* nearing completion, it would soon be time to begin construction of the *campo*; it suddenly came to him to create an elaborate mosaic, depicting the struggle between good and evil, based largely upon the images from his dream. He felt certain that through Fra Danilo he could obtain the materials he needed. Three times each week he rowed out to Boccasante, unfolding his plan to visitor after visitor after visitor. Finally, as August slackened into September and the white summer sun eased down to an autumn glow, he received a message that Fra Danilo had found what he was looking for and that he should hasten to the monastery immediately.

"Sior del Ponte is one of the richest men in Venezia," said Fra Danilo as he introduced the wealthy merchant to Piero just a few hours later. "His palazzo on the Canal Grande is the new pride of the city."

"It is a beautiful creation," said Eduardo del Ponte, a rather stocky gentleman dressed in heavy brocades. "I would be honored if Your Grace should care to visit it someday." Eduardo del Ponte referred to everyone within the walls of Boccasante as "Your Grace"; fawned over by most of Venetian society because of his tremendous wealth, he gained a keen sense of pleasure in humbling himself before the quiet circle of monks, a circle in which, by friendly association, he seemed to include Piero. "The entire *salone* is in mosaic: the walls, the floors, the ceiling. It creates a most satisfying effect. Something like the Basilica di San Marco, if Your Grace will permit me to make such a comparison."

"It sounds magnificent," said Piero. And with great tact and the utmost precision, he launched into a description of his own "little project." He tried not to make it sound too ambitious, and he tried not to make it seem as if he were asking for anything, but before he had even outlined the dragons, Sior del Ponte offered to donate twenty-seven crates of Murano glass tiles left over from the elaborate depiction of the del Ponte family being received into heaven, which graced the upper *salone* of the Palazzo del Ponte. His only requirement was that Piero promise to prominently display the del Ponte family crest within the final design.

"Everyone in Venezia, I'm sorry to say, is out to imitate my *salone*," explained Eduardo del Ponte. "If Your Grace does not take the tiles, I will simply have to dump them into the Canal Grande. Besides, it will be amusing to imagine a tiny splash of del Ponte color at the outskirts of the lagoon."

All that Piero need do, he continued, was send someone to Venezia to pick them up—and it was this that Piero was contemplating as he circled the Chiesa di Maria del Mare on the following morning. He could not go himself; with Gianluca's obvious intentions toward Miriam, he would not allow himself to be away from Riva di Pignoli for more than three hours at any given time, and a trip to Venezia would take at least half a day, or even more. He could ask Giuseppe Navo or Gesmundo Barbon to get them on their rounds of the lagoon, but he feared that with their rough manners either one of the old fishermen might say something to spoil the entire affair. It had to be someone innocuous. Someone honest, and trustworthy, and easy to deal with. And the name he'd awakened with on his lips was Albertino.

Piero had no question as to where he might find him: since the violation of the radicchio heads, Albertino had begun sleeping in the vegetable garden. With the exception of the time he contributed to the construction of the *campanil*, he could always be found between the onions and the celery, beside the turnips and the broccoli, beneath the almonds and the pears. Now Piero found him upon a ladder, picking apples from one of the five trees the Tonolo brothers considered their orchard. To his consternation, however, Albertino was not alone. Stretched out against the trunk of the tree was Gianluca. And Piero felt certain, from the light in his gaze and the dreamy fluidity of his gestures, that the subject he was discussing was Miriam.

"*Buongiorno*, good brothers," said Piero, eager to interrupt the conversation before he could hear what was being said.

Albertino and Gianluca both turned to him with a start, Gianluca's expression twisting from rapture to malice.

"*Buongiorno*, good brother," he said with sarcasm. "Lost the way to heaven?"

"I've come to speak with Albertino," said Piero.

"With Albertino!" said Gianluca. "Little brother! I never knew you entertained such holy guests!"

"Be quiet, Gianluca," said Albertino. "Piero's done nothing to harm you."

"*In nomine Domini Dei*," said Gianluca, rising into an elaborate bow. "Say what you like. I won't stop you."

"I'd like to speak to Albertino in private," said Piero. "If you don't mind."

"If I don't mind!" said Gianluca. "If I don't mind being kicked out of my own fields! And what if I do mind, my little builder monk? What if I mind very, very much?"

"Oh, stop it, Gianluca," said Albertino. "You're late for market anyway. Get going."

"Do you hear that, good brother? *My* good brother suggests I go to market and leave you two alone. Well, as I always follow *my* good brother's instructions, I won't argue." He bowed again, quite deeply, to both Piero and Albertino; then, slipping into his usual, arrogant posture, he sauntered off.

As soon as he was gone Piero began to describe his encounter with Eduardo del Ponte and the offer of twenty-seven crates of mosaic tile with which they would be able to ornament the *campo*.

"But why me?" asked Albertino as he climbed down the ladder.

"I need someone I can depend upon," said Piero. "Someone I can trust as I trust myself."

"Why not go yourself?"

"It's a question of propriety," said Piero. "Sior del Ponte thinks I'm a member of the order at Boccasante. It would seem undignified for me to go. It's terrifically important, Albertino. It would be a tremendous favor."

Albertino rested the basket of apples he had been carrying on the ladder and offered one to Piero; Piero declined, so Albertino took it himself.

"I don't know, Piero. As it is, I've been giving an awful lot of time to this project of yours. And it's been an exceptionally busy season for us. I just don't know if I can sacrifice a whole day to go into Venezia."

Piero saw the concern in Albertino's face as he looked out over the vegetable garden. "I'll look after the vegetables for you," he said. "I promise that nothing will happen to them."

Albertino slowly chewed his apple. "But twenty-seven crates? How can I possibly carry twenty-seven crates in my boat?"

"They aren't large crates," said Piero. "They aren't really crates at all. They're more like boxes, really. Boxes filled with tiny mosaic tiles."

Albertino stopped chewing. "Boxes?" he said.

"Boxes," said Piero.

"When would I have to go?"

"The day after tomorrow — the last day of summer. He'll be waiting at the Ponte di Rialto at midday."

Albertino thought hard before giving his answer. "All right," he said. "I'll go. Gianluca won't like it, but I'll go."

"*Grazie*, Albertino," said Piero. "*Grazie tantissimo.*"

Piero took a few moments to explain carefully to Albertino the particulars of his mission; then he thanked him again and began to make his way back to the Chiesa di Maria del Mare. His spirits were very high as he walked

through the low fields that backed the vegetable garden
and led, in a graduated curve, toward the Calle Alberi
Grandi. As he looked up, the sky seemed to shimmer in a
great mosaic of blue and gold and white. Just at the edge
of his sight, however, he noticed something quite peculiar:
high above the north rim — above the field of wild thyme
where he'd buried the swollen body — a black bird hovered
motionless in the faint wind. Piero blinked his eyes and
shook his head, but the bird remained hinged on the horizon, poised like a dark star over the island.

Perhaps the day after tomorrow wasn't soon enough.
Perhaps they should begin the *campo* while they were still
finishing the *campanil*. Piero could not help feeling, as he
stepped up onto the trodden path that led through the
clutch of pine trees, that there wasn't a moment to waste.

# Chapter 8

ON THE MORNING after the morning after Piero had come to see him, Albertino set out for the great city of the winged lion. He left at dawn, dressed in his best tunic and his cleanest pair of hose, a feeling of hopeful anticipation perched lightly in his breast. As he rowed out into the open waters of the lagoon, he tried to push all thoughts from his mind — the needs of the vegetables, his strife with Ermenegilda — and concentrate only on the cleansing impressions that widened in the white morning light. The soft streaks of cloud against an azure sky. The continual changing of the pale green water, its moment-to-moment transformation from shade to shade to shade to shade to shade. The expanding and contracting of a speck into a boat or a bird into a speck, the hushed illusion, as his movements became mechanical, that rather than him moving across the plane of these images, they were passing, at their own perfect pace, past his motionless form. In time he lost all sense of being separate from what surrounded him. It was he who was rising, and widening, and warming — he who was humming, like a mill wheel, on the surface of the day.

To Albertino there was nothing quite like the smell of the lagoon. Flavorful, expansive, slightly sour, it gave him the feeling that the waters were as rich and fertile as the soil that nourished his vegetables. He imagined himself a farmer of sea vegetables, submerged beneath the green-gold surface, at work with a shovel and hoe on the floor of the lagoon. He felt a pleasant awareness that beneath the water the islands were connected, that even while moving through liquid he was passing over land.

Albertino could have stayed in his boat forever. Yet as he moved past Burano and Mazzorbo, past Ponte di Schiavi and Borgomagnolo, past Puntalupa and Pescatorno and Terra del Pozzo di Luna, he began to feel the excitement of Venezia luring him to land. Past San Cortino, as the pale outline of the churches and palazzi grew more and more distinct, past Murano, and San Michele, until the energy of the throbbing metropolis washed over him like a sudden wave. Approaching the city from the north, he circled out around the eastern edge of the island — past the Quartiere di Santa Elena — past the vineyards and the orchards and the pastures that lay along the outskirts of the isle — past the Lido, and the Isola di San Giorgio — until at last he entered the basin of San Marco and the open arms of her piazza. Albertino was always dazzled by the city's entrance. The twin columns that rose like the frame for a puppet-show masquerade. The Palazzo dei Dogi, which seemed like one of Siora Bertinelli's Christmas pastries: so light, so airy, you doubted it had substance until you felt its flaky sweetness on your tongue. And San Marco itself, that splendid apparition that at any moment might shrug its shoulders and slip, laughing, beneath the foam. That was the trick of Venezia's beauty to Albertino: he was never entirely certain she would not suddenly disappear.

Aware that the hour of his appointment was nearing, Albertino continued on toward the Punta della Dogana and into the curving passage of the Canal Grande. As he headed up the waterway, past the countless glittering buildings, he heard the *campanili* strike the chorus of *mezzogiorno*: heavy bells responding to light bells, the myriad overlapping voices brightly sounding out the hour. His appointment with Sior del Ponte was for *mezzogiorno* — at the western foot of the Ponte di Rialto a red boat with a yellow flag displaying the del Ponte crest in black would be waiting for him. Sior del Ponte had given Piero a handkerchief with the del Ponte crest stamped into its silk: an enormous bird with the head of a dog devouring a tiny rabbit. Albertino now spread that handkerchief upon the floor of his boat, convinced that such an odd insignia would be easy to spot, and before the bells had returned with the dry clang of the half hour he came upon the great pontoon bridge and the bright red, flat-bottomed rig piled high with wooden boxes that awaited him. Two men stood on the dock beside the rig: a rough-looking fellow with a ruddy complexion, a nose that made a sharp turn toward the Lido, and a gaily striped scarf tied loosely around his throat; and a robust gentleman with a well-formed stomach who, despite the heat, was swathed in a velvet robe and whom Albertino took to be Sior del Ponte.

"How good of Your Grace to come within the hour," called the latter as Albertino tucked his boat into an adjacent slip. "We were fully prepared to wait until sunset."

Albertino was surprised at the gentleman's respectful, almost reverential tone; he spoke to him as if he were someone quite other than Albertino.

"I left just when I needed to," said Albertino. "It generally takes as long to get here as it takes."

"Your Grace speaks like a man of God," said Sior del Ponte.

Albertino was convinced that the man was confused, but nevertheless he adjusted his hose and climbed up onto the dock beside him. There was so much color spinning past his eyes, so much maddening, dizzying movement, he could barely concentrate on what he had come for. The canal was swarming with boats either loaded down with cargo or carrying passengers from one bank to the other. People flocked across the bridge in gaily patterned silks and pointed-toed boots, their laughter following behind them on the tails of their pet monkeys. It was hard for Albertino to believe that such a festival went on each day while he went quietly about his business on Riva di Pignoli. It seemed too fantastic — too animated — not to wear itself out.

Albertino asked if the boxes on the rig were the ones he was to transport back to Riva di Pignoli; Sior del Ponte confirmed that they were. But when he stepped down onto the floor of the rig in order to begin loading them into his own boat, the wealthy merchant insisted that "His Grace" leave the labor to "the servant." The rough-looking fellow

seemed to resent this: Albertino gave off not even a whiff
of the Holy Spirit to his well-trained, workaday senses.
But one by one he transferred the crates from the rig to
Albertino's boat, while Albertino answered Sior del
Ponte's questions in his direct, inimitable way.

"Your Grace has a remarkable manner," said the merchant after several minutes of conversation. "Such a cryptic, almost Oriental way of expressing himself. I would be
so pleased if he would come and dine at my palazzo this
evening."

Albertino looked up at Sior del Ponte, not comprehend-
ing. "But it's only midday," he said.

"All the better," said Sior del Ponte. "Venezia is the
most ravishing city in the world. You'll have all day to
explore her charms."

"But what about the tiles?"

"I'll have my man take Your Grace's boat to my palazzo.
It can remain there until you're ready to leave."

"But how will I get there without my boat?"

"I'll send someone to fetch you — say half-past seven?"

Albertino stared down at his *barca da pesca*, now laden
with the boxes of tile. He could not think of any other
impediments, but he still felt reluctant to accept Sior del
Ponte's offer; it was a long time to stay away from the
vegetables, and he would most likely be required to speak
with Sior del Ponte's wife, if not his son or his daughter
as well. On the other hand, a free afternoon in Venezia
sounded delightful — and he was sure that there would
be either meat or fish with dinner — so he shrugged his
shoulders and agreed to the plan.

"*Splendido!*" said Sior del Ponte. "It shall be an honor!"

Albertino was now certain that Sior del Ponte was mis-
taken as to his true identity; surely such fuss could not all

be for him. But as the decision was made, and Albertino could not see that there was anything else to be said about it, he confirmed the hour for half-past seven and then hurried off into the teeming midday throng.

※

BACK ON RIVA DI PIGNOLI, Miriam was preparing for a very different sort of assignation. For she'd promised herself that if Gianluca's and Piero's attentions did not cease by the end of summer, she would have no choice but to stop them herself. Now, on the final day of that languid, liquid season, she gathered her resolve and set out across the island to find them.

Piero, who was faithfully fulfilling his own promise to keep watch over the vegetables, was propped against a fig tree, reading a copy of Marcus Aurelius and trying to shake away the insistent image of the bloated, blackened corpse, when she quietly entered Albertino's and Gianluca's gardens. So engrossed was he in what he was reading, he did not notice her until she bade him *"Bon dì"* — and when she did it so stunned him, he forgot to stand up.

"I hope I'm not disturbing you," she said. "Beppe Guancio told me I would find you here."

Piero was too startled by her presence to speak. So Miriam took a step closer and continued.

"What are you reading?"

"Marcus Aurelius."

"Is it interesting?"

"It's sublime."

"I'll have to borrow it, then," she said. "If you'll allow me."

Seeing that he was not going to rise, Miriam lifted her skirts and joined Piero on the ground; Piero felt grateful to have the book in his hands to keep him from reaching out to touch her.

"Do you read?" he asked.

"A little," said Miriam.

"How extraordinary. Here on Riva di Pignoli most people can't even recognize their own names."

"There was a man in my village, a very old man named Obediah Bocconcini, who offered to teach anyone who wished to learn how to read. Most of the village came at first, but only a few stayed on. I stayed for five years. When Obediah died he gave me this." Miriam drew a small, pearl-encrusted volume from a pocket in her skirt: the second of the objects contained in her mysterious bundle. "I carry it with me wherever I go."

"*The Praise and Glory of the Virgin*," read Piero, opening the ornate cover to reveal the elaborately scripted title page. "It's very beautiful."

"It's the only thing I read," said Miriam. "Besides the scriptures, of course."

Piero was distracted, as Miriam spoke, by the almost imperceptible swelling of her lips. They seemed to expand with her devotion in a way that he found devastatingly erotic; it took every bit of his will to keep from kissing her.

"May we walk?" she asked, slipping the book back into the folds of her gown and turning to face him.

"Yes," said Piero. "Of course."

She drew herself up. Piero followed. Then together they walked in silence along the ordered lines of Albertino's handiwork. The sun was penetrating; it burned away the last of the dew and the carefulness between them.

"Why do you follow me?" she asked.

"I can't help myself," said Piero. "Which disturbs me terribly. I've always been able to place mind before body. That's the way to God."

"Sometimes the body has a mind of its own."

"Perhaps," said Piero. "But how can I allow myself to listen to it when my spirit is so diseased?"

"Why do you say that?"

"I reach for good, but my grasp falls short. I fail again and again."

"But the tower you're building — your concern for the people — "

"You don't see what lies beneath those things. Vanity . . . desire . . . fear."

"You're too hard on yourself," she said. "You're a good man, Piero."

He closed his eyes at the sound of it: the first time she said his name. Yet despite the pleasure it gave him, he could not keep his thoughts from circling back to the body. It was like a stone upon his conscience, a weight that pressed down as if he'd murdered the poor fellow himself.

"Is it good," he said, "to conceal a death?"

"It's neither good nor evil. You cannot conceal a death from God."

"What about a body?" Piero hesitated for a moment. "One of the brothers from the monastery where I was raised found a dead body washed ashore. He buried it quickly, without telling anyone. Except me, that is."

"If he gave it a proper burial, he did all he could."

"A proper burial?"

"The appropriate sacraments, a placement in hallowed ground. I'm sure your friend knew what to do."

Piero thought of his hasty shuffling of the carcass beneath the sandy soil at the edge of the island, and he suddenly knew why he had not been able to shake off the shadow of its death.

"Of course," he whispered.

"Are you all right?" asked Miriam.

Piero looked up. "Yes," he said. "I'm fine."

They walked a few paces farther; then Miriam paused and looked out toward the water. "I have to ask you something," she said.

"Anything," said Piero.

She turned to face him. "Stop following me," she said.

"I've tried to stop."

"Try harder. We can speak again if you like. But I need my shadow to be my own."

Piero flushed at the thought that they might meet again, speak again — possibly even touch. "All right," he said. "I promise."

They continued on until they reached the low wall that bordered the edge of the garden.

"It's time for me to return to work," said Miriam.

"I understand."

"Thank you for the walk. I hope we can speak again soon."

She held his eyes for a long moment — that thrilling, tempting farewell — and then turned to walk away through the sun-drenched fields. Piero watched as her golden form grew brighter and brighter, until, like a spark before a flame, she was absorbed into the light. Then he went back to the broccoli patch to see what Marcus Aurelius had to say on the subject of a proper burial.

[ornament]

FOR THE FIRST hour or so, Albertino buried himself in the spinning, chattering mob that thronged the *merceria*. He followed up and down bridges, moved left and right over smooth cobbled *calles*, as an endless line of shopkeepers urged him to buy everything from satin hose to sanitary tubing to salt fish and cheese. The streets remained crowded even though it was lunchtime; Albertino stopped to have a roasted sausage, a hunk of bread, and a glass of exceptionally good ale at a small stall that was wedged between a fertilizer concession and a shop that sold hand-painted scarves.

After lunch he doubled back across the Ponte di Rialto and headed toward Campo San Polo, home of the city's best fruit and vegetable market, which Albertino always liked to examine to see if he could learn anything. Today the stalls seemed less overwhelming than usual because of the endless abundance of the Riva di Pignoli spring, but he still noted that eggplants had more brilliance when placed beside pale summer squash, and that carrots stacked horizontally created an impression of unusual elegance. For a while he sat in the grass near the stout stone *pozzo*, munching a handful of sorbs and medlars and enjoying the splintered music of the passing conversation. Then he shuffled back out into the streaming crowd and set about to do what had propelled him to accept Piero's offer in the first place: to find himself a new box.

As with everything else Albertino did, there was a perfect science to finding the right box. One dared not be impetuous. One dared not rush headlong into a purchase based upon the excitement of the moment or a quick rush of the senses. (That was how he'd ended up with that hideous monstrosity with the squat gnomes for feet and the sad little sacrificial lamb perched piously on top. He'd paid a whole summer's wages for that one, only to give it away to the Vedova Stampanini, who placed it in her garden to scare away the hedgehogs.) He began with a slow scanning of the city's central zone; the finest shops tended to be scattered along the eastern side of the Ponte di Rialto and out beyond San Marco. When he passed a window that held something of interest, he made a mental note of it. If he turned and retraced his steps in order to look at it again, he tied a piece of colored ribbon, which he'd purchased from a milliner, around his finger. No matter how much it attracted him, however, he would not enter the shop and ask to see it until he'd beribboned every last digit from pinky to thumb back to pinky again.

By three o'clock his fingers were rainbow strung. By five he'd managed to narrow the field to three particular boxes: a cask of brass with the story of Noah carved into the lid, a coffin of pewter etched over with flowering hieroglyphics, and a chest of rosewood with a group of sowers and a group of reapers painted lovingly on the front and back. He returned to each shop three times, each time asking the keeper to draw the treasured object from the curtained window and place it on a square of velvet on the shop counter. But even as he traveled back and forth on his methodical tour, he knew which one he would ultimately take. The reapers and sowers seemed to be rejoicing in the Riva di Pignoli spring; how could he refuse such a delightful reminder of what had so miraculously happened on his island?

When he'd bought the box and had it carefully wrapped, he found that there was still a good bit of time left before his appointment at the Ponte di Rialto — so he used the opportunity to wander off the main pathways and explore the coiling, twisting, mind-changing, labyrinthian side streets. A whole other facet of Venetian life disclosed itself to him as he followed down shoulder-width *calle* and under low, jutting *sotopòrteghi*. The clatter of children playing games in hidden courtyards. The curses of the boatmen, stripped to the waist and sweating at the *squeri*. The conversation of tunics and tights stretched taut over narrow canals. It was as if the great city wore a rough, peasant face beneath its glamorous public mask, which Albertino found all the more charming for its simplicity.

He reached the Ponte di Rialto with the seven o'clock bells and seated himself, near the leafy plane tree where the horses were tied, to watch the last of the light fade from the last-of-the-summer sky. It was gray-violet black when the half-hour chime struck; Albertino could barely make out the design of the del Ponte crest on the flag that rose from the slender gondola that was gliding toward him like a ghost upon the water.

A gondola!

On Riva di Pignoli one spoke of gondole the way the educated Venetian spoke of the coaches of Prague or the camels of Jerusalem. It was one thing to cross the canal, standing, with a pack of bored Veneziani, on a *traghèto*; it was another entirely to be guided down it like a doge in the cushioned splendor that awaited him now.

Albertino stepped down into the hull and placed his box and himself upon a satin pillow. The torches that were being lit along either bank cast a series of nervous reflections upon the water; Albertino was grateful for the open sky and the familiar stamp of the stars above him. As the boat made its rhythmic passage down the curving length of water, he abandoned himself to the shadowy impressions that moved in and out of his sight: doorways that opened on moonlit water risen up to flood what it entered upon; side canals leading like secret tunnels toward realms that vanished by day. To Albertino, the canal at night was both beautiful and ominous. He felt lost in the grips of a fabulous whim that might lead him almost anywhere.

They approached a great building streaming light from every window, set with blazing torches against the water. Albertino knew instantly that it was the Palazzo del Ponte and that — to his horror — there was a celebration going on. At least two dozen boats were lined up between the massive poles that stood at varying paces beside the central portcullis. From the second-floor windows he could see the candles of an enormous chandelier glow brightly and could hear horns and flutes and voices tumble out upon the cool evening air.

The gondolier took him not to the front gate, but to an entrance farther on that led to a small chamber, where he was instructed to change his clothes. He was met by a servant who gave him a crisp linen blouse and a pair of blue silk tights, a lavender tunic and a pair of soft black boots — all of which made him feel not so much elegant as simply not Albertino. The servant escorted him out into a lavish garden with billowing fruit trees and a great fountain, and then up a wide stone stairway to where the revelry awaited. Albertino felt as if he'd stepped into a ballad: ladies dressed in marbled silks stood languorously beside exquisite tapestries; peacocks wandered past strolling lute players; great goblets of wine were offered up like draughts of well water. But what dazzled him the most was the long, satin-draped table overflowing with a variety of foods that went beyond anything Albertino could ever have imagined: miniature fish pastries in the shapes of the figures of the Tarot deck; gilded meat tiles arranged in a bold mosaic; roasted capons, sliced venison, papered partridges, poached pike, glazed duck, grenadined geese, pit-charred quail, split lobster; beets in a green sauce, beans in a pink sauce, peas in a yellow sauce, leeks in a white sauce; custard and jelly and aspic and pudding and muffins and junket and fruit.

"I see Your Grace admires the table," came the voice of Sior del Ponte from just behind Albertino.

"I was expecting something simpler," said Albertino. "A lot simpler."

"I suppose I forgot to mention that we were having a few others to dinner. But it's common custom here: the Palazzo del Ponte has been host to members of every profession, and to citizens of no less than fourteen different countries. Your Grace does not by any chance possess a trace of foreign blood, does he?"

"I don't think so," said Albertino.

"Well, even if you were a marauding Hunsman, you'd be welcome at our dinner table. At the Palazzo del Ponte, tolerance is the byword."

Albertino was about to say that it would require at least a tolerant stomach to contain all the foods he saw before him, but he was interrupted by the sudden sounding of a great gong.

"Ah!" said Sior del Ponte. "Time to tear oneself away from gazing at these delights and take oneself in to taste them. Please follow the others into the next room. You'll find a place marked for you at the table."

Albertino joined the rest of the group as they oozed into an adjoining chamber that centered upon a magnificent table set for at least forty. As he made his way down the length of it, he was transfixed by the play of the candlelight upon the spun-glass bowls of fresh-cut flowers and the tiny platinum-and-ebony moors' heads clasping the names of each of the guests. As "Albertino" was the only word Albertino could-read, it was not difficult for him to find his place among the dozens of otherwise indecipherable scribblings; he eased out his chair in the hope that with so many people at the table he would not even be noticed. But just as his strangely swathed bottom made contact with the hard wood seat, his fantasy crumbled into a tiny heap of ashes before him. For there, on the seat directly across from him — strapped in satin and steeped in candle-light — sat none other than Ermenegilda Torta: guest of the tolerant del Ponte graces and Albertino's apparent dinner partner for the evening.

WHILE ALBERTINO had sat waiting at the Ponte di Rialto for the boat that would guide him, unknowingly, toward Ermenegilda, Gianluca stood bent over the empty fruit bins at the market, securing their muslin covers. It was early evening. The same light that Albertino had watched fade away over the Canal Grande was still softening in the Riva di Pignoli sky, and most of the market sellers had packed up their wares and gone home. The pastries were wrapped in cloth, the hacked torsos of goats and pigs slung over tired shoulders, the dresses folded, the eggs placed in straw, the fish toted off in barrels of ice or left to the grinning cats. Gianluca, however, had decided to wash down his stalls before closing up, so he was still there, alone, when Miriam came to find him.

He neither heard her footsteps nor saw her splendid figure as she softly approached him — he knew she was near only from the sudden pounding inside his chest. When she paused just a few paces behind where he crouched over the boxes, and actually addressed him, he felt that newly identified, weightless part of himself rise up with a cry to relinquish all ties to reality. Only the ludicrous distension of his tights drew him firmly back to earth.

"I'd like to thank you for the delicious gifts you've brought me," said Miriam. "I was embarrassed until now. But the melons are sweet. And the music is lovely. So — thank you."

Gianluca, like Piero, was so surprised that he could not speak. With a startling aggression he gave a sharp squeeze to his swollen member, draining it instantly of its vigor, and then stood to face his angel in the fading light.

"I was hoping we might walk together," she said. "It's a beautiful night."

Had Miriam's words been one shade less simple — less perfectly transparent and light emitting — Gianluca would have thought that she was mocking him. Her manner, however, was so direct that he could find no way to interpret it other than as it was presented. Still without speaking — without even bothering to finish covering the strawberry bins — he nodded and followed her out through the fields toward the western shore.

"How long have you worked the market?" asked Miriam.

"Fourteen years," said Gianluca.

"That's a long time."

"It doesn't seem it. It hardly seems any time at all."

"It must suit you."

"I like the noise. And the arguing. And I like the work. We've done well this year; the crops should bring us more than the last two summers put together. But it isn't the money that matters. It's the work."

" 'Wealth gotten by vanity shall be diminished; but he that gathereth by labor shall increase.' "

The formality of Miriam's words cut short the sudden, genial flow of Gianluca's. He felt too rough, too educated, to rise to the level of her righteousness.

"What is it?" she asked, sensing the change in his manner.

"You — aren't like the other women I've known."

"How do you mean?"

"When I'm near you — it's — hard to explain. You make me feel . . ."

"Yes?"

He paused. "Holy."

Miriam lowered her eyes, and they continued walking in silence. In time they reached the western docks, but Gianluca was so dazzled by Miriam's presence that he could not fathom how they had got there. Had they floated on a breeze? Had they disappeared within the flames of their exchange to rematerialize, halfway across the island, as the smoke cleared? He only knew that the sun was gone behind the horizon, that the sky was cracked with pink beneath the lowering darkness, that the golden hairs on Miriam's upper lip were traced with tiny pearls of perspiration.

"There's a part of you that craves what any man craves," said Miriam. "A dry bed. A plate of sardines in the evening. A woman. But there's another part — the part that stops when you're carrying a heavy load and listens for the sound of crickets, and finds it, and follows it. That part craves something else. That part is holy."

"You've watched me?"

"I've watched everyone, these past months. It's a small island. A difficult place, I think, to keep secrets."

"I don't have any secrets," said Gianluca. "Everyone here knows me for what I am."

"And what is that?"

Gianluca studied the planes of her face, washed of color now as the light escaped from the sky. "I've been with many, many women," he said. "I never gave it a thought until you arrived."

" 'There are sixty queens and eighty concubines, and maidens without number, My dove, my perfect one, is only one. . . .' "

Gianluca raised his hand and placed his fingertips against her cheek; for the first time, Miriam felt a trace of the same desire he felt for her.

"I must go," she said. "It's late."

"I was going to sing you a new ballad tonight. I've been working on it for over a fortnight."

Miriam realized then that she had been about to leave without saying what she'd come for. "I don't want any more ballads," she said. "And I don't need any more cantaloupes. We can meet again. But you must stop coming to see me every day."

"But what will I do when the song starts rising up in my throat?"

Miriam smiled. "Swallow."

Gianluca smiled, too. And though he wanted to protest, he gave in to Miriam's request. "All right," he said. "No more ballads."

"And no more cantaloupes."

"Not even a honey melon?"

"Not even a honey melon."

Gianluca shrugged and nodded, then escorted Miriam

back to Maria Luigi's hovel. They did not say much as
they walked, and they did not touch again. When they
reached Maria Luigi's door, Miriam whispered a soft
*"Bona notte"* and then crept to her darkened alcove to
prepare for bed.

No more cantaloupes. No more ballads. But the feel of
Gianluca's hand against her cheek would remain in her
mind for days and days to come.

FOR ERMENEGILDA, the evening was just beginning. From
the moment she looked across the table and saw Albertino,
trimmed in bright silks and satins like a wayward capon,
she knew her carefully laid out plan for revenge would
travel toward its ultimate end. There was no accident in
his suddenly appearing on the seat opposite her at the del
Ponte supper; Ermenegilda had been responsible for every
step that had guided him toward his fate.

Once a month Beppe Guancio came to the Ca'Torta to
get a fresh supply of candles for the Chiesa di Maria del
Mare. On his latest visit Ermenegilda informed him that
he could only have them if he helped her find a way
to ensnare Albertino. At first Beppe refused — but when
Ermenegilda threatened to have her father take back the
marble he had donated for the new village monument, he
gave in. The following day he came to her with the news
that Piero was looking for mosaic tiles for the *campo*, and
Ermenegilda sprang into action. She went to visit Eduardo
del Ponte, who was a client of her father's, and deftly
arranged his visit to Fra Danilo, his offer of tiles to Piero,
and the elaborate supper to which she would lure Al-

bertino. Getting Albertino to the supper was the most difficult part; Ermenegilda was depending on her sense that Piero would not wish to fetch the tiles himself. Her instincts proved correct — so on the night after he'd spoken with Sior del Ponte, when he was trying to decide whom to send in his place, she crept to his bedside and patiently repeated "Albertino" from midnight until dawn. Piero awoke with the name echoing in his head, and the rest went according to schedule.

Albertino knew none of this and so did not know what to make of Ermenegilda's presence before him. That she would be invited to dine at an elegant Venetian palazzo didn't surprise him. That she would appear, however, directly opposite him, at the only such dinner to which he'd ever been and most likely ever would be invited, seemed a joke too malicious for anyone he'd ever have considered to be an inhabitant of heaven. For the first three courses — the pastries, the pike, and the goose — he kept his eyes upon his plate in an effort to block out her presence. When the raspberry ice arrived he prayed that his torment was over, but it proved to be only an interval before the quail, the lobster, the partridge, the venison, and an assortment of purees Albertino could not identify. It became more and more difficult, amid the chatter and the music, to ignore the silent fire that burned across the aspic. But somewhere around the partridge he was aided by a rumpled, fluty voice that piped up to his right.

"Do not tell me. You're a painter of icons!"

"Excuse me?"

"Those are the hands of a painter of icons. I'm certain of it."

Albertino looked first at the startling face from which the startling voice had emanated: the incarnadine lips, the plucked eyebrows, and the hair that seemed to have been frightened by the abundance of courses. Then he looked down at his stubby, soil-stained fingers, which thrust gingerly at the succulent food upon his plate.

"No, no," he said. "I'm a vegetable farmer."

The woman let out a rich, gurgling laugh. "Of course!" she cried. "And I'm the Holy Virgin!"

Albertino kept his gaze upon the moist wedges of partridge that dangled between his thumb and forefinger. He was certain that this woman was not the Holy Virgin, but he was grateful nonetheless for the rousing manner in which she drew his attention away from Ermenegilda.

"I knew you were an artist. I'm always right. I could have been a witch, you know. My cousin is a painter of icons—or should I say 'was'? Poor Bertoldo. So much talent simply swept away like a few crumbs on the *terrazza*. They say it's some kind of awful sickness, you know. Half of Naples dead, bodies everywhere. But I don't believe nine-tenths of what I hear these days. The Neapolitans eat too much garlic. In that kind of heat you pass out for three days and they bury you before you wake up again. I only hope poor Bertoldo was actually dead. Imagine yourself a great artist, a man of excruciating sensitivity, waking up in a wooden box because you ate too much garlic. Between you and me, it's what he deserves for going to live with those animals. 'The light,' he says—or said. 'You cannot imagine the light.' Well, light is light and Naples is Naples, and now the poor fool has nothing to paint but the inside of a wooden box. If I were you, I'd keep my apostles in the Veneto. You agree with me, don't you? I just know you agree with me."

Albertino was fascinated by the way the woman's head bobbed above the thick strand of pearls wrapped tightly about her neck. He imagined that if he were to remove those pearls, the head would topple onto the floor — all the while continuing to talk about his hands, the light, the cousin in the box.

"I once met a Russian painter of icons," she said. "He was very, very handsome, but he refused to paint the crucifixion. Absolutely refused. Which seemed somewhat cowardly of him. Don't you agree?"

Albertino was on the verge of saying something, any-thing, when he became aware of an odd pressure against the inside of his ankle. As the woman continued talking — about Greek versus Roman statuary, about the inability of the eye to perceive the subtleties in a fresco without the aid of direct sunlight — he felt it move its way up to his knees, push in between his thighs, poke up under his tunic, and press quite firmly against his crotch. Once there it began moving back and forth in a rhythmic manner that rendered Albertino utterly speechless. It was all he could do to keep from moaning or from flinging up strips of dripping partridge to sizzle in the chandelier.

For the remainder of the meal Albertino remained trapped between the embroidered musings of the shock-haired matron and the maddening ministrations of Ermen-egilda's foot. By the time the mulberry custard was served he had forgotten the tortured cabbage leaves and the ru-ined artichokes — indeed, everything that had happened since their idyll in the graveyard — and could only think of where, and how, he might be with her again.

Ermenegilda had to fight back the feelings of arousal her footwork stirred inside her. She was not there for pleasure, and she resented the tingle of satisfaction the hardness beneath the sole of her stocking gave her. The feeling was so delicious, however, she decided it made no difference if it pleased her. So she downed her custard in a series of quick spoonings, reached across the flowers to take up Albertino's serving, and breathlessly excused herself from the table to accelerate the encounter. As she moved away from him, Albertino felt his modest organ fairly rip through his tights. Without even a nod to the shock-haired matron — who had advanced to theories concerning the overabundance of flies in the Adriatic in August — he rose from his seat and followed Ermenegilda out of the room.

She led him down through the gilded mansion to the shadowy gates where the boatmen waited. Then she whispered something into one of their ears, stepped down into his gondola, and spread out her skirts as she seated herself. Albertino followed, and the boat set off.

He hadn't the slightest idea where they were going. He was barely able to breathe. For as soon as the gondola began to wind its way down the canal, Ermenegilda placed her hand in the bowl of mulberry custard and lowered it into Albertino's tights. Albertino thought he would die from the sheer bliss of it — either convert into liquid and pour off into the lagoon or explode into fire and add a bead to one of the lesser constellations. Before the ecstasy could outrun itself, however, the boat stopped and Ermenegilda withdrew her hand. Albertino regained awareness of the stars, the smell of the torchlight burning, the sound of the water lapping against the stone shores of the fabricated island. When Ermenegilda climbed up out of the gondola he climbed out after her, his tunic smeared with mulberry juice, his tights stained and dripping with the clotted cream. He followed her as she moved through the enormous marble columns. He followed as she entered the piazza, a pawn trailing his queen across the ordered field of an Olympian chessboard. He followed as she approached the magnificent facade of the glorious basilica, until the great leaping horses and the kneeling saints and the majestic mosaic deities loomed like phantoms overhead. Then she lay back on the steps, tore down his demolished tights, and pulled him — custard-covered and gleaming in the moonlight — inside her.

For Albertino, it surpassed their first encounter as a comet does a campfire. The unexpectedness of seeing her, the subtle workings of her foot, the slow torture of the cream inside his tights — all led him to a state of desire from which he knew he could never again retreat. No more resistance. No more denials. Only Ermenegilda — thighs and knees and hair and arms and all.

And she — whose deft manipulations had drawn him back to her bosom — whose still aching heart had only that morning set to flame an entire patch of parsley and half a dozen rotten pears — who would have given anything to have him inside her again as late as June or even into early July — was carefully laying the trap that would ensnare him. For Ermenegilda's heart could stretch only so far without snapping. And Albertino had more than earned what she was about to do.

# $C$ *h a p t e r*
## 9

A S THE CAMPANÌL began to take its place among the zigs and zags of the Riva di Pignoli landscape, the roosters, pigs, and ducks discovered it cast an altogether different shadow in sunlight than by the light of the quisling moon. Had they been able to describe it, they would have called it a flatness versus a roundness, a smooth-honed edge versus a scalloped irregularity. For as the stones and the wood and the mortar rose up by day, Piarina, in all her longing, rose up by night. Each evening she left her bed at precisely the hour at which she'd set out upon her fateful circuit of flame; each morning Piero found her sitting upon the uppermost stone, her fragile countenance like that of a banished monarch: slack, eviscerated, waiting for some sign from the forces of heaven to indicate what to do next. She was generally covered with birds: they sat on her knees and her shoulders like a gaggle of gossips and perched in her wispy hair as if it were straw. Piero had to fetch the ladder to bring her down, and though he removed it immediately once he had done so, she always managed to find her way back to the top again each evening without it.

On recent mornings, when Piero placed Piarina upon the ground, she scampered off into the shadows as if she were afraid of what the rising light might reveal. Autumn had come to Riva di Pignoli. The fruit tree boughs sagged heavy to the ground or sprang back slender and empty. The triumphant greens lost their conquering vitality and began to make way for the ginger, rust, and blood that would succeed them. Even a spring-that-outdid-all-other-springs had to end sometime. The villagers only hoped they could preserve some of its richness to last throughout the winter.

The *campanil* rose like a stone vine of ivy creeping up the side of the church, until finally, around the first week in October, it was finished. The villagers smoothed out a slightly domed roof over the rough walls and placed a small iron cross at the top; the only thing left to do was hoist the bells. The brothers of Boccasante, at Fra Danilo's insistence, had donated three great bronze bells to the island. They were to have been used for a second *campanil* that was to have been built along the south wall of the monastery, but after having procured them from an order on Elba (which had closed the previous summer because of a scandal concerning the chief prelate and a neighboring flock of goats), the monks decided that a second *campanil* might seem prideful. So they offered them to Piero, who accepted them gratefully and had them delivered to the Chiesa di Maria del Mare before the brothers could change their minds.

Though the completion of the *campanil* constituted only a third of the projected work toward the construction of the new town center, the people of the island felt a celebration was in order. And as the excessive spring had led to an exceptionally abundant harvest, it was decided that the raising of the bells should coincide with an enormous *pranzo della vendemia*. The Feast Day of Flavio Ubaldo was chosen: on that afternoon, in the third week of October, the entire island would gather to watch the bells be lifted into place, to hear Piero's plans for the new *campo*, and to feast upon the best of the season's bounty before storing what was left away. Calendars were marked, and the villagers began to make plans for the festivities.

Only Piarina remained outside the busy web of preparation and anticipation. For her the magic season of plenty had meant the loss of Ermenegilda. For her the completion of the *campanil* meant she could rise no higher above the horror of her matricidal fantasies. There was nowhere to go but deeper inside. No place to find refuge but within the confines of a body that was growing thinner, and brighter, with each successive night's climb.

❦

FOR EVERY OUNCE that fell from Piarina's frame, a dozen were added to Ermenegilda's.

"More shrimp tarts," she declared when Romilda Rosetta came to clear away her breakfast tray. "And don't forget the cardamom jelly."

Romilda Rosetta was happy to comply. Since returning from her recent trip to Venezia, Ermenegilda had dismantled her stinking vegetable pyre and had adopted so sweet a tone (relatively speaking) that it seemed almost a pleasure to be at her beck and call; Romilda Rosetta felt that her suffering had turned a corner — that she had moved up from the fiery rings of Inferno to the more somber shadows of Purgatory. What she did not understand was that the cause of Ermenegilda's good cheer was the satisfaction she felt at having finally wrought revenge on Albertino.

On that fateful night, as they lay upon the steps of San Marco, the taut Venetian sky dropping graceful benediction on their spent and sweaty bodies, Ermenegilda had briskly moved her plan into action. After slipping out from under Albertino's sleeping body, she carefully removed his boots, his tights, his tunic, and his blouse until he lay naked as a plucked pea-fowl. Then she lowered her satin underskirt to the ground, tore it quickly into a series of slender ribbons, and began trussing up her inconsistent lover: she tied his left hand, on a leash, to the door of the great basilica; she drew his right arm across his chest and bound it tight to his body; she pulled his left ankle back and wrapped his shin to his thigh; she knotted half a dozen ribbons together and strung his right leg to the base of a nearby flagpole. Then she fashioned a bow around his limp little penis and left him to the pigeons.

Albertino, as he was wont to do, slept on. It was only toward dawn, when an elderly woman who came to sweep the *piazza* found him lying there and gently shook him by the shoulder, that he became aware of his situation.

"Is it some kind of penance, *amore?*" asked the woman.

Albertino swallowed. "In a manner of speaking."

She looked at him for a moment and then shrugged. "Seems a good way to catch cold," she said.

She began to walk off, giving a sweep to the stones with every few paces, when Albertino called her back.

"Do you think you could untie me?" he asked.

She turned and looked at him again. "If you like."

And with a terrific nonchalance she returned to where he lay and began to loosen his various bonds. When she had finished, and Albertino sat rubbing the dull cramp in his sore left calf, she pointed to the bow between his legs.

"I wouldn't call attention to it if I were you, *amore*," she said.

Albertino looked down at the sad little bow tied fast to his manhood, but even humiliation couldn't dampen his desire for Ermenegilda. She had finally broken though his defenses, and nothing she either said or did could ever turn him away from her again. While the old woman shuffled off across the piazza to begin her morning labor, Albertino lowered the heraldic banner that flew above the flagpole, wrapped himself up in its colorful folds, and hailed a passing dairy barge to take him back to the Palazzo del Ponte. When he got there, the servant who answered the door seemed not in the least surprised to find him barefoot and bedraggled, wearing only the Lion of San Marco; Albertino wondered what had become of the other guests of Sior del Ponte's parties. With little fuss the servant found Albertino's clothes (still hanging in the changing room), his box (on a shelf by a window in an antechamber of the dining salon), and his boat (tied to a blue-striped pole by an entrance to the garden down a side canal), and within an hour of waking naked on the steps of San Marco, Albertino was rowing back to Riva di Pignoli across the open waters of the lagoon.

When he arrived at the island he docked his boat and headed straight to the vegetables. Piero was pacing between the parsnips and the rutabaga as he quietly entered the north end of the garden.

"Albertino!" he cried when he saw him. "How did it go? Did you meet Sior del Ponte? Did you bring back the tiles?"

Albertino nodded. "They're in my boat," he said. "Twenty-seven boxes. I'll help you unload them later."

"That's wonderful!" cried Piero. "But where have you been? What took so long?"

"I don't have time to explain," said Albertino. "But perhaps you can tell me if you've seen Ermenegilda?"

"Ermenegilda? She's probably still sleeping. You know how the Tortas love to stay in bed."

Albertino considered explaining that at least on this particular morning, Ermenegilda had good reason to want to stay in bed. But instead he simply turned and walked away. As he crossed the fields, he passed Siora Scabbri cleaning out the seed bins for the hens.

"Have you seen Ermenegilda?" he asked.

"I'm afraid not, Albertino," she said. "Has she been at your vegetables again?"

But Albertino did not stop to reply. He did not know whether Ermenegilda was at home or if she had even returned to the island, but he could not control his need to see her. He strode past the still sleeping market stalls and crossed the open fields that backed the Chiesa di Maria del Mare until at last he arrived at the door of the Ca' Torta.

"I'd like to see Ermenegilda," he said to the servant who answered his knocking, a grizzled fellow who had been with the Tortas exactly two weeks and had already posted his notice.

"One moment," said the servant, who passed the message to Romilda Rosetta, who passed it to Ermenegilda, who laughed so hard that the swinging bed began to corkscrew.

The carved oak door was shut firmly in Albertino's face — but the following day, and the day after that, and every day since the morning after the evening of their passionate second encounter, Albertino rose as soon as the sun peeked over his east wall, took his tiny *barca da pesca* across to the shores of the main island, made the small trek through the wet fields to the door of the Ca' Torta, and promptly knocked on it again. He did not seem to notice when the servants changed; he simply cleared his throat and said in an even voice, "I'd like to see Ermenegilda."

It was this message that was once again delivered to Romilda Rosetta on the morning she went to replenish the empty tray with shrimp tarts some two weeks after the incident at San Marco. And when she returned to Ermenegilda with both tray and message, the great girl's response was no less mirthful than it had been at each previous morning's announcement.

"He'd like to see Ermenegilda!" she giggled, sliding down between the goose-down quilting and the satin sheets. "He'd like to see Ermenegilda!"

Romilda Rosetta watched as she lifted a steaming shrimp tart from the polished silver platter. But before putting it into her mouth, Ermenegilda paused. "Hold out your hand," she said.

Romilda Rosetta did as she was told — and with a red

fist Ermenegilda squeezed the savory tart into a tight clump, and a tricolored ooze of pastry, fish, and fat drizzled out into her hand.

"Give it to him," she said. "With love — from Ermenegilda."

Romilda Rosetta hurried from the room, and Ermenegilda reached for another shrimp tart. But the smell of the hot pastry suddenly made her feel sick. So she threw the tray across the room, buried her head beneath the pillows, and tried to keep her laughter from giving way to the wail that was forming inside her gut.

❊

PIERO ONLY HOPED that his haste in burying the swollen body could be corrected by a more intentional second effort. He'd found little in Marcus Aurelius to guide him — nor Cicero nor Livy nor Dante nor Aristotle nor Ovid. There was much mention of death, and a surprising number of dead bodies, but nothing indisputable on the subject of "a proper burial." So he decided to treat it as he would have treated any ordinary citizen of Riva di Pignoli: by taking it to the cemetery, giving it a small formal service, and leaving the rest to God. He waited until the new moon, when even the cats had a hard time telling one passing villager from the next, and then went to the north rim of the island, where he set about to dig up the body.

He had not ventured out to the field of wild thyme since just after the spring had come. Yet even on a moonless night, in the heart of an encroaching autumn, he could tell when he'd reached it by the delicate sweetness that laced the air. He dug for over an hour, careful as he reached the body not to nick or disfigure it with the sharp mouth of his shovel, and as he removed the final layers of soil the most horrifying smell rose up. Piero could barely keep from retching, and it was only after he'd torn the left sleeve off his tunic and had tied it securely over his nose and mouth that he could allow himself to climb down into the grave to loosen the stinking fellow from the earth. Without a moon he had nothing to go by but torchlight, and in the wildly flickering shadows he often could not tell what he was grabbing. The body seemed unfathomably heavy; he tried and he tried, but he could not make it budge. Then, suddenly, it wrenched free — and he found to his surprise that it was both lighter and more malleable than when he'd first come upon it some six months earlier. It gave in his arms, was stiff in places and like jellied mush in others. And when he finally pulled it from the ill-fashioned plot and laid it on the cold, damp ground, he found that it was covered from head to toe with snails. For the next hour — taking periodic intervals to walk a good distance away, slip off the sleeve, and take in deep draughts of the fresh night air — he sat snapping their hard shells off its face, its chest, its legs, and its back and out of the tangled mass of its slimy hair. Then he filled up the gaping hole and dragged the sad, reeking mess to his waiting boat.

It was an agonizing trip across the small stretch of water. Piero had no explanation to offer as to why he was moving a partially decomposed body from one shore to the other; if some insomniac islander had chanced to come upon him, he would have been as frightened by the look on Piero's face as by the creature lying fetid at his feet. When he reached the shores of the cemetery island, he proceeded with caution past Albertino's room — though had he tossed the body over the east wall, to land on his blankets beside him, Albertino would have just rolled over and continued dreaming of Ermenegilda.

He managed to drag the body through the rusted-open gate, past the still flowering rose bushes, and over to the south wall and a patch of unused earth that sat waiting between Sineraldo Saccardi and Apollonia Ambrosiana Barbon. As quickly as he could (and by now he was quite exhausted), he dug another plot and lowered the body in; then he softly recited a brief Latin mass, scattered a handful of pignoli over the corpse, and covered it back over with earth.

When he returned to the main island and his broad stump near the Chiesa di Maria del Mare, he gazed up to the top of the *campanil* to see if Piarina was there. The night was so dark he could barely tell; he could just make out her ragged form as a patch of blackness blocking out the October stars. He felt a peacefulness at having reburied the body, which he wished he could communicate to her; he somehow felt that if she knew what he had done, it would ease her troubled mind. But Piarina was too deep inside her trance to receive anything he might have shared with her, so he curled himself up beneath a blanket and slipped off into sleep.

MIRIAM'S SOLACE CAME from the solitude of her home-made altar. She knelt before it when she rose in the morning, when she returned in the evening from her chores in the henhouse, and just before she lay down at night to sleep. As the weeks went by, however, it became harder and harder to kneel: even with the strip of satin beneath her knees, her growing belly demanded a more relaxed position. So, like Ermenegilda in her splendor before her loom, Miriam took to propping herself up on a series of large pillows, leaving one hand free to hold *The Praise and Glory of the Virgin*, the other to comfort the restless child inside her.

"Easy," she said to it now as it bucked beneath her fingers. "If we're patient — if we're quiet — it'll come."

Ever since the baby had begun, Miriam could see a thin veil of light around things, a kind of luminous skin that made the objects themselves seem ephemeral. It began with the altar: the statue of the Virgin suddenly lost its hardness and became fluid; the bolts of linen started to glow; the straw at her feet began to pulse with an inner fire. It lasted only an instant, but for the span of that instant her longing dissolved — so Miriam found herself longing for the return of the glow. At first it came only when she knelt before her altar, but then she began to experience it throughout the day. She would be gathering the eggs and one would suddenly begin to vibrate in her hand — it would cease to be an egg, would become a ball of fire, an expression of pure energy — and by the time she'd laid it inside her basket, her entire morning was transformed. Sometimes it happened with the water jug, or the pine trees, or the Vedova Stampanini's face: like a loosened mask, the features would slip away until all that remained was radiance.

And always, at the moment of the glow, she would feel a keen awareness of the child. Expanding like a sea sponge placed in well water. Absorbing warmth, and life, from the inside of her womb. And since the glow was so lovely, and since she was afraid that when the child moved out of her and into the world it would end, Miriam waited as long as she could to tell the people of Riva di Pignoli that she was pregnant. Because somehow the thought of telling them made the birth, and the loss of the shimmer, seem that much closer. She waited until her loose white gown could no longer camouflage the thickening of her waistline. She waited until her place in the hearts of the villagers was so secure, they would never be able to set her on a raft and send her out into the lagoon to give birth to her baby alone.

"*Non preoccuparti,*" she said, giving a stroke to her belly and then reaching up to the cutting table to pull herself to a standing position. "Perhaps we'll get a glimpse of it later."

She placed *The Praise and Glory of the Virgin* on a crate near the entrance to the alcove, then reached for the dark blue mantle Maria Luigi had made her for the coming winter. She could wait no longer, she thought. No matter that the villagers might be shocked, that the veil of light might blacken into shadows and come no more. The time had come to share her secret with the people of Riva di Pignoli. And as she walked out into the morning light, she felt nothing so much as a tremendous sense of relief.

ON THE MORNING of the *pranzo della vendemia*, Piero rose as usual to find Piarina sitting quietly atop the *campanil*. When he fetched the ladder, however, and climbed up to bring her down, Piarina wouldn't budge.

"It's almost dawn, Piarina," he said to her. "You'd better get home before your mother wakes up."

Piarina blinked twice and brushed a pigeon off her left

knee. "A lark's wing," she said. "A piece of wet parchment."

Piero, like everyone else on Riva di Pignoli, knew that Piarina spoke only when she was summoning up a cure. So as he felt particularly well that morning, and as he did not wish to force her to move against her will, he simply climbed back down the ladder and left her there.

There was much to do to get ready. Piero wanted it to be a simple affair; he did not want this celebration to eclipse the fact that there was still a tremendous amount of work ahead. But the people of Riva di Pignoli were so flushed with the bounty of their extraordinary spring and summer, they gave it a bit more zest than Piero had intended. Maria Luigi brought eight lace cloths to cover the tables. The villagers brought their own bowls and plates, but the Vedova Scarpa supplied two silver pitchers for wine (which she had not used since her husband, Luigi, mysteriously rowed off into the lagoon some twenty-six years earlier), and Orsina, thought she refused to attend, sent several dozen pewter goblets to pour it into. Giuseppe Navo and Gesmundo Barbon provided the fish, which the Vedova Stampanini and Siora Bertinelli prepared; there would be *brodetto di merluzzo, baccala, seppie,* cauliflower, turnips, and a series of *dolci* made from every kind of fruit Gianluca and Albertino could deliver. Silvano Rizzardello offered to play his lute, and Cherubino Lunardi promised to bring his reed pipe.

By late morning the field was abuzz and an atmosphere of boisterous good cheer had ascended. Paolo Guarnieri and Brunetto Fucci spent close to an hour placing the tables at even distances across the grassy field. When Armida Barbon arrived, however, she insisted they be placed lengthwise from east to west in order to guarantee good fortune for the *pranzo*. For much of the time the villagers bustled back and forth as if they were not quite certain what to do with themselves. But when Beppe Guancio arrived in a cloud of nutmeg and coriander, carrying the cauldron of steaming soup from the Vedova Stampanini's hearth, the milling ceased and the celebration began.

"What have you come up with this time?" asked Fausto Moretti, always eager to taste the Vedova's culinary magic.

"Just an old cod broth," said the Vedova. "Don't get your hopes up."

"She calls it an old cod broth," muttered Giuseppe Navo, "but she makes it taste like sweet-sea nectar!"

As the soup was ladled out into the variously shaped vessels, the villagers began to seat themselves at the tables. There were no assigned places, and when seats were taken they were rarely held for long; someone was always rising to refill his plate or to share a sprightly story with another table.

"Bindaccio Ferrelli claims he met a Venetian last week who saw a horse for the first time," said Siora Scabbri.

"What did he say?"

"He didn't say anything. But before he got on, he raised his handkerchief to test which way the wind was blowing!"

The energy grew more expansive as the meal went on. Armando Guarnieri went from table to table demonstrating his impression of the doge being attacked by a fleet of Barbary pirates. Maria Patrizia Lunardi got an attack of hiccups that lasted for over an hour. The Rizzardello twins hollowed out the *pan di casa*, placed one loaf each upon their heads, and began running, in opposite directions, around the base of the Chiesa di Maria del Mare.

Everyone took note of Piarina — it would have been

difficult to ignore her as she hovered silently over the supper from her post atop the *campanil*. There was little Piarina could do, however, that could surprise the people of Riva di Pignoli. Ever since she had begun curing their San Barnaba fever or drying up their aguey eyes, she'd sat sweetly outside the circle of their speculation. For the most part they now assumed that she had been set atop the tower as a part of the harvest celebration. The Vedova Scarpa whispered that Piero had chosen her especially to be the first to ring the bells. It was only when Valentina appeared, red-faced and ranting at the edge of the field, that they realized something unusual was taking place.

"*Cinque*, Piarina!" she shouted as she raised her right arm high into the air. "That's how long I'm going to give you to get your skinny little rump off the top of that tower and down here on the ground. *Uno. Do. Tre. Quàtro. Cinque!*"

Everyone looked up to see how Piarina would respond, but she merely sat there — wide-eyed, loose-limbed, lost inside a distant reality.

"Don't you ignore me, girl!" cried Valentina as she moved closer to the crowd. "I said get down here! And I don't give a pounded crayfish tail who hears me say it!"

Piarina remained motionless; the villagers remained rapt. And then, in her faint, otherworldly voice, she cried:

"A heron's claw . . . a gram of angelica . . ."

Valentina marched straight to the base of the tower. "Don't you start talking birds and black spices to me! I know your tricks, and I don't need no home remedy. I said get down here!"

But Piarina remained where she was, and Valentina had no choice but to back down. Without even casting a glance at the fascinated observers of her wrath, she gave a sharp kick to the tower and then stormed her way back to her hovel.

Valentina's wild display became the talk of the supper. The people of Riva di Pignoli had had more than a few suspicions as to what went on between her and Piarina, but they had never seen it brought so dramatically to light. They wondered whether Piarina planned to stay at the top of the tower forever; they wondered what her words were meant to cure.

"Seems to me she's awfully clever to get where Valentina can't reach her," said Armida Barbon to Siora Scabbri as they helped replenish the pitchers of wine.

"A body can sit atop a tower only so long," said Siora Scabbri. "Even Piarina'll have to come down sooner or later."

"Wonder what the cure's for," said Giuseppe Navo to Ugolino Ramponi as they stood urinating behind a pine tree fifty paces from the supper.

"Maybe she's come up with a curse to make Valentina's other hand fall off," said Ugolino Ramponi.

The conversation gradually wound its way back to a more casual array of topics. Maria Patrizia Lunardi and Miriam helped clear away the plates, scraping the uneaten food scraps into a bucket for the pigs and then wiping them down with a muslin rag and returning them to the tables for the *dolci*. While the Vedova Stampanini served heaping portions of gooseberry tart and peach-pear-strawberry pudding, Siora Guarnieri recited a poem she'd written:

> *When the grape descends*
> *And the summer ends*

*And the fruit trees grin*
*And the days grow thin*
*And the leaves turn gold*
*And the air turns cold —*
*Harvest, harvest, harvest, harvest, harvest.*

Just as the meal was ending, Ermenegilda and the three
Marias appeared from behind the sloping herb patch that
lined the north wall of the Chiesa di Maria del Mare. They
walked in a straight line between the tower and the tables,
neither slowing their pace nor in any way acknowledging
the festivities. But though Ermenegilda, in her fixedness,
did not see Piarina, and Piarina, in her dazzlement, did
not see Ermenegilda, it took Gianluca, Giuseppe Navo,
and Silvano Rizzardello to hold down Albertino. Long
after the Torta girls had passed, he was still wrestling with
them to let him follow after Ermenegilda.

Of all people, Gianluca understood his brother's dis-
tress. For if Albertino had to bear the momentary apparition of the object of his deepest desire, Gianluca had to
sit, and eat, and endeavor to retain his sanity, as the object
of his stood a falcon's cry away throughout the entire
afternoon. Gianluca's feelings for Miriam had only become
more complicated since she'd begun talking with him; the
exchanges they shared increased his understanding of
God, but the nearness of her body still inflamed him.
And though they were now on more intimate terms than
Gianluca had ever expected, the meaning of their relation-
ship was confused by the fact that she was every bit as
intimate with Piero. On a Monday she might appear at
the Vedova Stampanini's hovel and walk with Gianluca to
market. On a Wednesday she might bring Piero a dozen
fresh eggs on her way home from the henhouse. Gianluca

fought against his innate sensuality in an effort to feel holy. Piero grasped at his ingrained religiosity in the hopes of not feeling his desire. And neither one of them considered that, but for the flip of a florin, their situations were essentially the same.

It was therefore somewhat ironic when the impassioned monk and the illuminated satyr joined forces for the raising of the bells. Piero would have liked to be able to raise them himself, but as they were far too heavy he agreed to let Gianluca help him. Late in the afternoon they climbed the ladder and lowered themselves into the belfry; once there, they attached the hoisting ropes to the pulleys, and while Paolo Guarnieri, Beppe Guancio, and Cherubino Lunardi heaved down on the ropes, they hoisted up the bells and fastened them carefully in place. Despite their animosity they worked together as a team, a pair of interlocking wheels in the simple machinery that would ring their island to life.

When the last bell was lifted into place, and Piero and Gianluca appeared at the window of the belfry, the crowd below burst out in a rousing cheer.

"May they ring in another spring like the one we had this year!" cried Armando Guarnieri.

"May they only ring out the hours," cried Siora Scabbri. "And spare us the noise of anybody's death!"

The prayers and benedictions rippled through the crowd; there were wishes for fat cows and flaky pie crusts and golden afternoons to lie on the docks and daydream. To Gianluca and Piero, however, they were only a mass of voices playing a playful *contratempo* to the sweet soundlessness of Miriam's beauty.

"What do *you* wish for, Miriam?" asked the Vedova

Scarpa. "From the looks on their faces, it seems as if they've raised them just for you!"

"Tell us, Miriam," called Gianluca.

"What do you wish them to bring us?" cried Piero.

Miriam closed her eyes and tried to resist giving way to the glow. She could feel it pressing in at the edges of her being — she knew that with the slightest encouragement she might relinquish all form and cast herself into a sea of pulsing light. Yet she couldn't help feeling that at that moment it would have been an act of cowardice. The village was offering her the chance to share her secret with them, and even the radiance was not enough to keep her silent.

"A baby," she said in an even voice. "I wish them to ring in the birth of a healthy baby."

"What a lovely thought!" said Siora Bertinelli. "That's just what Riva di Pignoli needs!"

"I wish I'd had a bell to ring each of mine in," said the Vedova Stampanini, "and a bell to ring each one out."

"The trouble is," said Maria Luigi, "no one's having babies these days. I've got five *strasordenari* christening gowns at home, and I can't even give them away!"

Miriam raised her hand to her belly and whispered good-bye to the light. "I'll take one, Maria Luigi," she said. "I'm going to have a baby this winter."

If in that moment winter had come, as miraculously as the previous spring had come — bringing frost, and chill, and a spreading, dulling darkness — it could not have frozen the crowd at the *pranzo della vendemia* any more completely than Miriam's words. So startled, so silenced, was the entire gathering, they did not even notice when Piarina slipped down off the edge of the tower, crawled into the belfry behind Gianluca and Piero, and reached for the thick, twisted cords that hung from the bells. They only noticed when the birds took flight as the thundering peals sang out across the island.

Ringing Birth! and Death! and Freedom!

Ringing Father! Son! and Holy Ghost!

Ringing Spring is gone! The leaves have fallen! and *Finalmente*, Riva di Pignoli is here!

# *C h a p t e r*
# 10

THE ANNOUNCEMENT Miriam made at the *pranzo della vendemia* had a profound effect on the people of Riva di Pignoli. Siora Guarnieri covered her eyes when Miriam passed by her at the market. Cherubino Lunardi stopped buying Siora Scabbri's eggs. Ugolino Ramponi crept up to Maria Luigi's hovel one foggy midnight and tacked a dead partridge to the door. Most of the villagers, however, seemed to take it less as a judgment of Miriam than as a simple proof that nothing was as it seemed — that angels without wings were not really angels at all.

The only thing that managed to take the villagers' minds off the subject of Miriam's baby was the need, now that the *campanil* was finished and the sonorous bells were in place, to begin the work of laying the foundation for the *campo*. Over the next few days the field was razed and the earth beneath it beaten flat; a wooden frame was erected, and a thick layer of rubble was laid down; a mixture of powdered brick, lime chalk, and linseed oil was spread evenly over the rubble, scored and crosshatched so that it could receive a second layer into which the bits of colored glass would be set.

When Piero finally opened the twenty-seven boxes of tile that Albertino had brought back from Venezia, he felt like an Arabian sultan before a store of looted gems. They were not so much tiles as they were cubes, or fragments; they shimmered in the sunlight with a thousand glittering winks. When he thrust his hands down into them, however, they cut him like tiny knives—which sent a flicker of pain to his heart and made him think of Miriam. For close to a fortnight Piero had holed himself up in Beppe Guancio's hovel, amid the smell of cod and the sound of dripping fat, trying to translate his smoldering vision of Miriam and the dragons into two-dimensional form. After studying the elaborate tilework at both San Marco and Torcello, he realized that it was easier to create a harmony of geometric patterns than successfully to depict the human form; he was nevertheless convinced that with attention to gradation of color and the balance of light and shade, he could come up with an image that would be as satisfying to the soul as to the eye. When the design was complete he divided it into a hundred equal sections, enlarged each section to its actual dimensions, and then divided each enlargement a hundred times again, carefully indicating, in the end, where each and every tile should be placed.

The people of Riva di Pignoli were as fascinated by

Piero's diagrams as they were meticulous about adhering to them. Since few of the villagers could read, Piero marked the squares with tiny dots of wine and blood and strawberry juice, of indigo and crushed pansies, of mustard seed, of cabbage pulp, of mud and dung and pitch. As the diagram for each day's work revealed only a small portion of the overall design, the project soon became a guessing game: someone could always be found peering over the shoulder of whoever was working to announce the discovery of a snout, a claw, or a wing. The *campo*-in-progress became a gathering place; the villagers set up chairs on the unfilled spaces and waited to see what the workers would lay down next. The Vedova Stampanini brought her broad beans to snap. Maria Luigi brought her sewing. Siora Bertinelli set up a stand by Piero's stump and began selling capon pastries and cod-liver crisps.

And every so often, when no one was looking, Piarina would slip down into the belfry and ring the bells. She had not left her perch upon the tower since the morning of the *pranzo della vendemia*, despite the repeated threats and the ever-louder shouts of Valentina. Each morning Piero would climb up to leave her a plate of salt herring and a cup of dandelion tea, twice a day she would call out her cryptic cures, but mostly she either sat stone still or rang the bells. She rang them in no particular pattern and for no particular length of time. The people never knew when their work or their meals or their slumber would suddenly be interrupted by the round, ringing peals of Piarina's impulse. Beppe Guancio became convinced that an evil demon had taken over her soul; he began strewing bones and rubbish around the base of the church in an effort to protect it from her influence.

About ten days into the laying of the tiles, as the eastern and southern edges of the design were beginning to piece to life, Piero looked up to find Miriam standing beside him. He had not seen her since the *pranzo della vendemia*, but as he looked at her now he could not imagine that only a few weeks earlier he had failed to see that she was pregnant. It shone from her like the faint scent of milkwood or the heat of a summer night. It whispered from the strands of her fire-bright hair and sang from the tightened fullness of her rounded belly.

"I need to speak with you," she said.

Piero tried to hide the obvious passion she aroused; it seemed unfair that while bearing another man's child she should be so beautiful.

"What do you wish to say?"

"I can't tell you here."

"Where, then?"

"Wherever we can speak in private."

For a moment Piero actually imagined that she was going to tell him the child was his — that in a sleeping trance he had come to her, and lain with her, and left himself inside her. But Piero knew no trance could have been so deep that upon the touch of her skin he would not have awakened. He knew it was only a fantasy. He knew the child was Gianluca's.

"Perhaps we could use the *chiesa*," she suggested. "What I have to say is as well said there as anywhere."

They moved across the field and entered the little chapel. After the bright sunlight it offered them a shadowy intimacy: the altar was covered, the candles were half-burned, the walls smelled damp from the fog still trapped between their stones. A breeze that entered behind them shuffled a few dry leaves in at their feet, where they were likely to remain until they'd resolved themselves down into a faint winter dust.

Miriam moved down the aisle and stood before the altar. The piece of white cloth was in place, and someone had strewn a few pinecones along its surface. As she looked at the image of scattered dark against light, she thought about the reaction of the villagers to her announcement that she was going to have a baby. For herself she did not mind the fall from grace; it was easier to be considered human than to be thought of as an angel. But for her child, who had no place in the community — who might be thrust from the island as the bastard of a *straniera* — she was concerned. So she waited until the talk had died down and then came to see Piero.

"We haven't spoken since the *pranzo*," she said, reaching out to pick up one of the pinecones. "I imagine you must be upset about what I said."

"Not upset. Confused would be a better word."

"I don't blame you. A stranger comes to your village, makes herself a part of the life of that village. And then you find she's not what you thought she was."

"I haven't made any judgments, Miriam. It's just — confusing."

"Then I should explain it as clearly as I can," she said, turning now to face him. "I'm going to have a child. I'm going to have it on Riva di Pignoli. I want it to be accepted as a member of the community."

"If that's what you wish, I'm sure it will happen."

"I need to be certain," she said. "I'm a stranger here. If anything should happen to me, I need to know my baby will be taken care of."

"The people will treat your baby like any other child of Riva di Pignoli. I assure you."

Miriam looked down at the pinecone in her hand. Each segment held a tender, pale *pignole*. "What about you?" she asked.

"What do you mean?"

"How will you feel toward my child?"

Piero flushed at the question. "What does that matter?"

"It matters to me," she said. "A child needs a father."

"The entire village will be its father," he said, flustered. "Every one of us will be its father."

Miriam paused for a moment, looking down at the straw-covered stones at Piero's feet. When she looked up again, her eyes were filled with a new radiance.

"I want you to be my child's father," she said. "You — and Gianluca."

"Me — and Gianluca!"

"I want my child to learn everything," said Miriam. "To read and write. To plant and fish. If it's a girl, I want her to learn sewing and astronomy and architecture. If it's a boy, I want him to write poetry and chop down trees. No one can teach all those things by himself. But together you and Gianluca can offer my child the most extraordinary education in the lagoon. Say you'll do it, Piero. Say you'll be my baby's father with Gianluca."

Piero did not know how to respond to Miriam's words. He could have imagined almost anything, and he never would have come up with what she was suggesting to him now.

"What does Gianluca say about this?"

"I haven't spoken to him yet. But I'm certain he'll understand what I mean. I'm certain you both will."

Piero was astonished at Miriam's offer. He was certain that the child was Gianluca's, and he could not fathom why she would ask him to share its fathering. Yet he could not help but think that it would offer him a chance to remain close to her, and that it might even help to lead him back to the piety he'd strayed from since Miriam had first arrived upon the island.

"It's a big decision," he said. "You'll have to let me think about it."

"Of course," said Miriam. "The baby won't be here for several months yet."

Piero nodded, and they left the chapel; then he quietly returned to the laying of the tiles while she went back to her various chores in the henhouse. That evening, however, when he prepared himself for sleep, he found that he could no longer bear his place beneath the stars beside the Chiesa di Maria del Mare. So he returned to Beppe Guancio's hovel and asked if he could once more make his bed upon the thin pile of straw that lay in a mound in the corner.

For a scholar, or a sculptor, an exposed tree stump was a fine place to slumber. But for an expectant father, it simply wouldn't do.

❧

UNLIKE PIERO, Albertino was content to face the damp November nights without a roof over his head. Lately, however, he found his bed to be unbearably lonely. He cursed the times he'd forbade Ermenegilda to enter his room and lay beneath his blankets; perhaps if he'd let her, a trace of her odor would still be trapped between the chestnut and the azure or wound around the emerald, the rust, and the gold. His only solace was the knowledge, each evening, that when morning finally came he could go to her door and wait for her to reject him again.

One night he decided he could not wait until morning. He kicked down his blankets, threw on his clothes, and made his way across the water and over the fields to the gates of the Ca' Torta. In the generous glow of the three-quarter moon, the great house rose up like a temple; as Albertino moved toward it, he felt as if he were being drawn by some elaborate ancient spell.

When he reached the door, he looked up to Ermenegilda's window. He imagined her deep in a comforting slumber, eating sliced beef with horseradish sauce and a soup made of pulverized almonds. He heard the rustling of the satin coverlet he imagined lay beneath her, and the faint whisper of his name as she wished him to her side. And though he knew the difference between what he imagined and what was real — and that any attempt to be with her might well be met by his execution — he could not resist his impulse to climb to her window and find his way into her dreams.

He continued looking up, the cold, predawn mist wetting his cheeks and throat and seeping into his light wool tunic. From his vantage point beneath the first-floor *terrazza*, it seemed an easy enough maneuver; Enrico Torta had built his jewel box to dazzle and had given little thought to protecting it from intruders. First he stood upon one of the marble pigeons that flanked the columns that flanked the doorway; from there he stepped upon the moor's-head knocker and hoisted himself to the ledge above the doorway by clasping the small bas-relief of the Virgin and Child that jutted out just beneath the *terrazza*; from the Virgin and Child he lifted himself to the *terrazza*, and from there it was just a toehold on the Lamb of God to the casement of Ermenegilda's window. He knew which one was hers from the dozens of times she'd pointed it out on their walks up the Calle Alberi Grandi. She'd shown it to him in the very hope that he might someday do precisely what he was doing now — though the irony of that went completely over Albertino's head.

When he reached Ermenegilda's window he pressed at the bubbly glass, but Ermenegilda had sealed it tight and it wouldn't budge. The damp air was beginning to soak into his skin, so he drew up his courage and rapped sharply upon the window several times. Ermenegilda's sallow face suddenly appeared — but the irregular glass so distorted it in the moonlight, he could not tell whether she was angry or elated. After a long moment she opened the window, leaned out over the ledge, and sank a soft, wet kiss onto his lips. Then she drew back, heaved the contents of her night bucket over his head, and slammed the window fast against his face.

Albertino crouched there for a moment, caught between horror and bliss; then he slowly began to work his way back down the facade of the building. He lowered himself to the Lamb of God and from there to the first-floor *terrazza*. But when he reached the Virgin and Child he misjudged his footing and fell flat upon the hard stone entrance, bruising his right shoulder and breaking his left leg in three places.

Ermenegilda dispatched Romilda Rosetta to attend to him before his howls of agony woke the entire island. The maid ladled half a bottle of *grappa di radicchio* down his throat and then went and fetched Gianluca, who carried him back to the Vedova Stampanini's, where he was trussed up tightly and coddled into sleep.

In his dreams Albertino felt himself falling again and again and again. But never for a moment did he blame Ermenegilda, nor wish to undo the climb that had led to the kiss that had led to the slime that had led to the fall.

IT SOON BECAME CLEAR that Albertino would have to remain in bed until at least the Immaculate Conception of Maria the Virgin, leaving Gianluca to do both their labor himself. By this time there were only the parsnips and a bit of lettuce left to lift, but with the digging and the manuring that had to be done before the ground became too hard, and his regular market tasks, he found that he needed to rise two hours earlier and continue working until well after nightfall. He was so busy, in fact, he almost managed to drum Miriam out of his mind — until the Vedova Stampanini stopped him with a message that proved such efforts were hopeless.

"She wants to see you," said the Vedova. "She wants you to go visit her at the henhouse."

Gianluca didn't answer, but from the way he shifted his tights the Vedova had little doubt that he would go.

Gianluca had a problem. After months and months of ignoring *Il Bastòn* in pious devotion to Miriam, he was nearly mad with the excess energy that flooded his system. He had not been with a woman in close to six months, his longest period of abstinence since his first encounter with Maria Patrizia Lunardi at the age of fourteen. As a result, *Il Bastòn* was at a constant state of attention, and Gianluca's only recourse — if he wished to show himself on the Calle Alberi Grandi without causing people to drop their teeth in the mud — was to strap it tight against his left leg with a sturdy piece of muslin and dare anyone to cast their gaze below his waist.

Now, however, as he crossed the island on his way to Siora Scabbri's henhouse, Gianluca worried that a confrontation with Miriam might make him burst his fetters. Like Piero, he had not spoken to her since the *pranzo della vendemia*, and like Piero, he was absolutely certain that his rival was the father of her child. The difference was that where Piero accepted his speculations with a valiant resignation, Gianluca found his own assumptions maddening. To think that she had been with Piero, to imagine that she now carried his child, came as close as anything could possibly come to driving him insane.

When he reached the yard where Siora Scabbri's hens roamed free, he was stopped by the smell of chamomile and spearmint leaf; as he pushed open the gate and entered the yard, he found Miriam, in a clean apron with her hair gathered off her face, pouring the contents of a kettle into a series of shallow bowls.

"Do you serve them black bread and *conserva di pesca* as well?" he said.

Miriam smiled but did not turn; even without looking at him she was overwhelmed by the power of his sensuality. "It's for their stomachs," she said. "It makes the eggs taste sweeter."

Gianluca watched as she filled each of the bowls half-full and then, bit by bit, with a pinewood ladle, added water from the well bucket. When she was satisfied that it was cool enough, she stood, wiped her hands against her apron, and turned to face him.

"Thank you for coming," she said.

Gianluca bowed his head somewhat formally.

"I trust your work at the market is going well?"

"My brother had a small accident. He broke his leg. I expect to be quite busy until he's better."

"I'm sorry to hear that."

"He'll be all right," said Gianluca.

Miriam knelt down to take up the kettle, the bucket, and the ladle, which she'd laid at her feet, and then carry them to an open shed near the rear of Siora Scabbri's hovel. Then she gathered some dry crusts of bread inside her apron and returned to where Gianluca was standing.

"I wanted to speak with you about what I said at the *pranzo*."

"About your baby, you mean."

"About my baby. Yes." She reached into her apron as she spoke, crumbling the crusts into tiny pieces and scattering them to the hens. "The people here have been good to me. But my baby doesn't 'belong' to Riva di Pignoli. Not yet. I'm hoping you'll help me overcome that."

"How do you mean?"

Miriam paused for a moment — and then proceeded to ask Gianluca the same thing she'd asked Piero: to put aside his anger and jealousy and share in the fatherhood of her child. Where Piero's response had been surprise, however, Gianluca's was utter amazement.

"You can't be serious," he said. "You can't really be asking this."

"You told me you wanted to find your soul. What better way than to care for a child?"

"A child can't have two fathers. It's ridiculous. It's insulting."

"I'm asking for your help, Gianluca. I'm asking for your blessing."

"My blessing," he snarled. "Mine and Piero's."

As Gianluca said Piero's name, Miriam understood what he thought: that she had slept with Piero and that the baby inside her was his. In that moment she realized that Piero thought the same thing about Gianluca, and that the entire island most likely believed that one or the other of them was the father of her child. It had not occurred to her that by waiting so long to tell the people of Riva di Pignoli that she was pregnant, they would assume she had become so *after* her arrival upon their island. Yet as she stood there now, alone in the hen yard with Gianluca, Miriam saw no reason to tell them otherwise. She was going to have a baby, and perhaps it was better if the people of Riva di Pignoli believed it was one of their own.

"I want you to be a father to my child; to teach it, to help guide it, to love it. Is that so much to ask?"

Gianluca measured the look of innocence upon her face against the restless throbbing of *Il Bastòn*. He tried to gauge the love in her eyes, a love that offered to lift him beyond his jealousy to a place of peaceful acceptance. But the thought that Piero had been with her — had known the sweetness that he himself had been too dazzled to reach for — was like the diamond-edged blade of the hangman's ax slicing cleanly between passion and reason.

"No," he said. "It's impossible."

"Gianluca — "

"No! I won't even consider it!"

And before Miriam could dissuade him, he ran out of the henhouse and across the fields like a pheasant marked for supper.

For the rest of the day, Gianluca threw himself into his labor. He hacked at the soil where the fennel would be planted, pitched late November apples into the baskets of startled customers — in short, did all he could think of to vent the fever that burned inside him. And when the day had ended, and the energy was still as strong as when he had just started out, he knew that he would have to find a way to keep it away from Miriam. So while Albertino lay in his bed at the Vedova Stampanini's, Gianluca set up quarters across the water in Albertino's room.

With the wind on his face. And the dead for neighbors. And that slim width of water to keep him from his desire and his rage.

❧

FAUSTO MORETTI could feel that rage when he passed Albertino's room on his way to the cemetery. He was going to visit the grave of his wife, Brunella, who had died from a ruptured spleen some thirty years earlier, when a blast of cold wind rose up from the stones and spat at him across the radicchio patch. For a moment he paused and looked over the wall to the rumpled blankets Gianluca had lately slept on; then he hurried to the graveyard to place a cluster of sweet william on the muddy spot where only memory and a few bones remained.

Fausto never failed to visit Brunella's grave on the anniversary of her death; he wore the same gray tunic, which had grown tighter and tighter over the years, and he always sprinkled a little hyssop and hornbeam in his beard. Fausto's beard was extraordinary: it started up under his eyes and ran down, in a great, white waterfall, to just below his belly. He felt that it lent him an air of mystery; he'd seen detailed engravings from Constantinople of wise men with facial tresses not half as elegant as his. He even

*174*

believed that it was on account of his beard that Miriam had chosen to live with him and Maria Luigi.

When he reached the grave he placed the sweet william at the foot of the marker and then sat on the ground and began recounting the events of the past year. This took a bit longer than usual, as he had the remarkable spring and the arrival of Miriam and the discovery of Miriam's condition to add to the old quarrels and new kittens that peppered his annual report. There had been no births — except for the kittens — and the only death had been Vincenzo Bassetti, who had been buried the previous January just a few paces down and a bit to the south of Brunella's narrow plot. Fausto had considered leaving something on Vincenzo's grave, as they had often played cards together and had known each other since they were boys, but he knew that Brunella would be wildly angry if he spent his visit with anyone else but her (including his mother, who was buried beside Arriguccio Forbi, and his sister, who was somewhere near the Furian family, though he could not quite remember where).

It had been early afternoon when Fausto had left the main island to cross over to the floating graveyard; by the time he was ready to leave, the sun was half-sunk in the watery embrace of the lagoon. The light was so muted as he moved toward the gate that he almost did not notice the freshly dug mound lying snug between Sineraldo Saccardi and Apollonia Ambrosiana Barbon. When he stepped closer to the south wall, however, the signs were unmistakable: someone had been buried within the month.

He clasped the ends of his flowing beard and tugged down sharply. How could there be a grave without a body? How could there be a body if no one had died? Yet there was the fresh gravesite, as plain as could be, sitting hushed in the fading light.

He returned to his boat and started back across the water. When he reached the main shore he was greeted by a thin, spectral cry.

"A boar's head . . . a bowl of mashed chickpeas . . . a potful of phlegm stirred lightly in the morning mist. . . ."

He knew Piarina's voice as he knew the flatness of the bed that he lay down to sleep on each evening. Yet coupled with the inexplicable grave, it sent a flash of fear down his spine. It was nowhere near Brunella, not even close to Arriguccio Forbi, and on the other side of the cemetery from the Furian family. Yet something in his heart could not help but feel that the grave he had just discovered was his own.

# Chapter 11

HE AUTUMN RAN out like the rivers of rain that gushed from the roof gutters of the Ca' Torta. As the days grew shorter, the villagers began to prepare for both the coming of winter and the celebration of the birth of their Savior. Siora Bertinelli began making *stufoli* and *ambrosina* and *pan di Natale*; you could smell the delicate fragrance of milk and almonds from almost anywhere on the island. Romilda Rosetta began her annual practice of quietly clenching a prickly soursop in either fist; she hoped to create the impression of stigmata by at least the beginning of Advent. Maria Luigi began tying up bundles of sage and tarragon to nail to the villagers' doors. Even Piarina seemed to adopt a holiday air — her cures were filled with the sweetmeats of the sea-the season, and the Vedova Scarpa was convinced she was actually leading up to a spectacular recipe for *pan casalin*.

Work on the new *campo* continued with speed and precision; the coming of Christmas seemed to add a touch of glee to the islanders' toil. As Piero's dark vision began to reveal itself, however, the people of Riva di Pignoli became concerned. Maria Luigi let out a shriek when she discovered she was laying the tiles for a newt's tail. Siora Guarnieri had to lie down in the Chiesa di Maria del Mare when she found she was working on the triple penis of a grinning, two-headed dragon. The villagers had faith in Piero's piety, but more than a few of them worried that this time he had gone too far.

Piarina stared past the devils that were forming below her with the same vacant intensity with which she looked beyond everything. The murderous schemes that had driven her from her bed still danced their goblin fugue inside her brain. Yet now that she had settled into her perch upon the *campanil*, they mingled with tender daydreams of Ermenegilda. She imagined that she and her former friend were the only ones left on the island. She imagined them laughing and swimming, playing hiding games along the banks of the canals, sleeping curled in each other's arms like a pair of cats. The only time she left these fancies was when Piero brought her her breakfast, when her woeful heart urged her to either ring the bells or call out another cure, and when Valentina appeared at the base of the tower to torment her.

"Six cakes a day, Piarina! That's how much you're costing me — six cakes a day for forty-seven days now. That's two hundred eighty-two cakes, Piarina! Two hundred eighty-two today, two hundred eighty-eight tomorrow, two hundred ninety-four the next day — are you listening, Piarina? Do you hear what I'm saying?"

Piarina gave no answer — in her dreams she was on a cushion before a fire in the drawing room of the Ca' Torta counting the sparks that flashed as she tossed pomegranate seeds into the flames.

"Because someday you'll come down, Piarina. Someday you'll get fed up with being an undernourished nest for birds and you'll come crawling down the side of that thing and come back to my door to beg for shelter — and you know what I'll give you?"

Piarina saw the door to the drawing room open — she saw Valentina enter and move toward the fire — and she felt the sting of her hard, horrible hand upon her body.

"Two hundred eighty-two!" cried Valentina as she slammed against the side of the *campanil*. "Two hundred eighty-eight! Two hundred ninety-four!"

Piarina knew that she was safe. Valentina might assail her with a thousand whacks, but with only one hand and a worn-out heart she could never climb up to get her. She nevertheless managed, through wood and stone and iron, to feel each and every one of her mother's blows.

Piero was too busy working on the statue for the *campo* to take note of Valentina's tyranny. As the centerpiece of the new village center, it demanded his finest, most focused energies. Yet even though he'd worked upon it steadily while building the *campanil*, while designing the *campo*, while following Miriam and laying the tiles and reburying the decaying corpse, it was only now, when all the rest of those tasks were very nearly done, that he turned his full attention upon the statue.

Miriam, in a cloud of light. Miriam, daubed with honey,

dusted with dry snow, naked, breasts shining, arms floating, eyes glistening.

It wasn't going to be easy. It was going to require more
concentration, more talent and inspiration, than anything
Piero had ever done. And no matter how glorious it might
seem when it was finally unveiled on the morning of Epiphany, the only thing Piero felt absolutely sure of was that
Gianluca was not going to like it at all.

❦

MIRIAM SPENT much of the month knitting a blanket for
her baby, a blanket made of bright, iridescent seaweed.
She'd been out one morning for a walk along the eastern
shore when she came upon a great deposit of the stuff, its
slick green tendrils snaking in toward her feet. When she
bent down to touch it, it felt wonderfully strong, so she
gathered up as much of it as she could and carried it back
to Maria Luigi's hovel.

Miriam had tried doing countless things to win back the
affections of the people of Riva di Pignoli. She took water
to the Guarnieris when their well ran dry. She brought
fennel cakes to Armida Barbon when she came down with
the grippe. She worked extra hours at the henhouse, she
read scriptures to the Vedova Stampanini, she swept the
Calle Alberi Grandi from its southernmost tip to where it
ran out past the Rizzardellos' salt shed. But eventually she
realized that those who had truly taken her into their
hearts were not going to turn her out because she was
expecting a child, and those who were inclined to judge
her were not going to change their minds no matter what
she might do.

Miriam accepted these judgments — and reaffirmed her desire for self-sufficiency. But as Christmas approached, she found herself returning to thoughts of Piero and Gianluca. Her plan to ask them both to father her child had backfired; Gianluca's rage had shown her that she was tampering with dangerous emotions. What confused her, however, was the complexity of her own emotions: she found herself thinking of Piero one day and Gianluca the next, when she did not wish to be thinking of either one of them.

So she sat before her altar and knitted her blanket. Maria Luigi insisted that it could not be done. Seaweed turns brittle when left out of water, how could a pile of dried grass keep a baby warm? But Miriam's seaweed did not turn brittle as it dried. It turned into soft, ropelike strands that felt like goose-feather down and held like links of iron. While the villagers followed the feast of San Nicolo and the celebration of Santa Lucia, Miriam knitted her blanket for her baby. So that no matter how few or how many fathers it had, it would always be warm, and always be safe, and always belong to the sea.

A QUIET JUBILATION built throughout the month. There was more eating than usual, more laughter, more song. Yet it was only when the Novena began, those nine nights before Christmas, that the joyfulness spilled through the cracked chimney pots and spread out over the fields and docks and canals. It was as if the spirit of Saturnalia still buzzed in the air: that atmosphere of blissful, giddy abandon. The Vedova Scarpa and Armida Barbon walked up and down the Calle Alberi Grandi singing shepherd's carols. Ugolino Ramponi and Armando Guarnieri tied their livestock to a series of posts behind the Chiesa di Maria del Mare to create the mangerlike effect of a *presepio*. Candles were placed in the hovel windows; torches were lit by the docks; tarragon and bay laurel were burned in the hearths to send a musky perfume out over the island.

The Christmas revelry even penetrated the walls of the Ca' Torta. Enrico managed to remain in Verona for the better part of the month, but he sent partridges and pheasants, enameled vials of perfume, and enough silks and satins to make holiday gowns for Orsina, Ermenegilda, and the three Marias. The women of the Ca' Torta were planning a Christmas Eve celebration. Each of the girls was to invite an available member of Venetian society to an elaborate midnight supper. But while Orsina and the three Marias sat together in the main *salone* trying to choose among the span of wealthy bachelors, Ermenegilda sat propped before her loom in a state of despair. Ermenegilda had found that her recent acts of enmity toward Albertino were not nearly as satisfying as she had anticipated. It had been different when he had ignored her and rebuffed her; she cherished the destruction of the vegetables as one of the high points of her life. But ever since their encounter in San Marco, when his bitter indifference had been transformed into uninhibited yearning, she found that her attempts at humiliation and revenge left an acrid, unpleasant aftertaste. So unpleasant, in fact, she could not eat the ringlike breakfast pastries that lay stacked before her on the loom — nor the *sopa di ghiozzo*, nor the pheasant with cinnamon sauce, nor the special Advent cake Romilda Rosetta had brought her from Siora Bertinelli. Her appetite had become as erratic as her emotions: she would eat and not eat, starve herself and gorge herself, and had little control over whether she did either one.

Now, while her mother and sisters were conferring about the selection of suitors and the choosing of fabrics for the dresses they would wear, she sat propped behind the loom playing games with her vegetable dolls. Ermenegilda had fashioned tiny likenesses of Albertino, Piarina, and herself from the vegetables she once set flame to. There was not much to work with in mid-December, but she managed to gather some carrots, a few turnips, some dried figs, and a handful of beans and lentils and worked them into vegetables versions of herself and her two loves. She spent hours creating fantasies between them, not un-like the fantasies of Piarina atop the tower: she and Al-bertino selecting furniture for their country villa; she and Piarina taking boat rides about the lagoon; the three of them chasing peacocks across the garden of the Ca' Torta. They were always gentle and kind with each other, and the Ermenegilda doll always went to great lengths to see that the Albertino doll and the Piarina doll were happy.

Today they were out hawking, the Ermenegilda doll graciously allowing the others to take their turns first. Their play was so pleasant that Ermenegilda tried to ex-tend its contentment into reality by reaching for something to eat. When she lifted the nearby *miel-pignole* pastry to her lips, however, its sweet fragrance nauseated her, and she was reminded of the falseness of her game. She was grateful when Romilda Rosetta's rap on the door inter-rupted her.

"Your mother is waiting for you," she called through the door. "I told her you'd be right down."

Ordinarily Ermenegilda would trounce the tiny maid

for saying anything that went against her will. But she was so relieved to avoid the taste of the pastry, she thanked her and went down to join the others.

The four women were engrossed in discussion when Ermenegilda entered the room.

"What about the Count Capocchio?" said Maria Seconda as she held a bolt of lemon silk up to the light.

"Too vain," said Maria Prima. "All he ever talks about is himself and that ridiculous villa he has in Favaro."

"I'm inviting Francesco Montanaldo," said Maria Terza as she tested the strength of a rippled chiffon between her clenched fists.

"Francesco Montanaldo!" cried Maria Seconda. "He'll never come to Riva di Pignoli!"

"Oh, yes, he will. Papa arranged for him to borrow twenty thousand florins from a bank in Siena on the condition that he be my dinner companion."

"Papa always makes the best arrangements for you," said Maria Prima, tossing down a bolt of turquoise satin. "I hate being the oldest; everyone expects me to do everything myself!"

"Stop it!" said Orsina. "Your father has never failed any one of you yet — at least when it comes to coercing people to dinner. Have a seat, Ermenegilda. There's a case of fabric by the fireplace that hasn't been opened yet."

Ermenegilda took a place in the circle and began absentmindedly fingering a bit of gold-and-cerulean brocade.

"Then I'm inviting Teobaldo Spumi," continued Maria Seconda.

"Teobaldo Spumi!" cried Maria Prima.

"And I just might tie him to one of the supporting columns in the *androne* and never let him leave."

Ermenegilda winced at Maria Seconda's words; her fantasy about trussing up her dinner guest brought painful memories to her mind.

"What do you think of this?" asked Maria Prima, stretching an olive-and-cream-striped silk across the broad landscape of her bosom.

"Terrible," said Maria Seconda.

"Try the marbelized magenta," said Orsina. "You can never go wrong with magenta."

The women continued to shuffle and compare, holding up bolt after bolt of the fabulous material to flatter themselves. But though Ermenegilda nodded, and smiled whenever it seemed appropriate, it soon became evident that her heart was not really in it.

"What about you, Ermenegilda?" asked Maria Terza as she coiled a bit of lavender ribbon in her dark, aggressive hair. "Who are you going to invite?"

"Are you going to ask that banker you met on your trip to Venezia?" asked Maria Prima. "The one who kept you out so late?"

"I don't know," said Ermenegilda. "I haven't decided yet."

"Well, you'd better choose soon," said Orsina. "It's only a week away, and you know how precious these noblemen become during the holy season."

"You choose, Mama," said Ermenegilda. "You choose for me."

"Ermenegilda!" cried Orsina. "It seems hardly like you to let me make such an important decision!"

"It's fine, Mama. Just choose someone. I'm sure he'll be handsome and rich, like all the others."

"You must be ill. Maria Prima, call Romilda Rosetta. She must be ill."

"I'm not ill!" cried Ermenegilda. "I just don't really care

who I have dinner with on Christmas Eve. Pick someone and then stop talking about it already!"

And she threw down the brocade she'd been holding in her lap and hurried out of the room.

"What's the matter with her?" asked Maria Prima.

"She'd getting ruder every day!" said Maria Seconda.

"I'll bet she's just jealous that I'm inviting Francesco Montanaldo," said Maria Terza. "She probably has her eye on him herself."

But Ermenegilda — who had fled to the pantry to see if there were any *crostini alle olive* left over from lunch — simply could not bear to think about dining with a stranger when Albertino was so close at hand.

❧

WORK ON THE village center tottered toward completion amid healthy breaks for *vin marzamin* and the Vedova Stampanini's *bagna cauda*. Only Piero remained hardworking throughout the holiday revels, laying the last of the mosaic and adding the final touches to the monument. The *campo* now resembled the smoky plains of his darkest nightmare; without Miriam at their center, the ruby-lipped dragons and glittering snakes seemed an awfully hellish way to praise the island. But when Piero moved the statue into place on the morning of Christmas Eve — with the help of Beppe Guancio and Paolo Guarnieri and with a canvas tarpaulin snugly shielding it from view — he felt a quiet sense of completion and pride.

With over six months of work behind him and the unveiling not due until Epiphany, Piero decided to pay a visit to Boccasante. There was always a particular feeling about the monastery around Christmas; he felt the need to sit, for a few hours, in the gentle company of his former brothers. He arrived at the great gates as the vesper bells were chiming. Fra Antonio informed him that Fra Danilo was in the scriptorium, and as Piero knew his way, and Fra Antonio was expected in the chapter hall, he allowed him to climb to the second-floor chamber unescorted.

Piero was grateful to have a few moments alone within his solemn childhood home. His work on the new village center seemed strangely unreal when set against the abstract nature of the world in which he'd been raised. As he ascended the stone steps that led to the chamber where the manuscripts were kept, he felt the breeze of other Christmases blow over him. When he was eight, and Fra Matteo had allowed him to light the candles for the midnight mass. When he was twelve, and Fra Rinaldo had placed a sculpture he'd made of the Holy Family in an archway of the northern corridor. Even the chastisement that followed the discovery of his obsessions and his not-long-after eviction from the order produced a sudden feeling of warmth and a tender wistfulness.

When he reached the scriptorium he found Fra Danilo poring over a series of intricately detailed illuminations.

"I've come to wish you the good blessings of the season," he said.

"Piero!" cried Fra Danilo. "How good to see you!"

"Are you busy?" asked Piero. "Should I wait for you downstairs?"

"No, no," said the monk. "I'm just trying to decide which manuscript to use for tonight's mass. Fra Teodoro has done some extraordinary figurework in the gospels this year. His use of gold leaf is extraordinary. But we've always used Fra Crispino's manuscript — which is, of course, magnificent, though in a less spectacular way. It's a difficult decision."

Piero looked at each of the manuscripts that lay open on the rosewood stand. "They're both beautiful," he said. "Perhaps it's time to honor a new vision."

"Yes," said Fra Danilo. "I tend to think that myself." He studied the manuscripts a moment longer, then shifted his attention to Piero. "Come. Help me get my mind off it for a little while. Tell me how you've been."

"I've been well," said Piero, pulling up a bench and sitting. "Busy and well. We've finished the project."

"Finished!"

"On the morning of Epiphany we'll unveil the monument. And then it's done."

"Are you pleased with it?"

"Very. If Sior Bon could see it, he'd have a completely different opinion about the 'existence' of Riva di Pignoli."

"That's wonderful, Piero. I must come see it myself. As soon as the holidays are over — I give you my word."

"Thank you, Fra Danilo. You've always been a great supporter of my work. It would mean a lot to me to have your opinion of it."

"You have a great talent, Piero. I've always said that. I hope the people of Riva di Pignoli appreciate what you've given them."

"Yes," said Piero, picturing his vision of dragons and demons. "I hope so, too."

Fra Danilo turned back to the manuscripts, lifting the newer of them up toward the light. "And in other respects," he said, "has it been a good season for you?"

"It's been a time of challenge," said Piero. "And a time of warnings."

And with careful attention he proceeded to tell Fra Danilo

the saga of the dead body: his chance discovery of it in the springless spring, his rather hasty burial of it in the field of wild thyme, and his recent transference of it across the darkened water to the sacred ground of the cemetery.

"It was as if I'd removed a pair of stone weights from my shoulders," he said. "As soon as I'd said the prayers, and had covered it over, I felt as light as a gull feather in the wind."

Fra Danilo lowered the manuscript he'd been holding aloft and closed its heavy cover.

"What's wrong?" asked Piero.

"Nothing."

"I know you better than that. What is it?"

Fra Danilo hesitated.

"Please, Fra Danilo. Tell me."

"Perhaps it's just superstition. Perhaps it means nothing at all."

"*What?*"

The old monk turned to him. "As a member of the order of San Gerolamo nel Bosco, it was deeply ingrained into me that once a body is buried it must not be moved."

Piero closed his eyes. "Why not?"

"Because the body is placed into the ground in order to sanctify it," explained Fra Danilo. "And in order to mark the spot where the soul can find it again on Judgment Day."

"But surely it's better for a body to be moved than to remain in unhallowed ground without a prayer upon its head."

"I don't know, Piero. Imagine if everyone went shifting bodies about after they were buried. It could wreak havoc of the highest order."

"Surely God will know which souls belong to which bodies."

"Come Judgment Day, Piero, God will have quite enough to keep him busy. You'll have to hope the angels get it right."

Piero stood and walked to the window. "Is there some kind of law about this? Something I can look up?"

"No. If it's a law at all, it's an unwritten one. But what's the point in talking about it? It's been done. If the soul was virtuous, it will undoubtedly find its way back to itself come Resurrection. Please, Piero, don't let it ruin your good spirits."

Piero looked down upon the courtyard of the cloister, where Fra Claudio was spreading sprigs of juniper and ivy along the rim of the small stone fountain.

"I won't, Fra Danilo," he said, turning back to him. "I won't."

"Good. Now come help me decide about these illuminations. I think you're right about Fra Teodoro's work — but take one more look with me before I make up my mind."

Piero returned to where Fra Danilo was standing, and together they compared the two manuscripts. But though he gave his opinion, his heart was not in it; it had already hurried down the stone stairs and across the lagoon, through the graveyard gates and into the unmarked grave with the twice buried body. Where it was likely to remain until Judgment Day. Or at least until he could think of what to do next.

❧

THE REVELRY OF the Novena focused down to a bright humming with the arrival of Christmas Eve. The carols were abandoned, the torches extinguished, and the bustling up and down the Calle Alberi Grandi was replaced by a gentle stillness within the island's homes. The night before Christmas was a time of solitude for the people of Riva di Pignoli. A light fog descended over the huts and hovels, and even the most curious of the island's inhabitants would have been unable to peek through a low window to see how his neighbor observed the night. Only the darkling spirits of the Riva di Pignoli dead, had they risen from their graves and floated out over the island — had they passed, like an insistent whisper, through the thatched roofs and the pebble-and-mud-brick walls — would have been able to describe both the fever and the calm that permeated the tiny village.

They would have seen Siora Bertinelli, sitting naked beneath a hemp blanket, asking God to grant her the capacity for gratitude. They would have seen Siora Scabbri describing Christ's passion to her chickens, Ugolino Ramponi beating himself in a corner with a switch, and the Vedova Scarpa, alone at her table, pouring *vin santo* for the Holy Ghost.

They would have seen Giuseppe Navo and the Vedova Stampanini, sharing a candlelit supper of *vongole, scungili, cozze,* and *capitone*. They would have seen Maria Luigi and Fausto, full of pig-and-blood pudding, sleeping peacefully on their chairs before the fire. They would have seen the Guarnieris eating the salt fish the Rizzardellos had given them, and the Rizzardellos eating the Guarnieris' pork. They would have seen Brunetto Fucci preparing a bed of herbs, and Beppe Guancio fashioning a Christ Child out of pinecones to place upon the *presepio* at midnight.

They would have seen Albertino, in Gianluca's bed, dreaming blissfully of Ermenegilda, and Ermenegilda, at the Ca' Torta supper, dreaming likewise of Albertino.

They would have seen Miriam, on her cushions before her altar, singing softly to her child. And Piero, with a shovel in his hand, fighting the bitter taste of rust from the fog and the stench of putrid flesh, as he once more exhumed the rotted body and returned it to the field of wild thyme.

They would have seen Gianluca whipped up — between the whispered rumors about the soon-to-be-revealed statue and the pent-up energy of *Il Bastòn* — into a priapic rage that sent him storming across the island, praying that he could resist his desire to destroy the six-months' labor of the island's dreams.

And they would have seen Piarina — a faint gargoyle, eyes blazing beacons through the fog — wishing a strong wind would blow in from the north and bring the entire structure crashing down on her mother's head.

# Chapter 12

B Y EARLY MORNING the fog had thickened into
an unstirred soup that completely covered the
island. You could not see the henhouse from
Siora Scabbri's gate, nor the boats from the
dock, nor your right hand stretched straight out before
you. The Ca' Torta dissolved like a snow crystal in a warm
breeze, and the Chiesa di Maria del Mare vanished into
the haze like a shrine before an unbelieving pilgrim. The
damp gray mist even entered the hovels: when Maria Luigi
woke she thought that Fausto had abandoned her, and
Siora Bertinelli, for the life of her, could not find her
clothes. All across the village the Christmas Day plans for
feasting and celebrating were canceled. The island had
simply disappeared.

Toward late morning, a heavy wind came up. This cleared away the fog but brought new problems: snapped branches and severed well buckets began flying through the air. Pinecones spiraled up off the ground and catapulted through blown-in windows. When the wind was joined by rain, in the early afternoon, the villagers began to huddle into dark corners hoping that the worst of it would pass quickly. But the rain only increased, beating hard upon the thatched roofs and overflowing the narrow canals. The straw floors became flooded; the villagers had to crouch upon their trestle tables and straddle the sides of their washtubs. The docks disappeared beneath the rising lagoon. The Calle Alberi Grandi became a muddy river, floating uphill through the trees.

The sky grew darker. Day became night. And then, with a cry of anguish, the heavens exploded. Wild streaks of fire blazed through the blackened storm clouds, huge gusts of wind tore the doors off huts, enormous waves splashed mud and muck across the gardens and footpaths and fields.

Trees were uprooted.

Bridges were wrecked.

Chickens and pigs were sucked up into the sky, never to be seen again.

It was not until almost morning of the following day that the winds quieted down enough to allow Piero to journey out to the Chiesa di Maria del Mare to view the damage. There was still quite a gust going, but the rain had slackened — and in the strange filtering of the premorning light he almost imagined that the project had been spared: he saw banners flying from the height of the *campanil* and the statue of Miriam stretching out in the gradually thinning shadows. As he moved in closer, however, his fantasy dissolved, and he found himself face to face with the awful reality.

A heap of stone. A sprinkling of tile. A mud-soaked ruin where he'd hoped a town would rise.

The new village center, still cradled in its infancy, had been smashed to pieces like a child's clay kingdom by the swipe of a cranky hand. All the wrath and the longing and the frustration and the desire that had curled about the gatepost — and cowered behind the roasting spit — and coiled around the careful feet of the island's hot citizens — had finally taken its toll.

# Chapter 13

WHEN THE SUN came out — not long after Piero had returned to Beppe Guancio's hovel and curled himself up into an unconscious ball — the villagers felt as if God had sneezed and their world had come flying apart. There was so much muck on the footpaths and mud in the gardens, they had to remove their boots to exit their hovels. Bits of debris were scattered everywhere, and the entire island seemed to sag under the weight of heavy water. But what troubled them most was the fear that a pattern was forming: just as there had been no spring in the spring, there was now no Christmas at Christmas. The day had come and gone without a glimmer of grace.

The damage to the island's huts and hovels was less

devastating than it was disorienting. The Vedova Stampanini's chimney wound up on Brunetto Fucci's roof. Maria Luigi's flower pots landed in the Rizzardellos' garden. Siora Scabbri's sundial hurtled clear across the island to surface in Giuseppe Navo's boat. Only Ugolino Ramponi had to actually vacate his home, since one of his goats had butted its way in during the storm to explode its bowels in his bedchamber. The rest were content to live, for a few weeks, without a door, without a well, or, in a few cases, without a roof, grateful that their four walls were still standing. After all, Albertino had been living that way for years.

As they began to pick their way through the damage, the people discovered rats in their washtubs, rabbits down their wells, and bits of colored tile in their boots, their beds, their hearths, their sheds, and their night buckets. Giuseppe Navo found a square of scarlet in his *sopa di legumi*. Maria Patrizia Lunardi brushed bits of damask and damson from the roots of her hair. Orsina encountered a sea of heliotrope and citron on the stairs that led from the main *portego* to the *piano nobile*. Piero's elaborate mosaic was strewn across the island; only the trace of a hoof and the remnants of a tail remained.

When Gianluca first awoke on that unusual morning, he felt light as a fistful of fennel seeds. The terrorizing winds had swept him clean; the power of their hot breath had got down inside him and had neutralized the power of his rage. He felt relaxed; released; almost giddy. The soft earth had never felt so comforting, the air had never smelled so sweet.

Gianluca had been in a state of torment on Christmas Eve that he had neither wished for nor could control. So when the rains came up, and the wind, and the hail, he

went out to the docks along the western shore and invoked
the elements to move their way through him like angry
music through a clotted reed pipe. When the lightning
flashed he hurled curses after it. When the water rose up
he hugged the trunk of a pine tree and let himself be lashed
by the waves. About midway through the deluge he began
a low keening sound, which gradually rose into a great
cry. He drew all the mad railing of the heavens into his
body, in the hope of eradicating the wildness that had
seized his soul.

He raged and wailed until the storm had run its course.
Then, purged of his wrath and desire, he slept the most
delicious sleep — as if he were lying on the surface of a sea
of ambergris that was melting in the wan December sun.
When he awoke and found himself half-naked beneath a
pine tree, he slipped back to the Vedova Stampanini's
hovel, where he found the Vedova and Giuseppe Navo
huddled under a blanket beneath the chopping table, and
Albertino, between the bed and the night bucket, tangled
up in one of his old tunics. After the intensity of the storm,
they slept like infants; Gianluca stayed just long enough
to steal a couple of cold *capitone* off the Vedova's plate and
to trade his tatters for a pair of warm hose and a dry
muslin shirt.

When he left the hovel his mood was so light that he
did not notice the glass-eyed fish lying strangled in the
mud or the blasted branches and blown roots that scattered
his path through the village. He moved past the Guarnieris'
porkhouse and the Rizzardellos' salt shed and Siora
Scabbri's henhouse, completely oblivious of the missing
door and the torn-up garden and the three-quarters crash-
ed-in roof. He wandered through the chaos and calamity
in a state of dumb grace, until he came to the clearing

beside the Chiesa di Maria del Mare and saw the *campanil*-that-was-no-longer-a-*campanil*, and the *campo*-that-was-no-longer-a-*campo*, and the statue-that-had-once-been-Miriam-but-was-now-merely-rubble.

And he fell to his knees.

And he covered his face.

For though he'd tried to prevent it, it seemed clear to him that his rage had lit the heavens — and that the storm had done precisely the damage he'd feared to do himself.

❦

HAD EITHER PIERO or Gianluca taken the time to examine the rubble, they would have found a slender girl lying slumped at the core of the confusion. For when the *campanil* came crashing to the ground, so did Piarina. She landed in a heap on the broken mosaic, amid the scattered tiles and the shattered stones and a few pieces of Miriam's left leg. No bones were broken, but between the wind and the rain and the shock of her fall, she was torn from her trance and plunged into a wild fever. She rolled and writhed on the *campo* floor as if Piero's mosaic demons had sprung to life. She shouted out such a succession of cures, the Chiesa di Maria del Mare began to quiver. It was only when the storm had ended that she fell back into a trance that left her motionless and speechless, this time including her cures.

It was thus that Valentina found her when she came to look for her after the terrible winds had died down. She had prepared a lengthy speech, which she'd repeated to herself over and over again as she marched up the Calle Alberi Grandi, about how stupid the girl was to stay out

in a storm and how lucky she was not to have been dashed
to pieces. But when she arrived at the ruined *campo* and
found that she *had* been dashed — if not to pieces, to pulp —
she could only stand there, staring, another bit of debris
upon the map of disaster. For a long while she circled
Piarina like a crow, her lone hand clenching and opening
involuntarily. Then she scooped her up, tossed her over
her shoulder like a sack of steaming coals, and carted her
back to the hovel. Where she threw her into the low straw
bed. And waited.

❧

WHEN MIRIAM HEARD about the destruction of the new
village center, she hurried out to the field beside the Chiesa
di Maria del Mare and began trying to piece it back together again. For the most part the stones were too heavy
for her to lift, but she did what she could in an earnest
attempt to organize the disorder. About an hour after she
had begun she felt a hand on her shoulder and looked up
to see the Vedova Stampanini.

"And you think you can't lose a baby as easily as you
got it?" she said.

Miriam neither answered nor argued. She simply put
down the stone she was holding, took the Vedova's hand,
and followed her back out into the confusion of the day.

AS SOON as the storm had ended Albertino knew that he
had to return to his room. His leg had been healed since

the third or fourth day of the Novena; he had remained in his brother's bed only for the *brodo di pesce* and the *pan da pistor* that the Vedova Stampanini had served him throughout his convalescence. He felt nervous, however, about returning home after an absence of over six weeks. In the first place it had been an entirely unplanned absence: he'd flung himself out of his bed with such vehemence on the night he'd gone to Ermenegilda's window, he'd hardly had time to pull on his tights, let alone smooth down the blankets or sweep the floor or take the boxes to the cemetery and hide them behind the cypresses. In the second place there was Gianluca, and in the third the storm, and though Albertino was not sure which was more dangerous, he knew that between the two his room was certain to be in a different state from when he'd left it, those many weeks ago, in a moon-drenched moment of passion.

As he made his way to his *barca da pesca* and across the narrow width of water, he took note of the behavior of the other villagers as they reacted to the storm. He saw Anna Rizzardello on the Calle Alberi Grandi, plucking goose feathers from the grain of her wash barrel. He saw Gesmundo Barbon on the center plank of his *sandolo*, struggling to remove the scythe that was lodged in its prow. When he reached his little island, however, and crossed the slumbering radicchio patch to stand before the east wall, he was surprised to find that barely a stick on the hearth or a slug in the mud seemed altered. There was a slightly higher drift of dirt against the base of the north wall, the emerald blanket was between the violet and the rust instead of between the crimson and the ocher, but his boxes sat precisely where they ought to — not a hinge, a latch, or a lid seemed to have been touched by the violence.

When the storm had come, and had knocked the shelves off Gianluca's walls, and had caused his bed to jump up into the air and land with a thud on its back, Albertino had thought of only two things: his boxes and Ermenegilda. He trusted that the Ca' Torta had been able to withstand the pummeling of the elements; he only prayed that the battering winds had remagnetized Ermenegilda's heart's compass, sending its fragile needle spinning from hatred back to love.

He climbed over the east wall and hobbled toward the bed of blankets; his left leg felt like a piece of broken pottery pasted together in all the wrong places. After lowering himself to the ragged stack, he carefully removed his boots. Then he dropped to the ground and crept to the line of boxes.

For years they had sat there, from the chest of sun-bleached sandalwood to the cask of hammered brass, as free and as empty as his ever-uncomplicated heart. That heart, however, was no longer uncomplicated — and the boxes only reminded him of Ermenegilda. So one by one Albertino removed them from the south wall, opened their lids, and whispered his deepest apologies into their carved-out bellies. Then he piled them into his *barca da pesca* and carried them across to the main island, where he left them — as an offering to love — on the doorstep of the Ca' Torta.

WITH BEPPE GUANCIO gone off to the docks to try to separate his boat from the mud, Piero was left in solitude. He tried not to think about what had happened — he tried to hollow out his mind until it was a void — but the image of the ruined *campo* kept flashing before him, and he could not help making certain connections.

It was because of the dead body. He knew it. How could he be allowed to build a tribute to higher understanding when he could not even properly dispose of a swollen corpse? He'd been careless and fearful, and God had brought down his fist to punish him. What troubled Piero was that in punishing him, God had also punished the people of Riva di Pignoli.

He tried once more to close down his consciousness. He hugged his knees and pressed his chin down into his chest. He tried to let his thoughts splinter and shake free like bits of straw off the tail of an old broom that the rats would then scatter into careless piles in the far corners of the hovel. But just as he began to give himself over to this fracturing of his perception, a rapping on the door brought him back to focused awareness. He opened his eyes and lifted his head, and as the door slid open a panel of light cut into the darkness, inside of which stood Gianluca.

"Do you know?"

"Yes."

"Have you seen for yourself?"

"Yes."

Gianluca remained motionless in the doorway; Piero sat silent against the wall. Then the door opened wide — bright sunlight mocked the shadows — and Gianluca entered the room. And when he closed the door behind him, returning the hovel to its quarter-light dimness, Piero felt a sorrow in his bearing that made him almost doubt it was Gianluca.

"I want to fix it," he said.

"Fix it?"

"Rebuild it. The whole thing. From start to finish."

Piero looked at him for a moment as if he were mad. Then he lowered his head back to his chest.

"Get out of here."

"I mean it," said Gianluca. "The *campanil*. The *campo*. How long do you think it would take?"

"To rebuild it?"

"Exactly as it was the day before yesterday."

Piero leaned his head back against the damp wall but did not respond.

"How long, Piero?" repeated Gianluca.

"If all the materials could be found, if anyone would bother to help with the labor — probably not much less than it took the first time. Six months. Five, maybe, if the foundations are still intact."

"I'll do it in three."

"Impossible."

"In less than three. I'll do it by Easter. By spring."

Piero gazed through the thick light into Gianluca's eyes. "Why?"

"Because it's my fault."

"How can it be your fault?"

"Because I wanted it," said Gianluca. "I willed it. And now I want to rebuild what I've destroyed." He paused for a moment, the intensity of his declaration like a third, immovable presence in the room. "Except the statue. That you have to do yourself."

"The statue."

"The monument. Of Miriam."

Piero closed his eyes. "I can't."

"Yes," said Gianluca, "you can." He crouched down and inched his way closer until he was practically whispering in Piero's ear. "Another three months with her body beneath your fingers? Another three months making love to her day and night? Standing close to her — concentrating on her — perfecting her hands, her hair, the light in her eyes? You can do it, Piero. Believe me. You can do it."

Piero turned to Gianluca, their faces separated only by a few breaths. "You think you can win her by doing this," he said. "That's what this is about, isn't it? She won't choose between us, no matter what's happened, and you think this will make her decide."

"I think I can rebuild your *campo*. If it should please her, that's fine. But that's not why I do it."

Piero looked hard into that face, which possessed all the confidence he had never known. "Why do I believe you?"

"Because I tell the truth, my little builder monk. I'm going to rebuild your *campo*, and you're going to help me do it. I'm going to need your plans, your sketches, your eye for detail. And your artistry: you're going to have to make me another monument."

"What about your own work?"

"It's winter. I go crazy from nothing to do. Please, Piero — let me rebuild it."

Piero pressed his feet down into the straw. "No," he said.

Gianluca stood. "I'll start clearing tomorrow," he said. "You'll change your mind."

Then he turned and left the hovel.

For a long while Piero remained just as Gianluca had left him: alone in the corner with the rats and the straw and the shadows. Then he lifted himself up and went to the shabby worktable where he had sketched the plans for the *campanil*, the *campo*, and the monument. The designs were all there, stacked in a neat bundle beneath a heavy brass pestle — the measurements for the scaffolding, the gridwork for the laying of the tiles, the differing perspectives for the statue he'd made of Miriam. The only question was whether he could summon the energy to breathe them to life a second time.

Gianluca seemed to have enough energy, not just for Piero but for the entire village — and Piero realized that the main obstacle to the rebuilding of the village center would be his having to allow him to lead the project. There had not been a trace of hostility in him as he'd crouched on the floor of Beppe Guancio's hovel — and not a trace of the familiar swelling of *Il Bastòn* — and Piero knew that if he could feel the change in him, Miriam was bound to feel it as well.

He lifted the pestle and spread the sheets of sheepskin out on the rough-grain table until he came to the sketches of Miriam. That he had been able to capture even a glimmer of her beauty had seemed a miracle. That the work had been destroyed before anyone had seen it seemed a sign. Perhaps he'd been rash to create so rapturous, so stark, so uninhibited an impression for the center of a village square. If he went along with the reconstruction — if he allowed Gianluca to become the sweaty hero his efforts were bound to make him — it would afford him the opportunity to design a new statue, something easier to bear in the light of common day, something closer to the hearts and minds of the people of Riva di Pignoli.

He closed his eyes and tried to imagine the villagers clearing away the rubble and allowing the spot beside the Chiesa di Maria del Mare to return to the grassy field it had been before they'd begun. He thought of all the work that had been done, all the hopes and dreams that that work had embodied, and he knew that he could not let his feelings toward Gianluca endanger the island's fate.

Reaching for his quill, he drew a clean sheet of parchment from the bottom of the stack; then he curled his body around the edge of the table and began to let his imagination do its work.

# C h a p t e r
## 14

A S THE ISLAND crept back to its usual routine — the people gradually patching up their roofs, their wells, their gardens — Gianluca threw himself, with an adamantine zeal, into the reconstruction of the new village center. By the morning of Epiphany he'd managed to organize the village into four teams, led by Silvano Rizzardello, Paolo Guarnieri, Ugolino Ramponi, and Gesmundo Barbon; fueled by Gianluca's seemingly inexhaustible energy, they worked day and night to clear away the rubble, separate it into pieces of the *campanil* and pieces of the *campo* (making a special pile for pieces of the monument, which Piero placed in a burlap sack and had Giuseppe Navo bury at sea), and then find a way to put the whole thing back together again.

While Piero waited for the new piece of stone that Enrico Torta had promised for the new central monument (guaranteeing, in addition to the twin burial vault, a perpetual flame at the rear of the chapel to be attended, after his death, by Beppe Guancio), Beppe Guancio went around the island with a two-wheeled cart made of woven twigs and lined with a piece of satin to gather up the bits of scattered tile. After forty-two rounds — including a thorough scouring of every hovel on the island — he managed to collect over two-thirds of the lost pieces. Added to what Giuseppe Navo retrieved by dragging the lagoon along the perimeter of the island with a quarter-nail double-mesh wading net, that accounted for everything except an occasional patch, which Piero assured them he could fill in with painted stones.

Gianluca worked feverishly both day and night. His strong body seemed to thrive on the exertion, and his enthusiasm was so great that it managed to blind the other workers to the sudden change in weather. Winter had come to Riva di Pignoli. Fog rolled in in thick waves, filling the fields and footpaths with a soft gray uncertainty. The Bora blew down, penetrating the flimsy hovel walls with its chill. The colder weather created problems that had not been present during the late summer and early autumn construction: the dampness rusted the pulleys so that the scaffolding ropes jammed; the mortar work had to be covered with straw and wet dung each night to prevent it from cracking before morning; the workers' dry, chapped hands became easily cut by the sharp edges of the hard glass tiles.

"The pieces don't fit the same way they did in the summer," said Fausto Moretti. "Hot weather, cold weather — it's not the same thing."

"Yesterday my thumb got stuck to the tile," said Siora Bertinelli. "Maria Luigi had to ladle some *brodo di verzurra* over it get it free."

"Brunetto Fucci's spent so much time with his hands in wet mortar," said Maria Patrizia Lunardi, "his fingers won't bend. He can't even pick up a sardine."

No matter the complication, however, the villagers worked on, led by the spirit of renewal and the dash and diligence of Gianluca.

Of the handful or so of the villagers who did not participate in the labor — Orsina and the three Marias, Valentina and Piarina — the most obvious absence was Miriam. It wasn't that she didn't want to help; it was simply that having reached the final stages of her pregnancy, she had grown so large, she could neither stoop nor bend nor hoist nor lift nor carry. Her desire to be a part of the activity was so great, however, that Siora Scabbri let her leave the henhouse each morning and each afternoon to walk to the Chiesa di Maria del Mare and serve spiced cider to the workers. Gianluca pretended not to notice these visits, but everyone could see that he moved more quickly, shouted more loudly, and in general seemed more alive when Miriam appeared. For the rest of the villagers, it provided an opportunity to participate in what had become the island's favorite pastime: trying to guess the sex of Miriam's baby. Nearly everyone had a different means for determining what it would be, each equally emphatic that his or hers was the only reliable method.

"It's a girl!" announced Siora Scabbri after examining the shape of Miriam's belly. "Big in front, it's a boy; wide on the sides, it's a girl."

"It's a boy!" declared Silvano Guarnieri after pricking Miriam's finger with a sharp pin to bleed over a bowl of well water. "When it floats, it's a girl; when it sinks, it's a boy."

"It's a girl!" insisted the Vedova Scarpa after approaching Miriam with a goose bone suspended from a thick piece of twine. "If it spins to the right, it's a boy; if it spins to the left, it's a girl."

Gianluca did his best not to enter into these discussions; he refused to acknowledge that he was still in love with Miriam and that his incredible efforts to rebuild the village center were in large part for her benefit. He tried to work as diligently as he could, aware that sooner or later even he would grow tired. But as the weeks slipped by, and December became January and January became February, he found to his astonishment that his energy was only increasing — and one day, as he was crouching over the tilework to examine the missing pieces of a dragon's tail, he discovered the reason: his own dragon's tail had reawakened. While he hadn't been looking, *Il Bastòn* had roused to life again. And though it helped him to keep going when the energy of the other workers flagged, it also drew the feather of tranquillity from off his chest and led him back on the rocky path toward desire.

❦

GIUSEPPE NAVO THOUGHT the winter a fine time to fish. True, the fog made it more difficult to navigate, and the icy air made it less pleasant to venture out into the lagoon before sunrise, but as most of the other fishermen used these facts to stay in bed a bit longer or skip their work entirely, Giuseppe found it a time of more space, more solitude, and, ultimately, more fish. He often had to travel farther out from Riva di Pignoli — there were pockets of warmer water to the south and the east where the fish tended to migrate — but the satisfaction he felt when he returned from his journey was well worth the extra effort.

One morning, about three weeks after the devastating storm, Giuseppe started out toward Puntalupa for what he called "the quick catch": get there early, gather up a dozen in the first few hours, and hurry back to the island to stock the stalls, visit with the Vedova, or, in this case, help Gianluca with the reconstruction. When he reached the zone he'd aimed for, however, he found that the current had shifted and that the water was icier than the water close to home. So he continued south — past Terra del Pozzo di Luna, past Pescatorno and Murano, and even past Venezia herself — until he found a warmer region just north of Chioggia, where he dropped anchor and set up his poles.

The catch was as easy as any he could remember; the fish practically hurled themselves out of the water and over the side of his boat. By the time the first glow of light had begun to spread on the horizon, his little net was full, and he began to make his way back north.

Although it was not his home, the southern part of the lagoon was not unfamiliar to him. A lifetime of fishing had given him contact with nearly every patch of land that showed above the surface. One tiny groundswell was something of a haven to him: a shelf of rock that rose so gradually from the water, one could ease one's boat upon it and dock without using a rope. Many times Giuseppe had stopped there, pulled up his rig, and climbed out to sit like a happy pelican, his toes in the water, looking out over the lagoon.

Today, as he neared that groundswell, he gave an unconscious nod to the figure sitting just as he himself had sat so many times before. But it was not until he had almost passed it by that he realized that there was no boat beside the figure, and that it was not so much sitting as lying slumped on its side. The morning light was still faint and gauzelike, but when he came to within arm's length of the body, Giuseppe could see that it was swollen with death, and that where its clothes were shredded open it was covered with hideous black sores.

Easing his boat back out into the water, he dumped his entire morning's catch over the side. Then he headed back to Riva di Pignoli, grateful that such a thing was occurring well away from home and eager to see how he might best forget it.

THROUGHOUT THE BITTER WEEKS of building, Valentina and Piarina remained sheltered inside their hovel — for from the moment Valentina had scooped up the injured girl and carried her home to the low bed made of straw and pigeon feathers, she became as mute and immobile as the storm-tossed, star-crossed child. While Piarina lay on the ravaged bedding, eyes open and body rigid, Valentina sat on the cold dirt floor twisted up in a fisherman's knot. She rose only to stumble to the hearth and either crush down some peas or slice a few onions to make a thin *brodo corto* to keep them both alive. Once a day she would raise Piarina's head and feed her tasteless mouthfuls of the warm, watery gruel, forcing herself to take a few spoonfuls too before she returned to the dirt and slipped back into her rope knot. What stunned her, what froze her in place, was the awful awareness that, even as her child lay gravely ill, her desire to beat her was every bit as strong as it had ever been. The only thing that had changed was the awareness: suddenly, like Piarina, she saw her impulses and was horrified by them. So she sat in the dirt and stared at the wall, afraid that if she went about her chores, she might forget herself and whack the sickly child into death.

Piarina, whose already wispy hair had begun to shed and whose body temperature fluctuated between smoldering heat and trembling cold, made no attempt to rouse herself from her stupor. She was convinced that her murderous fantasies had finally gone beyond her control — that the terrible storm that had toppled the *campanil* had come because she'd prayed that it might fall on Valentina. So she lay on the bed, sometimes shivering, sometimes sweating, and tried not to move even a toe for fear that it might bring the roof crashing in.

They remained that way for over a month, growing thinner and weaker as the broth-filled days passed by. The people of Riva di Pignoli noticed their absence, but as long as a few ribbons of smoke continued to issue from their chimney, they figured it was best not to question their habits. They might have stayed that way, in silence and fear, until they'd wasted down to a pair of glowing skeletons, had it not been for Ermenegilda. One morning in early February, she was sitting at her loom staring dejectedly at the dozens of boxes Albertino had sent her, when Romilda Rosetta suddenly entered with a pitcher of fig juice and a plate of *sarde in saor.*

"I've brought you something special!" announced Romilda Rosetta.

"I don't want it," said Ermenegilda. "Take it away."

Albertino's plan to send Ermenegilda his boxes had tragically misfired: having given him most of them herself, she received them back as a blunt declaration of the end of his affections. After tying him to a flagpole and casting him from a third-floor window, Ermenegilda could not bring herself to challenge his decision; so she sat before the stack of boxes and refused the food that Romilda Rosetta tried daily to get her to eat.

"It's half-past one," said Romilda Rosetta. "You know what you promised: one meal at half-past one, and I won't tell your mother you haven't been eating the rest of the day."

Romilda Rosetta was amazed to find herself actually encouraging Ermenegilda to eat; for years she'd watched the enormous girl devour whatever was placed before her with unbounded glee. In the past six weeks, however, Ermenegilda had lost that extra layer of fat that made her still seem childlike, and Romilda Rosetta was afraid that if she stopped eating altogether, she would soon be out of a job.

"It can't be half-past one," said Ermenegilda. "It's not even *mezzogiorno*."

"I'm sorry," said Romilda Rosetta, laying down the pitcher and plate before her. "But the sundial shows half-past one. I can bring it here and set it by the window if you don't believe me."

"Don't bother," said Ermenegilda, poking through the onions to count the number of *sardelle* on her plate. "When are they going to finish that stupid tower? And start ringing those stupid bells?"

"I think they're working as fast as they can," said Romilda Rosetta. "And besides — no one's seen that little girl who rings them since the storm."

Ermenegilda had just picked up a *sarda* by the tail —

and there it dangled, dripping with sauce, as she froze at Romilda Rosetta's words. For close to a year she'd repressed her longing for Piarina while she'd busied herself with gaining revenge on Albertino. With what she now perceived as his ultimate rejection in hand, she shrank at the possibility of her little friend being in danger.

"Piarina?" she said.

"That's it. The one you used to like to visit."

Ermenegilda virtually leapt from the loom — sending spindles and bobbins and *sarde in saor* flying out toward the west wall tapestry — and fled across the island to the shabby hovel where Valentina and Piarina remained fixed. When she threw open the door the light revealed a dusty mausoleum with a pair of seeming corpses in its grasp — but Ermenegilda knew the flavor of despair as well as she knew the flavor of pignoli, and her sturdy heart was not remotely fooled.

"What's going on here?" she demanded.

Valentina and Piarina were so startled by the intrusion, they each turned a double hand's span toward the sudden light. But while Piarina remained paralyzed in her new position, Valentina turned instantly back toward the darkness — forcing Ermenegilda to go to her side and force her into an explanation.

She muttered about the storm, about "curses" and "magic," she rapped her wooden stump against the floor and shouted, *"Uno, do, tre, quàtro, cìnque!"* — until finally Ermenegilda left them and went back to the Ca'Torta, where she gathered up as much food as she could carry and threw it into one of the wheelbarrows from the rose garden, along with Albertino's boxes — the cask of ivory, the coffer of pewter, the chest of cherrywood, the caddy of quartz. Then she headed back to the broken hovel where her fragile friend lay perched between life and death.

For the next few weeks she kept vigil over the child, feeding her pickled dove and *fegato alle erbe* and slender strips of roasted goat with cherry sauce. In addition to that she strewed the hut with Albertino's gorgeous boxes, placing some upon the hearth and some upon the soap table, some in the straw and one at each corner of Piarina's bed. Finally, on the morning of the nineteenth day of Ermenegilda's succor, while Valentina puttered in the corner with a few cakes of soda soap and Ermenegilda stood over the hearth heating up a *sopa di tutti mar*, Piarina bolted up in her bed and began crying out in frenzy.

"A clump of chervil . . . a handful of dill . . . an owl's intestines . . . an ostrich plume . . . a bead of coriander . . . a bee's turd . . . a velvet glove . . . a gram of goat's blood . . ."

Ermenegilda dropped her ladle; Valentina dropped her knife; together they turned to where the cacophony of cures came streaming.

"A licorice stick . . . a basin of bile . . . an ox tongue . . . a sweet-sugar cake. . . ."

Piarina seemed fully restored to her former vitality. But fear still lurked in the dark corners of the hovel, and neither Ermenegilda nor Valentina had the slightest clue as to what she was trying to cure.

BY MID-FEBRUARY Miriam's baby was ready to be born. The people of the village didn't know this; had they bothered to count, they would not have been expecting the child before March or April, believing it to have been conceived sometime after Miriam's arrival. But everyone was too busy working to worry about counting, so when Miriam announced that the pressure in her abdomen had become so great that she feared she was going to explode, the only reaction was that it was time to start readying the swaddling clothes.

Word of the impending birth soon spread across the village. Maria Luigi began stitching fabrics together to make a coverlet for the cradle. The Vedova Scarpa began sending bowls of soup through the gradually thinning fog. And at the site of the reconstruction, where the *campanil* and the *campo* were slowly creeping back to life, the villagers began to quarrel over how to best determine when the long awaited moment would arrive.

"When it's cloudy for two days," said Siora Bertinelli, "then sunny for a day, then cloudy again. The baby will be born before nightfall."

"When she starts craving salt," said Siora Guarnieri, "and her feet begin to tingle."

"When the geese start coming to her door," said Anna Rizzardello.

But the Vedova Stampanini, who had had more experience with childbirth than probably anyone else in the lagoon, knew precisely how to predict when it would happen.

"As long as it still hurts, you're not ready. When the pain goes away — when you suddenly feel fine again — that's the sign. You'll deliver within two days."

Miriam had moved in with the Vedova Stampanini for the last weeks of her term — into the room, and the bed, where Gianluca usually slept. Gianluca, to accommodate her, moved back out to Albertino's, but Miriam could feel him with her as the birth drew near. His musky odor permeated the straw, his strong laughter lingered in the air like the fog lingered over the footpaths. She would not have admitted it to anyone, but his presence at this delicate time was a source of nourishment to her.

As the birth approached, Miriam began to sense that the arrival of the baby would finally take away her longing. The glow came so regularly now, she could not imagine it disappearing; it seemed only logical that the baby would replace it and that the aching inside her would finally be satisfied.

Around the third week in February Miriam announced the lightening of pressure that the Vedova had described, and almost instantly the hovel began to fill with women. They came from all over the island to see that the necessary precautions were taken to insure a safe birth. Siora Scabbri applied a sponge, soaked in morel, mulberries, and mandrake root, to Miriam's forehead to help her sleep; Maria Luigi gave her sage juice to drink to ease her into delivery; the Vedova Scarpa stood guard outside the hovel to prevent spirits from entering to snatch the newborn child. Miriam had never had *La Pica* — that strange craving for spicy sauces or salty cheese or tiny pieces of coal — but now, as her labor approached, she suddenly could not get her fill of *sopa d'osei*. Maria Patrizia Lunardi had to coax Ugolino Ramponi to set up a series of special nets to catch the fleet and tender birds, while the Vedova Scarpa worked well into the night stirring them into a fine broth of roots and herbs. Miriam always stacked the bones in a neat pile beside her pillow, which Siora Scabbri removed when she fell asleep and placed in the garden for the cats.

On the morning of the second day after the lightening of the pressure, Miriam awoke from a horrifying dream in

which she'd given birth to a child with a pair of bright
blue wings. She was so disturbed that the Vedova Stampanini had to brew a vat of mulled wine to sedate her, and
it was as the Vedova sat by the hearth, stabbing dried figs
with cloves to drop into the cauldron, that Armida Barbon
suddenly cried out that the process had begun.

*"L'aqua!"* she shouted as Miriam's waters soaked the
bed linens. "It could start any time now!"

The hovel swiftly prepared itself for action. Siora Scabbri began rubbing an ointment of chamomile and verbena
on Miriam's belly; Maria Luigi loosened Miriam's hair;
Armida Barbon ran about the hovel opening doors and
drawers and cupboards to encourage the opening of Miriam. By late morning the contractions had begun — from
the way Miriam grasped the Vedova Stampanini's hand,
the old woman knew that the pain was tremendous, but
Miriam did not let out so much as a whimper. For the
remainder of the afternoon, as the pains came and went,
she slept and read and sat propped up on pillows, helping
the Vedova pierce dried winter fruit with spice.

Around dusk the women helped her from the bed and
began walking her, in small circles, about the hovel. The
pressure grew stronger; there was less and less time between contractions. And as her body hurtled forward toward the moment of release, Miriam suddenly began to
fear for her baby.

"I'm frightened," she whispered to the Vedova Stampanini as Siora Scabbri and Maria Luigi began to rub her
arms and legs with clover oil.

"It's normal," said the Vedova. "Your body's about to
do something it's never done before."

"My baby's going to die!" she cried. "It's going to be
born with a pair of bright blue wings and die!"

"If that's what God decides, *cara*, there's nothing you can do to prevent it. But it's not going to help your labor to keep thinking about it."

"I have to think about it," she said as she gripped the Vedova's hand more fiercely. "Tell me. Tell me so I can survive it."

"Keep moving, Miriam," said Siora Scabbri. "It's getting close now."

"What do you mean, child?" asked the Vedova Stampanini.

"Your children. Tell me how you lost them."

"We have to move her to the stool," said Maria Luigi. "The pains are coming faster."

"It's not the time, *cara*," said the Vedova. "I'll tell you about it after."

"No!" cried Miriam as the three women led her to the birthing stool. "I want to know now. Tell me now — so I have the strength to face it if it comes."

As Maria Luigi and Siora Scabbri helped lower Miriam upon the stool, the Vedova Stampanini let go of her hand and clasped her bony arms about her waist. She stared off into the distance as if she were trying to visualize the separate sections of a huge tapestry that time had torn to shreds. Then she drew a deep breath that seemed to weave the pieces back together again, and spoke.

"First there was Bernardo. He had a thick head of curls and a cry that woke the entire village. The cry lasted six days; so did Bernardo. We buried him before the sound was out of the roof beams."

Miriam gripped the two women's hands as she went into another contraction.

"*Spingia!*" cried Maria Luigi.

"Tommaso was next. He lasted a whole year. Time enough for six teeth, three chins, and a wonderful fat bottom. I used to love to pinch that bottom — I'd sing, 'Tommaso, Tommaso, a baby made of clay!' He was bit by a rat. Six times, in his bed. He died within the hour."

"*Spingia!*" cried Siora Scabbri.

"Next came a spate of girls. Giovàna, with her black shining hair, who died of San Vitus' dance when she was four. Isabella, so delicate and frail, who couldn't stand the harsh winters. And Laura — such a strange child, with a bubbling laugh one minute and a face to the floor the next — who simply announced one Pentecost that she was through with eating and was gone before Tutti Santi."

"*La testa!*" cried Maria Luigi as the head began to crown. "*Spingia*, Miriam! *Spingia!*"

Miriam's body was now bathed in sweat, her gown unfastened, her face clenched tightly with her efforts.

"That's enough," said the Vedova. "You have to concentrate now."

"Tell me all of it," gasped Miriam. "Please — tell me the rest."

The Vedova cast a glance at Maria Luigi, who shrugged, and Siora Scabbri, who nodded, so she closed her eyes and continued on.

"Egidio came next. He lasted the longest. Sixteen winters to watch the baby become a boy and the boy become a man. To watch the tiny hand I used to hold between my finger and thumb grow big enough to swing a sledgehammer. It was hardest to lose Egidio — we'd given ourselves over to him. And all from a bad tooth — "

"*Spingia!*"

"But then Mario and Agosto were difficult, too.

Drowned in the lagoon. That was when I began to accept it. That was when I stopped sitting in the garden eating bitter herbs and crying myself to sleep at night."

"It's coming," cried Maria Luigi. "Don't stop now!"

"Go on," panted Miriam. "Go on."

"The next to last was Orlandino. Stillborn. His father didn't even want to name him, but after nine months inside me I knew him as well as I'd known the others, so I insisted."

"It's almost there!"

"The last was a baby girl. We named her Maria, hoping that maybe the Blessed Virgin would intervene and allow us to keep her, but she was gone before we could lay her in her cradle."

"That's it, Miriam! You're doing it! Here it comes!"

A silence came over the hovel as the tiny infant sprang out of Miriam's body and into Siora Scabbri's hands. There was a moment of prayer — and then a great, healthy wail filled the room.

"It's a boy!" cried Maria Luigi. "A beautiful baby boy!"

"Has he got wings?" whispered Miriam. "Has he got bright blue wings?"

"No wings, *cara*," said the Vedova as she reached down to lift up the slimy newborn to view it. "Just a milky-white caul over his head."

"A caul!" said Armida Barbon.

"That brings luck, Miriam," said Siora Scabbri.

The Vedova drew the sticky substance off the infant's head with the heel of her hand; then she lifted him up to Miriam's breast, where he eagerly sought the nipple.

"No wings," murmured Miriam. "No wings."

Siora Scabbri guided Miriam and the baby back to the bed. The Vedova Stampanini cut the umbilical cord with a sharp knife and placed a pair of sewing clips on the end. Then Maria Luigi took the baby into the other room, where she rubbed him from head to toe with salt, cleansed his palate and gums with acacia honey, and wrapped him tightly in swaddling bandages before returning him to Miriam.

*"Grazie,"* Miriam said to the Vedova, her cheeks damp and glistening.

The Vedova Stampanini said nothing. She merely sat by Miriam's side until both she and the newborn had fallen asleep. Then she went to the hearth and began dropping the studded figs into the kettle of dark wine — where they splashed like bits of sweet hail and then floated, calmly, to the surface.

# Chapter 15

THROUGH THE COLD gray months of January and February the people of Riva di Pignoli did their best not to think about the spring. They worked on the reconstruction of the new village center, they stumbled through the fog up the Calle Alberi Grandi, they hunkered beside their hearths over bowls of pease pudding and plate after plate of dried *baccala*. The spring was a fancy — a memory — a dream. After last year's game of hide-and-go-seek, they knew better than to count on its arrival.

As March eased the chill, however, and licked away the clouds of mist that swirled along the footpaths, they began to hear a faint singing. It started in the lagoon: beneath the surface of the winter waters the sea grass began to chant. The docks along the western shore began to stretch and sigh; if you listened closely in the early morning, or the hour between dusk and dinner, you could hear them creak a dry, plaintive melody upon the salty air. But clearest of all — if you paused beneath a pine tree for a quick rest or happened to wander into one of the sleeping fields, away from the voices of the village — was the low, rolling resonance that rose in a gentle arc from beneath the soil.

It gave a lilt to Siora Bertinelli's step as she moved about her hovel making pastries in the shape of swans. It caused Anna Rizzardello to do a shin dance as she scraped the salting racks, and it turned Gesmundo Barbon's daily ritual of untangling the fishing nets into an interpretive fisherman's ballet. When people passed on the Calle Alberi Grandi, they linked arms and did a quick jig; Giuseppe Navo sneaked into the Vedova Stampanini's twice a day to do a turn and a low dip before the broth pot. The spring might not arrive with all the whirring and popping and fierce drama with which it had exploded upon the villagers the previous year, but the urge to dance that came over them made it clear that it would come.

Albertino was determined that it come on schedule. So as the second construction of the *campanil*, the *campo*, and the monument moved toward completion, he suggested to Piero that they arrange a special event to attract the fickle season's attention.

"Perhaps we could light a bonfire," he suggested. "Or ring the new bells until at least a blade of grass appears. We can't take the chance that this year it might not find us at all."

Piero needed no convincing. The completion of the new village center, after so much difficulty, was a milestone in Riva di Pignoli history. Spring or no spring, he intended to honor it with as lavish a celebration as the island had ever seen.

Piero had worked hard the past two months. While the village had married itself to the reconstruction of the *campanil* and the *campo*, he'd burrowed himself away in his corner of Beppe Guancio's hovel and devoted himself to resculpting the statue of Miriam. Where the first statue had expressed his passion, however, this one expressed his piety: he carefully fashioned an elegant Madonna and Child, with Miriam and her newborn infant as his models. He had not actually seen the baby, as Miriam was still in her postpartum confinement, but he'd received detailed descriptions from Maria Luigi of the long, slender body, the abundant curls, and the slightly almond-shaped eyes, and he was sure that combined with his careful rendering of Miriam, his intentions would be unmistakable. How could the villagers reject an infant who graced their village center in the image of the Savior? How could Miriam reject a man who commemorated that village by dedicating it to her and her child?

The people of Riva di Pignoli had no money to pay for entertainment to be brought to the island, so Piero went to Fra Danilo to ask for his usual assistance.

"I want something the people have never seen before," he said. "I want music, and storytelling — a real public festival."

"Easter's coming," said the monk. "I'm sure I can arrange for a donation of services with the promise of a few paid engagements throughout the lagoon."

"Do you have a particular group in mind?"

"It depends on what you're looking for. I know a number of local guilds that provide excellent entertainment. There's a group of goldsmiths in Eraclea who do a splendid

Adoration of the Magi. There's a carpenters' guild in Pellestrina that offers a wonderful version of Noah's Ark. And there's a wine merchants' guild in Treviso that tells a riveting Marriage at Canaa."

"What about the Story of the Virgin?"

"The Story of the Virgin . . ." Fra Danilo pondered. "I believe there are some mummers from Padova who do that. They're primarily street performers — jugglers, acrobats, that sort of thing — but I've heard they do a very good Story of the Virgin."

"Perhaps they could do it all," said Piero. "We've never had a real festival on Riva di Pignoli. Perhaps they could do a bit of singing and dancing along the Calle Alberi Grandi and then present the Story of the Virgin on the new *campo.*"

"I've never seen you so enthusiastic, Piero! What's come over you?"

"It's a time for celebration," said Piero. "After all the troubles we've weathered this past year, I feel we should acknowledge our good fortune."

"You're perfectly right," said Fra Danilo. "I'll send word to Padova this afternoon and see what I can arrange for you."

Piero returned to Riva di Pignoli and sent word about the village: in celebration of the new village center and the coming of spring, the First Riva di Pignoli Street Festival — to take place on the only Riva di Pignoli street — would be held on the first day of spring.

Everyone invited. Wear masks. Bring pipes and tambourines.

That night Piero worked well into the darkness on the last touches of the monument: the folds in Miriam's hood, the curve of her wrist around the infant's belly, the traces of their lips and eyelashes. When he could work no more he laid down his chisel, crept to his bed, and fell asleep.

A short time after, he was awakened — or so he thought — by the sound of drums. They started in the distance like a heartbeat and grew louder, and more passionate, as they moved across the island toward Beppe Guancio's hovel. There were pipes and psalters, and there was singing, too, and a strange, dry clacking noise that Piero could not identify. When the sounds were just outside his walls there came a loud rapping at the door; Piero could not help but laugh thinking that the mummers had come too soon, that they had not been able to wait until the coming of spring to begin their joyful revels. He rose from his bed and went to the door, trying to formulate what to say to them; when he opened it, however, his words lodged in his throat. For there before him stretched a band of grinning skeletons — dancing wildly in the pitch of night and returning his own bright laughter note for note.

❈

MIRIAM TOO HEARD MUSIC while she lay in bed at night. It came in through the tiny window that let a bit of air into Gianluca's room at the back of the Vedova Stampanini's hovel. For Miriam, however, there was no need to go to the door to identify the sounds; even in her sleep she knew the searching, tortured-goat quality of Gianluca's singing.

"Such a terrible voice, Nicolo," she whispered to her baby, "in such a beautiful man."

Miriam had decided to name her baby Nicolo, after the

patron saint of the island. He was a serious baby. He hardly ever fussed, and he never cried. The women who attended the birth were quick to report that he resembled neither Piero nor Gianluca, but the truth was he did not even resemble Miriam. He resembled only himself. Nicolo. And even at a few days old he seemed to know it.

Nicolo delighted Miriam beyond measure — his perfectly shaped nostrils, his inquisitive gaze, his lean and noble toes. But he did not remove her longing. It sat like a sack of peas beside her heart as it always had. It still called for something to quench its fire, it still rolled back its edges and laid itself out in her prayers. And since Miriam now knew she could not expect anyone to take it away, it seemed harmless to allow herself her feelings for Gianluca. They'd barely spoken since that afternoon he'd bolted from Siora Scabbri's hen yard. But Miriam had seen the change that had come over him — how he'd practically chained himself to the Chiesa di Maria del Mare in order to rebuild the village center — and she was delighted to find him once again singing ballads beneath her window.

Gianluca's ballads soothed Nicolo to sleep. The moment he heard them he would close his eyes and begin a soft, mewling counterpoint that eased him into dreamland. So after a few weeks had passed, and Miriam had regained her strength, she asked the Vedova Stampanini to invite Gianluca in.

"Tell him Nicolo wants to meet him," she said. "And tell him — God help us — to bring his lute."

The Vedova delivered the message to Gianluca, and Gianluca entered the hovel.

"Nicolo likes your songs," said Miriam.

"I'm glad," said Gianluca.

"You must be nearly finished with the reconstruction if you have time for singing."

"We should be done any day now. We hoist the bells tomorrow, and spring isn't due for another week yet."

"You must be proud of what you've done."

Gianluca shrugged.

"You should be, Gianluca."

Gianluca stepped closer and began to study Nicolo. "He's a fine-looking boy," he said.

"He's very strong. He can already lift himself up."

"I suppose I'll have to teach him how to use an ax. People say there'll be a lot more building now that we've finished the campo."

Miriam looked up at him and thought about their conversation that day in the hen yard. "I think he can wait a few more months," she said. "For now I think he'd prefer another song. Do you know any lullabies?"

"I'll have to write some," he said. "What do babies like to hear about?"

"Nicolo would like to hear about the invention of the watermill or the discovery of the compass or the travels of Sior Polo in distant lands. Things which will stir challenge, and adventure, in his heart."

Nicolo yipped a little in agreement.

"I'll take him on a journey, then. To Malabar for pepper. To Tunis for wax and silver. Is tomorrow night all right?"

"Tomorrow is fine," said Miriam. "Come whenever you like."

Gianluca could not hide the blush that rose to his cheeks, but he bowed, and said, *"Bona notte,"* before Miriam could see the rising beneath his tunic. Miriam, for her part, was content with the thought that she would see him again the next evening, and that he'd finally offered to care for her child. The only thing that bothered her was that Piero had offered to do the same thing; that she'd asked him to do it; and that he waited across the island for an equal chance to prove his affection.

❧

ALTHOUGH ERMENEGILDA spent her days at Piarina's side, she made certain each evening to return to the Ca' Torta for supper. She knew her mother's temper; staying away from dawn to dusk might press it to its limits, but staying away for good would send it hurtling over the edge. Yet no matter how much Orsina nagged her, Ermenegilda would not disclose how she was spending her days. The hours she passed at Piarina's bedside were like pieces of another life; once she was back behind the walls of the Ca' Torta, she refused to taint them with discussion.

The women of the Ca' Torta, however, could hardly complain about the change in Ermenegilda's manner. Her appetite had returned, which relieved Romilda Rosetta; she no longer stamped and quarreled, which delighted Orsina; and she virtually acquiesced to every command of her astonished elder sisters. She would sit at the candlelit table like a painted screen image, neither flinching at the assorted digs that were hurled in her direction nor seeming to even notice when, in contrast, she was ignored. She ate her meals at a patient pace and went eagerly to bed the instant they were finished. The sooner she slept, the sooner she returned to Piarina.

Orsina was convinced she'd finally given herself to Albertino. She imagined them rolling over the dry fields where the carrots poked their crowns or heaving away in the brush on the eastern shore. The three Marias decided she was going off to Venezia to spend their father's money on potions and charms in order to win herself a suitor. Romilda Rosetta was half-certain she'd found an order of overweight nuns, as the glow she exhibited could only be the result of fanatical spiritual pursuits.

Romilda Rosetta came closest to the truth. For though Valentina and Piarina's hovel was hardly an abbey for prioresses, Ermenegilda's daily ventures there were softening something inside her. To care for her little friend was unlike anything she'd ever done; to watch her strengthen, to see her smile, was better than a dozen plates of red-deer stew. And though she was hardly aware of it, she even began to bear her loss of Albertino. Only now and then — as she traveled up the Calle Alberi Grandi at dusk or settled into her goose-down quilt before she drifted off to sleep — would his lopsided face appear to remind her that the world was a terrible place.

ON THE MORNING of the celebration the sun rose slowly into a pure, cloudless sky. As it lifted up above the lip of the lagoon, its light first struck upon the tiny cross on the roof of the completed *campanil* and then continued down over the arches of the belfry and the walls of the tower and the shrouded monument at the center of the *campo*, until it spread in a glinting wash over the finished mosaic. The griffins grinned, the circle of snakes expanded and contracted, the dragons and hell-sprites bristled down their fur as the river of light ran over them.

In the huts and hovels across the island, the villagers had risen and were preparing for the day's festivities. Most had nothing more than a clean tunic or a slightly less used gown to wear, but they donned them with pride and left their feelings of abandon to their masks. Siora Scabbri pasted chicken feathers to a matte of straw and fastened it to her head with red ribbons. Brunetto Fucci shaped a face from wet plaster and sprinkled it with an array of exotic spices. Maria Luigi wound a series of silk veils into the headgear of an Arabian princess. More than a few of the villagers harbored the secret fantasy that their mask would be so impressive, the mummers would invite them to join their troupe.

Albertino would have been willing to wear a boar's head if he thought it would help bring the spring, but in his heart he feared that all the fuss was for nothing. When the sun rose up over the east wall of his room, however, and shot across the floor to where he and Gianluca lay sleeping, it brought with it the unmistakable smell of hyacinth — and when he looked out over the *radicchio* patch he saw patches of green poking up through the dry March soil. So he quickly gathered some carrots, some pressed figs, and a handful of dried lentils and made the most euphoric piece of vegetable facewear anyone could ever have imagined.

When the sun had risen a slight head's tilt above the roof of Siora Bertinelli's hovel, the mummers arrived at the docks on the western shore. They poured from a series of large transport vessels dressed in bright masquerade. There were jugglers and fiddlers and acrobats; there were trunks of costumes and baskets of colored ribbons; there were children and monkeys and a few surreptitious rats.

Piero met them, in a skeleton mask made from the bones of a dead goat, and led them to the base of the Calle Alberi Grandi. As they started their procession, the people of the island rushed out of their huts to join them: the Vedova Scarpa in a mask of bright coins; Fausto Moretti with his beard painted blue; Maria Patrizia Lunardi with her hair full of grain-stuffed larks. They moved up the rough pathway in a state of exultation. One of the mummers juggled a trio of baked breads while another did a lively horn dance. Silvano Rizzardello tossed handfuls of salt into the air, and Gesmundo Barbon did an elaborate routine that involved slapping a pair of codfish against his shins, his thighs, and his belly.

When the boisterous procession finally reached the village center, Piero began to look around for Miriam. The Vedova Stampanini had assured him that she would make the celebration her first public appearance since the birth of Nicolo, but Piero couldn't find her anywhere. Just as he was about to give up hope, however, a whisper ran through the crowd — and as a pair of mummers walked the rim of the *campo* on their hands, the eyes of the villagers turned back toward the Calle Alberi Grandi and from behind the clutch of pine trees she appeared. She was wearing a mask made of seashells and swan feathers, and she was pushing a small cart, which Beppe Guancio had fashioned from an old cod barrel, in which Nicolo sat wrapped in his blanket of seaweed. He too had a mask — a scattering of *pignoli* on his cheeks and forehead — and together they managed to silence the revelry.

"*Che belo!*" cried the Vedova Scarpa.

"Our little king!" said Gesmundo Barbon.

Piero, who was no less dazzled by the impression they

made, took advantage of the suddenly focused energy. Moving to the center of the *campo*, he stepped up on one of the mummers' trunks and called for the villagers' attention.

"My friends," he said, "we are here today to celebrate the completion of a long labor."

"You aren't kidding!" shouted Ugolino Ramponi.

"Only a year ago," continued Piero, "our little island was so insignificant it took the spring an extra month to find us. We had no center, no identity. We hardly seemed to exist. Now we have a *campanil*, a *campo*, and a monument, and the spring has come to us right on time. I don't think it will ever forget us again!"

The villagers burst out in a great cheer.

"Show us the monument!" shouted Paolo Guarnieri.

"We want to see it!" cried Siora Bertinelli.

"Before I unveil the statue," said Piero, "I have to thank someone. Without his efforts we could never have recovered from the Christmas Day storm, and we wouldn't be celebrating today."

"Gianluca!" cried the crowd. "Gianluca!"

Gianluca, who was wearing a satyr's mask carved from a piece of pinewood, stepped forward to acknowledge the tribute; when his eyes met Piero's they were not without a certain humility.

"Let's just hope it stays standing this time," he said. "I don't think we could do it a third time."

Piero and Beppe Guancio approached the monument.

"I commemorate the new *campo* of Riva di Pignoli," said Piero. "May it guard us over demons and disaster."

They removed the canvas covering, and a second hush fell over the crowd. This time it was a silence, however, like the silence before the spring, which contained within it a singing. The villagers had not expected such a tender, reverent vision; they could hardly believe that Piero had sculpted it himself.

Miriam, who had remained until now at the back of the crowd, lowered her mask and moved through the hub to stand, with Nicolo in her arms, before the statue. Though the likeness of her was striking, she barely noticed it for the likeness of Nicolo. It brought tears to her eyes she worked hard not to shed and made her indecisive heart swing back toward Piero.

While the crowd absorbed the splendor of the new impression, the mummers began to set up the space for the presentation of their play. A wooden platform was wheeled into the *campo*, a pair of poles were set into its upstage corners, a large red curtain was draped between the poles. A few pieces of scenery were set out: a pair of large candelabra, a wooden palm tree, a mound of twigs and straw, a lavish-looking throne. The leader of the troupe had suggested that they also use something known as "the mouth of hell," a great dog's head that spouted fire and smoke ("It's our most popular piece," he insisted. "We always manage to work it into the story"), but Piero felt that there were more than enough images of hell in the floor of the *campo* and discouraged him from using it.

There were two actors for the role of the Virgin: a young boy to play her as a child and a teenage one to play her as a woman. They were dressed in light gowns and decked in simple wigs, the younger a pair of golden braids, the older a set of darker, free-flowing tresses. And though the former had a decidedly boyish ebullience and the latter a few traces of down upon his upper lip and cheeks, from the moment they stepped on stage they became the incar-

nation of the beloved Virgin to the people of Riva di Pignoli.

"A very long time ago," began the leader of the troupe,
"a girl was born in the land of Israel."

The villagers settled quickly into a spontaneous semicir-
cle around the edge of the platform as the players entered
in single file. They placed themselves at even intervals
before the curtain at the back and then one by one stepped
forward to enact the simple scenes. Piero, who had seen
such presentations at Boccasante as a boy, gazed over the
other villagers as they watched the proceedings: Albertino,
behind his carrots and his peas, tilted forward like a child
at a boat race; Gianluca, behind his satyr's broad grin,
astonished at what his efforts had wrought; Miriam, mask
still lowered, rapt at the beauty of the story unfolding
before her. They watched as the chronicle proceeded
through the Virgin's childhood and youth, through the
Annunciation, the Visitation with Anna, the Journey to
Egypt, and the preparation for the Birth of the Lord. They
listened to the rolling sounds of the actors' voices and
watched the flashing colors as they bent and bowed and
gestured. But as the actors moved toward the manger, and
the narrator began to describe the clarity of the night
and the brilliance of the lone star overhead, the villagers
noticed a change in the Virgin Maria. At first she swooned,
which they took to be the coming of the child. But then
she turned a distinctly unhealthy shade of greenish gray,
lurched forward, shouted *"Maledizión!"* clutched her side,
and fell before the manger in a heap. Even those islanders
who thought this was meant to be a slightly grotesque
representation of childbirth realized something was wrong
when the other actors rushed forward, removed the boy's
wig, and tore open his costume to give him air — revealing

a battlefield of angry blotches on his pale, youthful skin and a pair of fistlike swellings in his side.

The spring, this year, had come precisely on time. But what it brought with it made the people of Riva di Pignoli wish that it had stayed away for good.

# *C h a p t e r*
# 16

HE VILLAGERS did not know what to make of the collapse of the Blessed Virgin. The young boy was bundled up and taken to Brunetto Fucci's, where a poultice of barbasco and black mustard seed was applied to his hellish swellings, which not only lined his armpits and sides, but were embedded like stony apples in his groin. When it was explained that Riva di Pignoli possessed neither physician nor surgeon nor barber-surgeon, the mummers gathered up the boy; packed their trunks, their baskets, their platforms, and their poles; and set off into the lagoon to find him aid.

At first the villagers felt only concern for the poor lad, whose bitter wailing as the poultices were applied had sliced through the air like a cautering knife. Concern, and curiosity, and the subtle scent of something they did not yet recognize as fear. Reluctantly they removed their masks and returned to their various hovels. They cooked simple suppers over moderate flames and thought more about the excitement of the early part of the day than about the sudden disturbance of the latter.

Except for Piero. He alone among the people of Riva di Pignoli could not shrug off the sight of the dark swellings nor forget the image of the boy collapsing in pain. They were the same dark swellings he'd found on the body that had washed ashore a full year earlier, and he was horrified to see them again.

He had to talk about it with someone — but the only person who knew about the body he'd found before was Fra Danilo. So that night, while the other villagers tried to forget the ugly marks entirely, Piero took his boat and set out for Boccasante. There was not a trace of moon to guide him, and a low blanket of clouds blocked out the stars. Only a small torch and the frequency of his travel between the two islands over the years made his passage across the darkened water possible.

As he moved past the tiny cemetery island, he thought of how distant and foreign that place had always seemed to him. No matter how many times he'd visited there — including his recent journeys to bury and excavate the swollen corpse — he'd always passed through its shadowy confines as if he were moving through a dreamworld. Now, in the silence of the moonless night, the graveyard seemed as coldly real as any other part of the lagoon. Either that, or the rest of the world had grown as phantomlike as the graveyard.

He rowed on toward the shores of the monastery island.

He knew Fra Danilo would be able to advise him; the monk knew something of everything and was sure to understand what the black markings meant. He paddled slowly, careful to keep his direction clear in the blackness of the night. When he came to a distance of about three leagues from the monastery, however, he noticed a tiny spot of light floating over the water. It hovered, stationary, in the darkness — and it was only as he approached it that he could see it came from a torch, much like his own, which was fixed to the prow of a boat in which sat Fra Antonio.

"Stay back!" cried the elderly monk as Piero's boat drew near.

"It's Piero, Fra Antonio! I've come to see Fra Danilo!"

"Piero?" said the monk as he lifted the torch up overhead. "Piero who?"

"Piero Po. I used to live at Boccasante. Don't you remember me?"

Fra Antonio squinted into the darkness. "Go away."

"But I have to see Fra Danilo."

The monk's hands trembled, and the torchlight wavered wildly. "Fra Danilo is sick. The entire monastery is under quarantine. Go away."

"But —"

"Go away!"

Piero stared into the elderly monk's eyes and saw terror. He tried to look past him toward where he knew the monastery lay, but the blackness swallowed everything beyond the small circle of his flame.

"Will you tell him I need to speak with him? It's very important."

"There's no point in speaking with him. Go back to where you came from."

Piero tried to comprehend what Fra Antonio was saying. He'd seen Fra Danilo only the week before; the monk had been in perfect health, as had been all the brothers. Piero longed to press on and visit the island anyway, to see what was happening for himself. But he did not have the heart to upset Fra Antonio any more than he already was. So he thanked him for the information and then headed back through the darkness to Riva di Pignoli.

OVER THE NEXT few days the incident at the spring festival faded from the villagers' minds. With the *campo* completed and the spring at their door, the people were far too joyful to dwell on the illness of a veritable stranger. There were mattresses to be aired; there was planting to be done; there were violets and rose petals to be strewn across straw-covered floors. On the third morning after the festivities, however, a number of the villagers felt a weakness come over them. It started in their heads and spread down through their bodies until their limbs felt weighted with mud. Siora Guarnieri had to lie down under the smoke table and prop hunks of *prosciutto* beneath her neck, her knees, and her shoulders. Gesmundo Barbon could barely drag himself from his boat and had to stop six times on his way from the docks to his hovel.

"It's like I drank a case of *grappa*," he told Armida, "but forgot to take the pleasure of getting drunk."

When Siora Scabbri and both the Rizzardello twins discovered small greenish black marks on their sides, the villagers began whispering about "the sickness." Not ev-

eryone made the connection to the boy at the festival, but
the apprehension in the air increased.

Piarina knew without being told that illness had struck
the island. She leaned forward in her bed and groped the
air and stammered out her cures with new conviction.
Ermenegilda and Valentina could not help but notice the
change. For the past six weeks, as they'd settled into a
pattern of cleaning and feeding and caring for the child,
they'd become almost deaf to the endless litany that poured
from her mouth. For the first time there was a sort of
harmony in the hovel: Piarina knew that as long as Ermenegilda was there she would not try to murder Valentina;
Valentina knew that as long as Ermenegilda was there she
would not try to murder Piarina; and Ermenegilda knew
that, though her heart still pined for Albertino, her love
for Piarina was as selfless and true as anything she had
ever known. It was therefore somewhat disturbing when
Piarina began to behave in this new way. Not only did she
lean forward and speak with increased ardor, she began
to isolate items in her train. Her tongue would catch on a
consonant, then she'd return and repeat herself until a
single object emerged from the lengthy list. When this was
clearly identified she would lapse again into the flood. But
as the days went by, she gradually began to shift from a
random ranting to the specific voicing of a closed sequence
of objects. And eventually Ermenegilda and Valentina began to recognize their pattern:

"A scrap of seaweed . . . a strip of bark . . . a peacock
feather . . . a flask of mercury . . . a wasp's wing . . . six
pignoli . . . a bowl of sorbs set out in the midday sun."

Over and over again — as they stirred the morning
broth, and swept the straw, and dusted Albertino's

boxes — the list of articles came tumbling from Piarina's tongue:

"A scrap of seaweed . . . a strip of bark . . . a peacock feather . . . a flask of mercury . . . a wasp's wing . . . six pignoli . . . a bowl of sorbs set out in the midday sun."

Eventually it became imprinted on their brains, until they too began to chant it, until their three voices began to merge in a curative round:

"A scrap of seaweed . . . a strip of bark *A scrap of seaweed* . . . a peacock feather *a strip of bark* (A scrap of seaweed) . . . a flask of mercury *a peacock feather* (a strip of bark) . . . a wasp's wing *a flask of mercury* (a peacock feather) . . . six pignoli *a wasp's wing* (a flask of mercury) . . . a bowl of sorbs set out in the midday sun *six pignoli* (a wasp's wing) . . . *a bowl of sorbs set out in the midday sun* (six pignoli) . . . (a bowl of sorbs set out in the midday sun)."

But what Piarina intended did not occur to them until she grabbed Ermenegilda by the bodice as she was leaning over her to brush her hair, shook her as vigorously as her tiny arms could shake her, and shouted out the items one by one:

"A scrap of seaweed! A strip of bark! A peacock feather! A flask of mercury! A wasp's wing! Six pignoli! A bowl of sorbs set out in the midday sun!"

And then, in that old familiar voice, that trickle of steam, that strangulated weightless whisper, she added:

"Find them . . . bring them . . . now!"

Valentina, who was stitching together the pieces of a moth-ruined blanket, pricked her finger with the needle and screamed. Ermenegilda, whom Piarina still grasped by the bodice, nearly lost her balance and tumbled into bed beside her.

It was the first thing Piarina had said that was not a stick or a wing or a stone or an herb since that day Valentina had dragged her speechless from the well. And though Valentina and Ermenegilda still had no idea what they might be for, they immediately set out to gather the things she'd requested.

✿

THE FEELING OF FATIGUE raced over the village like a blast of sullen heat; in a matter of days nearly a quarter of the islanders had developed some sign of the sickness. The greenish black marks turned to swellings overnight. Fausto Moretti woke to the sound of his own screaming.

In spite of his visit to Boccasante, Piero tried his best to keep from panicking. There was no reason to believe that the sickness was serious; the reappearance of the ugly black swellings might well be just a gruesome coincidence.

"It's most likely some kind of blood fever," he said to Beppe Guancio as they sat by the fire eating bread and black olives. "The pain can be terrible, but it usually only lasts about a week."

"I've never heard of a blood fever that spread so quickly," said Beppe. "And I've never seen anything like those lumps."

"Whose have you seen?"

"Gesmundo Barbon's. He's got three of them in his left side — hard as rocks and black as soot. Armida says that if she stands there long enough, she can almost see them growing."

A chill ran through Piero; he wondered if this was the condition of Fra Danilo and the others on the monastery island. "It's the body purging itself," he said. "It's as it should be."

Beppe poked at the sticks of the fire with a pine branch. "You ought to tell that to the rest of the village."

"The people will see it for themselves."

Beppe looked up. "The people are scared, Piero. You should talk to them."

Piero stared into the fire. "What can I say?"

"What you've just said to me. Tell them not to be frightened. Tell them to have faith."

"Will they believe me if I do?"

Beppe placed his hand on Piero's arm. "I'll believe you," he said. "Tell me it'll be all right, Piero."

Piero looked at Beppe, at the fire, at the plate of black olives that sat on his crossed legs. He reached for an olive, but it suddenly repulsed him — so he placed his plate in the straw on the floor and turned back to his friend.

"Send word around the island to meet at the *campo* tomorrow at *mezzogiorno*. When *mezzogiorno* comes, ring the bells. I'll be there."

"*Grazie*, Piero. *Grazie tanto*. The people will be grateful."

Beppe reached for Piero's plate and then took it, along with his own, to a broad bucket that sat in the corner; Piero remained seated before the fire, frozen in thought. He could tell the villagers not to be frightened. He could say what he had to to raise their spirits and bolster their wavering faith. What he wondered was who would take away his own fears. And who would convince him that what was spreading through the village was merely a passing horror.

[ornament]

MIRIAM HAD BEEN GRATEFUL to remain in Gianluca's room after the birth of Nicolo. The bed was soft, there was light from the small window, and the Vedova Stampanini was close at hand to take care of her when she needed. As she had regained her strength, however, she had begun to miss her tiny altar. So on the morning of the spring festival, while the villagers were pouring out along the Calle Alberi Grandi, she placed Nicolo on his blanket of seaweed in Beppe Guancio's cart, wheeled him out through the gardens that lined the eastern shore, and settled back into the alcove in Maria Luigi's hovel. The cave of cloth was just as she'd left it; she paused only to empty out a basket of ribbons to make a bed for Nicolo before heading out to the *campo* for the dedication of the new village center.

When she returned to Maria Luigi's hovel in the late afternoon — after the disturbing interruption of the Story of the Virgin — Miriam wanted to pray for the boy who had fallen. In her alcove she knelt before the altar and lit a pair of tall tapers on either side of the Virgin. When she closed her eyes to pray, however, the tapers went out. She relit them carefully; again they went out. Only as long as her eyes stayed upon them would the tapers remain aflame.

For the next few days Miriam stayed before the altar — Nicolo at her breast, a plate of *sarde* and some maslin bread beside her in the straw, her eyes open wide to keep the tapers lit. Whenever she shut them the flames would go out, but she tried and tried, and by the evening of the second day she found that she was able to stop blinking. She replaced the tapers when they dwindled down to nubs, she nursed Nicolo and laid him in his basket, she ate, she slept, and did it all without closing her eyes.

On the morning that Piero had Beppe Guancio send word about the village to gather at the *campo*, Maria Luigi came rushing to the alcove. "It's Fausto!" she cried. "He's out of his mind with fever! We have to do something!"

Miriam laid Nicolo in his basket and followed Maria Luigi into the main room of the hovel. Fausto was spread out on the floor, his elderly body writhing like a piece of *panzèta* on the fire. His tunic was torn open, and his body was covered with the ugly black sores Miriam had seen on the fallen Virgin.

"Help me with his clothes," said Maria Luigi. "He's suffocating."

They removed his garments and lifted him into the washtub, which Maria Luigi had filled with cool water; then they sponged him down until the pain subsided and he fell into a heavy sleep. When she was certain that Maria Luigi was calm, Miriam fixed them both a dish of fennel tea and some black bread and honey and then returned to the alcove to resume her prayers.

As she settled back in, with Nicolo at her breast, she struggled more fiercely than she had all week to keep her eyes open wide to the flames. The heat she'd felt in Fausto's body was terrifying; it frightened her in a way she had not expected.

A short while after she'd returned to the altar, Nicolo began to squirm in her arms; her right breast was dry, and he wanted to change to her left one. Miriam moved him to the other side, but no sooner had she done so than she shifted him back. Nicolo was unhappy. He squawked a bit and scrambled in her arms, drawing Maria Luigi to the alcove.

"Does he need something?" she asked. "It's not like him to fuss."

"He's fine," said Miriam. "He must feel my concern for Fausto."

Maria Luigi nodded and returned to the other room. Nicolo continued to struggle to shift his little body, but Miriam stroked him, and slipped a finger into his mouth, and gently discouraged him from changing his position.

Nicolo was fine — Miriam had not lied to Maria Luigi. What she did not tell her was that when she'd shifted him to the left side she'd felt a painful pressure behind the breast, in the pocket of her arm, where the faint shape of a hard, dark swelling had begun to grow.

❀

WHEN BEPPE GUANCIO rang the bells at *mezzogiorno* the sound thundered across the island. With Piarina felled by the storm, the *campanil* under construction, and the spring festivities cut short by the illness of the mummer, the bells had not chimed since the last hours of dusk before the quiet of Christmas Eve. But where they were then the wild and improvised music of Piarina's longing, they were now the sober sounding of the island's fear.

Within minutes of the first peals the villagers began to gather at the new *campo*. The Vedova Scarpa, Brunetto Fucci, Siora Guarnieri, Giuseppe Navo, Silvano Rizzardello, Siora Bertinelli, Armida Barbon. They walked slowly and intently, their faces pale, their eyes ringed and hollow from lack of sleep. They carried spoons and switches and churning poles — whatever they could grab — in the hope that they might beat back this demon should he dare to show his face. The only demons they found, however, were the dragons that glittered on the floor of the *campo*; Piero's mosaic had taken on a new, grim meaning.

Piero arrived shortly after the others — an equal pallor on his face, a handful of wild thyme clutched tightly in his fist. As he approached the gathering he could feel the terror in the air; for a moment he considered running to the docks and racing off into the lagoon. But he knew that someone had to speak to the villagers, so he walked to the center of the *campo*, stood in front of his statue of Miriam and Nicolo, and tried his best to sound calm.

"I called you here because I know you're concerned. I know this sickness is spreading quickly. But we can't let ourselves be frightened by a few black lumps."

"Can't we, Piero?" said the Vedova Scarpa.

"We have to keep to the facts," he said. "Tell me who's been stricken. Tell me what you know."

"Cunizza Scabbri's in terrible pain," said Siora Bertinelli. "She keeps crying out that her hens' eggs are lodged in her side."

"The twins are spitting blood," said Silvano Rizzardello. "They have dark blotches on their bellies and they can't stop sweating."

"Gesmundo's got a crazy fever," said Armida Barbon. "His lumps have broke open and it's horrible what's coming out: black water, black sand, black pieces of sea scum."

"I've got one starting in my throat," said Siora Guarnieri.

"I've got it coming in my side," said the Vedova Scarpa.

"It's the mark of the devil!" said Giuseppe Navo.

"It's the end of the world!" cried Brunetto Fucci.

Piero raised his arms in the air and waved the sprigs of thyme like an olive branch.

"You mustn't panic!" he said. "We don't know what it means yet. We have to put our faith in God."

"God must be angry with us," said Silvano Rizzardello.

"He's punishing us for something," said Armida Barbon.

The people were silent for a moment — their arms hung limp at their sides, their heads sagged heavily to their chests.

"What about the girl?" came a voice from the back of the crowd. "Where's the little girl?"

The villagers turned to see who was speaking and found Orsina — her hair unpinned, her clothes in disarray, her sharp features softened by the obvious effects of fear.

"Maria Terza's got the lumps in her side. Maria Prima's feverish. And Ermenegilda's missing. She's been acting strangely for weeks now, disappearing from sunup till sundown. But the past three nights she hasn't come home at all. I have to find that little girl who can cure things."

A percussive ripple ran through the crowd as the people softly murmured, "Piarina."

"It's no use," said Armida Barbon. "I went there myself as soon as Gesmundo got sick. The door's bolted shut, and no amount of knocking will bring an answer."

"Some say the Devil's in there," said Giuseppe Navo. "But I think she and Valentina are finally having it out."

"If Piarina could cure this thing, she'd already have done it," said Silvano Rizzardello. "I think her powers have gone sour, and that's why she won't come out."

"Has anyone tried to get a physician?" asked Piero. "Perhaps there's a treatment. It could be quite simple."

"I've sent four servants out to bring back a surgeon," said Orsina. "Once they row off into the lagoon they never return."

"Maybe it's some kind of purification" said the Vedova Scarpa. "Maybe something black and ugly inside us has to come out, and then we'll be all right again."

"Maybe it's not a punishment," said Siora Bertinelli. "Maybe it's a cure."

Piero looked at the faces of the villagers and saw that if he were going to say something to soothe them, now was the moment. Their fear had relaxed. A breeze of hope had blown back across the *campo*, and a few strong words might build upon that hope. As he stood there, however — the sprigs of wild thyme hanging limp at his side, the faces of the villagers staring up at him in expectation — he realized that he had absolutely nothing to say.

"Do you think so, Piero?" asked Armida Barbon. "Do you think it's just a test of our faith?"

Piero tried to formulate a response — but before he could do so he was distracted by the sudden appearance of Maria Luigi at the far end of the *campo*. She moved slowly, with a fuguelike grace that made it seem as if she were absent from her body. Her face was expressionless, her eyes vague and emptied out; she traveled as if propelled by some mechanical, external force. When she reached the *campanil* she bent down, gathered up a handful of small stones, and began tossing them at the height of the tower. She threw in an easy, fluid manner, only stopping, when she'd emptied her hands, to bend down, gather some more, and toss again. The villagers watched her in fascination — the intensity of her concentration calming them, the careful elegance of her movements drawing them slowly out of their fear. There was no anger in her action, no willfulness, no blood. Only the determined intention to accomplish an aim that none of them could decipher.

"Maria Luigi," said the Vedova Scarpa, finally interrupting her, "what is it? What are you doing?"

Maria Luigi turned as if startled to find that anyone was there. "Have to — ring — the bells," she said.

"But the meeting's already begun," said Brunetto Fucci.

"Have to ring — the bells," she repeated.

"But why?" said Siora Bertinelli.

Maria Luigi looked down at the stones in her hand, then back at the faces in the *campo*. "Fausto's dead," she said. "Have to ring the bells."

She turned back to the *campanil* and began pelting it again. She tossed higher and higher, until she finally reached the open window of the belfry and a stone chinked lightly against the bronze. It was a tiny sound. A foolish, ineffectual sound. But it penetrated the hearts of the people of Riva di Pignoli like the sepulchral clanging of a cathedral bell tolling death.

# Chapter 17

THE PEOPLE OF Riva di Pignoli could no longer
hope that the sickness was not serious: by
nightfall Fausto's death had been followed by
Gesmundo Barbon's and Anna Rizzardello's.
Their pain at the end was so intense, they hurled themselves out of bed and began a frenzied dance before dropping, dead away, to the ground. The Vedova Scarpa
dubbed this "Beelzebub's dance," which the rest of the
island soon adopted as the malady's name. Over half the
villagers now had some sign of the sickness, which seemed
to follow a distinct pattern of development: the initial
feeling of heaviness in the limbs was followed by the appearance of the dark swellings; when these grew to about
the size of a fist, they began to ooze blood and a brackish

pus; this was followed by greenish black blotches across the arms, legs, and belly, wild fever, continuous sweating, and finally the lunatic dance that came before death. The entire process took only a matter of days, which meant that the victims had barely enough time to recover from the initial shock before the final stages were upon them.

Each villager had a different theory as to how the illness was communicated. Some said by breath, some said by touch, some said by mere proximity. Armando Guarnieri fled off into the lagoon. The Vedova Scarpa wrapped layers and layers of gauze, soaked in eglantine-and-lemon water, over her nose and mouth. Siora Bertinelli began burning everything she owned in her pastry oven.

More difficult were those villagers who insisted that someone be held to blame. That the sickness had been brought in with the mummers seemed obvious. The mummers, however, were gone — and for a handful of the villagers there was little satisfaction in hanging the responsibility on them. They needed someone who walked among them, someone they could focus their rage upon, someone whose very appearance on their island might contain the seed of this evil. And no one better fit their need than Miriam.

The group was small. It was made up, in part, of those who had never forgiven her for betraying her seeming purity: Siora Guarnieri, Ugolino Ramponi, Cherubino Lunardi. The rest were those villagers who had so little within them to face the rising horror, they let themselves be persuaded that this bright spirit they had held so high was really the Devil's messenger. It eased their anguish to have someone to blame. It allowed them to become victims, to remove the slightest possibility of responsibility from their own shoulders. So even as the dark swellings rose on their skin and the fever sapped their strength, they gathered in

Maria Luigi's garden, beating soup pots and skillets, hurling stones through the window, and demanding that Miriam come out and face their wrath.

Miriam, however, was barely aware of their presence. Each of her thoughts, every particle of her being, was focused upon the candles in her alcove. At first she had concentrated her prayers upon the mummer boy, had asked that his pain be soothed, that the black marks she'd seen be healed and fade away. When she found those marks upon her own body, however, she turned her prayers to Nicolo. She believed with all her heart that if she could keep her eyes from closing, keep the candles from going out, she could fortify her baby with the strength to resist the illness. That he not be touched was all that mattered; she would not cease praying until she knew that he was safe.

As the days went by, Miriam's ability to keep the candles aflame increased — and as her ability increased, she began to light more and more of them around the alcove. Two, six, twelve, twenty; they gradually filled the tiny space with a warm and nourishing light. But on the evening of the second day after Fausto had died — the first evening after the small band of vigilantes had appeared outside her door — Miriam felt a change come over her. The tension in her back and shoulders increased. Objects that had vanished reappeared suddenly to cloud her concentration. And the nagging choir of voices outside her window, which had seemed no more than the faint buzzing of flies, suddenly made its ugly chorus clear to her.

"Pox maiden!"

"Murderess!"

*"Strega!"*

"Whore!"

Miriam felt the words against her body like tiny blows, her prayer too deep for her to recognize that a fine shower of small stones accompanied the cries. For an instant her faith wavered; the tenuous thread of concentration that had allowed her to keep the candles aflame threatened to snap. But the warmth of Nicolo in her arms, the dampness of his skin against her skin, the ultimate urgency of her need to insure that he live — all these enjoined to see her through the trial. And when the thread was reconnected, and the sounds faded away again, she received the sign she'd been waiting for: her eyes closed as a brilliant stab of pain passed through her, and the candles stayed aflame. From that moment on they remained burning whether her eyes were open or shut — and Miriam knew that no matter what either the sickness or the voices outside the window might do to her, her little boy was going to be spared.

ERMENEGILDA AND VALENTINA learned of the illness as soon as they stepped outside the hovel. There was a frenzy in the air and a smell like rancid butter, and they each met someone who told them of the horror before they'd had time to consider the first of the items on their list.

"Have you got the marks yet?" called the Vedova Scarpa as Ermenegilda bustled past her garden.

"Is Piarina gone?" asked Armida Barbon as Valentina started up the Calle Alberi Grandi.

Both women quickly interrogated their interlopers and in a matter of seconds discovered what was happening, to whom it had happened, to whom it was about to happen, when it had begun, and how it had spread across the island. But though Ermenegilda and Valentina both recognized the fatigue and the slight tenderness in the side, neither of them was worried about what they were told. Piarina's cure now had its sickness; as long as they could locate the things she'd requested, they were certain they had nothing to fear.

Before leaving the hovel, they had divided the list in half: Ermenegilda took the first four items, Valentina the final three. So the first thing Ermenegilda did after speaking with the Vedova Scarpa was to travel out to the western docks to gather a scrap of seaweed. There were bits of it everywhere: clumped in the new grass, strewn along the edge of the shore, hugging the posts where the boats were tied. But as most of what she came upon had dried out in the sun, she lowered herself into one of Giuseppe Navo's boats, paddled out a short way toward Albertino's island, and fetched up a fresh, shining clump of the slimy weed.

The second and third items were easier. She did not know precisely what Piarina meant by a strip, but she gouged and hacked at the pine tree bark until she was satisfied she'd come up with a usable piece. In order to gather a peacock feather she needed only to return to the Torta garden — but as Ermenegilda did not wish to chance being seen by Orsina, she climbed the branches of the wisteria on the wall by the slender canal, raced up behind one of the peacocks, plucked a feather from its tail, and raced back over the wall before anyone had noticed her.

The only person who might help her with the final item was Brunetto Fucci. He had long ago transformed his apothecary's quarters into a spice shop, but as there was a good chance he still possessed the old elements of his trade, Ermenegilda set out for his hovel. When she arrived she found him tossing with the fever, midway between blackish green and greenish black. But when she explained that she had come from Piarina and that she was gathering the ingredients for a cure, he told her where to find a box of flasks and a cabinet that contained a bottle of mercury. Ermenegilda had never seen mercury before, and when she tried to pour it into the flask it ran off onto the floor of the hovel and separated into a thousand beads. She had to get down on her hands and knees and chase after it, but she finally managed to scoop up enough of it to take it back, with the other ingredients, to Piarina.

Valentina's task was in one sense easier and in one sense much more difficult. The six pignoli took minutes to gather; had she needed six hundred it would not have taken very much longer. The sorbs she found in Siora Bertinelli's fruit patch; she took them back to her hovel and laid them out on a piece of white muslin in the sun. In order to find a wasp's wing, however, she would have to find a wasp. So she took a long stick, traveled out to the marshy fields along the north rim of the island, and began poking around the grass until she stirred up trouble. When she passed the field of wild thyme she saw Piero curled up among the weeds. She considered prodding him with her stick — it had been a long time since she'd had that satisfaction — but as her task was urgent she continued on until she found what she was looking for.

It would be more precise to say that what she was looking for found her. For when she unknowingly struck the bowl-shaped object lying hidden among the rushes, a mass of angry wasps rose up and stung her. They bit her forehead and her forearm, her neck and her knees, but she swung her stick, and beat the ground, and finally managed to trap one beneath her broom-handle stump.

Then she bent down, removed one of its slender wings, wrapped it in a piece of cloth, and took it home to Piarina.

FOR TWELVE YEARS Albertino had carefully adhered to the standard calendar for sowing and planting: broad beans in April, eggplant in May, broccoli in June or July or even in August. This year, however, he decided to put down everything as soon as he could. Cauliflower and carrots. Sweet chard and onions. Parsnips and turnips and cabbage and fennel and peas. Whatever else happened, whatever fortune or destiny of the position of the stars decreed, he was determined to see that the vegetables went on without him. Albertino finally understood why the spring had been so reluctant to come to Riva di Pignoli the previous year. Why bring your bounty to a place of sickness and death? Why enliven the landscape with a sweep of brilliant color when the people are turning a blackish greenish gray?

Albertino did not feel the heaviness come over him until the evening of Piero's gathering at the new village center. He told himself that it was only fatigue, but when he woke the next morning and felt the soreness in his side he knew that the sickness had begun. So he gathered up his seeds and his bulbs and the sproutlings he'd begun in a series of shallow crates and set out across the water to do the planting. It was tiring work, and the lump in his side made the digging quite painful, but he wanted to put down the bulk of it while he still had the energy.

As he knelt before the trench he'd dug to lay down the fennel, he breathed in the smell of the fresh soil. He loved that smell, he couldn't imagine living without it; but he wouldn't be living without it, he would be dead without it; if he were living, he would still be able to smell it; but he wouldn't be, he'd be dead; unless you smelled things after death; although he doubted it; though on the other hand he imagined that there were lots of flowers in heaven; but it was better not to think about heaven and hell; and besides maybe it wouldn't happen after all; and so the best thing to do was to just continue laying down the seeds. That was as far as he ever got when he tried to think beyond the pain in his side: six paces down a twisted path that wound up in the mud. Planting the vegetables was the only thing that made sense; as long as he was doing that, nothing that might happen tomorrow really mattered.

Albertino worked through the morning. When he finished with the fennel, he began the cauliflower — bit by bit he sidled down the row, his fingers carefully sifting and patting, his eyes intent upon the placement of the tiny sproutlings. As he reached the middle of the row, however, he became aware of another presence in the garden — and when he turned to his right he found Gianluca, just a few yards away, placing sproutlings from a separate crate in the dark earth beside him.

"Gianluca!" he cried.

"*Ciao*, little brother."

"What are you doing here?"

"What does it look like I'm doing? Do you think I've forgotten how to put down a row of cauliflower?"

Gianluca did not look up as he said this; his attention remained on the simple act of placing the sproutlings in the trench and surrounding them with soil. Albertino was moved by his devotion and silently returned to his own work. After about a quarter of an hour, however, he turned back to his brother and spoke.

"You've got it, too."

Gianluca gave a quick nod.

"Right side or left?"

"Both."

Albertino could feel the sun blaze hot on his neck, his back, his shoulders. That he should have the sickness was one thing; that Gianluca should have it was entirely another. He could feel a rising in his throat, a thickening at the back of his tongue, a stinging in his eyes. But as he did not know what to do with these feelings, he turned back to the trench and continued on with his planting.

"We should do the eggplant next. And then the cabbage. I'd like to get everything down by tomorrow night."

"I'm here, Albertino," said Gianluca. "Just tell me what you want me to do."

They worked on in silence — row by row, vegetable by vegetable. Gianluca did not mention Miriam; Albertino did not mention Ermenegilda. They merely dug and planted, sifted and cleared, while the light faded, and the shadows crept in, and the darkness overtook them.

❧

AFTER THE GATHERING at the new village center, and Maria Luigi's ringing of the bells, Piero went out to the north rim of the island and stood in the field of wild thyme. In all the years he'd lived on Riva di Pignoli, Piero had seen the people bounce back from tragedy; famine or flood, they'd always demonstrated a remarkable resilience. What was happening now, however, could not be taken care of by a firm will and a hopeful spirit.

Piero knew that death was upon the island. He could see it in the eyes of everyone he came in contact with. He could smell it on their skin and hear it in their voices. And despite the brave calm he evinced for the benefit of the other villagers, he could not help but feel a shattering sense of responsibility for what was happening. What if he'd told the villagers about the body? What if he'd heeded the warning it had represented — the warning Nature had sent with the delay of spring and the devastating storm — instead of encouraging the people to pour their energy into the building of a useless *campo*? Perhaps he could have evacuated the island — averted the sickness — prevented the horror that was now spreading across the village like a fatal wave of gossip.

He stood there for hours trying to find some pattern in the horror, but nothing could help him make sense of it. Eventually he lay down upon the grave, hoping that understanding might come to him in his sleep. But when he woke the next morning his frustration and despair were as keen as when he'd closed his eyes.

When he returned to Beppe Guancio's hovel, Beppe informed him that Anna Rizzardello and Gesmundo Barbon had died, that Siora Scabbri and Maria Patrizia Lunardi and Paolo Guarnieri had reached the state of fever, and that he had found the first black lump in his side.

"It burns, Piero," he said. "It's hard to think about anything but the pain."

Piero instantly placed Beppe in bed and began laying hot and cold compresses on his swelling. He remained at his side for the rest of the day — encouraging him to drink a bit of broth, covering him with blankets when he became racked with chills, and pretending not to seem alarmed at how swiftly the illness accelerated. By nightfall the swelling had already burst and the blotches were beginning to spread across Beppe's belly. He whimpered like a small puppy and clutched Piero's hand and drew from him a strength he could not have drawn from himself.

Late in the evening Beppe's condition eased enough to allow him to sleep. Piero, who had sat by him and comforted him since early morning, was shaken and exhausted and longed for sleep himself. But before he could allow himself to crawl to his corner and lay down upon his bed of straw, he went to the worktable where he'd designed the *campanil*, the *campo*, and the monument, took a clean piece of parchment from beneath his drawings, and with his best quill pen, in his most careful hand, wrote *"Deus non est."*

God does not exist.

Before he'd even finished forming the final letter, he felt a wave of terror rush through him. He folded up the parchment as small as he could and placed it beneath his tunic and blouse where no one could know he'd written it. With careful steps he moved toward his bed, certain that he would be struck by lightning before he reached it or that the earth would open up to swallow him whole. But nothing happened. So he closed his eyes and waited for death to take him like the others.

Piero was not afraid of death. A part of him even welcomed it. The problem was that as yet he had no pain, no feeling of sickness, nor the slightest symptom of the disease.

[ornament]

WHEN ALL THE ITEMS had been brought to the hovel, Piarina began to inspect them. One by one she held her hands over them, closed her eyes, and awaited some kind of verification. When she received it — in the form of a light, high humming in her head — she placed a small stool before the hearth, stepped up onto it, placed the items in the cauldron, filled it three-quarters full with well water, and slowly brought the mixture to a boil. Then she took a spoon and began stirring it all together.

Ermenegilda and Valentina tried to busy themselves while Piarina stirred the hopeful broth. As the water evaporated she would replenish it: stirring and boiling, stirring and reducing, stirring and adding again. A new glow came upon her — she became transparent as the wasp's wing — but she continued to stir with an even stroke as the mixture gathered its potency.

Toward the end of the day both Ermenegilda and Valentina felt the tenderness in their sides begin to concentrate into hard centers of pain. By the following morning the swellings had appeared, but though they both felt concerned, neither one of them panicked. As long as Piarina stood stirring the broth, they trusted her cure would save them.

On the evening of the second day of her stirring, Piarina suddenly laid the spoon beside the fire and went to the corner where Ermenegilda sat nursing her pain. After raising her twinkling hands to her cheeks in their old, familiar embrace, she guided her friend to the steaming cauldron across the hovel, stepped up onto the stool, and began stirring the mixture in swifter, cleaner strokes. There was a sense of mission in her movements that made Ermenegilda feel certain the magic potion would work.

"Bless you, Piarina!" she said. "Bless you! To think you can save the entire island with a handful of nothing at all!"

Piarina continued stirring—but then she stopped and turned to Ermenegilda. She seemed puzzled by her words, her starry eyes a pair of vacant screens. Then she understood and began to shake her head.

"What is it?" said Ermenegilda. "You mean the cure doesn't work?"

Piarina shook her head more vigorously, and patted the cauldron, and pointed her finger at Ermenegilda.

"For me?" said Ermenegilda. "You want me to be first! What a sweet friend you are!"

Piarina began to become upset. She placed the spoon down and brushed a wisp of hair off her forehead. Then she patted the cauldron, and patted Ermenegilda, and made a motion with her hands that Ermenegilda knew only too well.

*"Basta così?"* she said. "What are you saying? You mean you made it only for me?"

Piarina smiled a contented smile and began stirring the broth again.

"But you can't give it only to me!" cried Ermenegilda. "The whole island is dying! You're the only one who can save them, Piarina!"

Piarina stopped stirring again, and again she looked perplexed. Then a torrent of tears flooded out from her eyes and she raised a tiny finger in the air.

"Heaven?" said Ermenegilda, thinking Piarina was pointing up. "We're all going to heaven?"

Piarina shook the finger wildly, and tapped it against the wall, and beat it against her chest, and raised it in the air again.

"One," said Ermenegilda. "Only one."

271

Piarina nodded.

"You mean you can only save one person."

Piarina nodded again, and again she pointed to Ermenegilda.

"You can only save one person and you want it to be me." Ermenegilda closed her eyes. "And what about you?"

Piarina raised her tunic, and when Ermenegilda opened her eyes she saw that she was covered with the black blotches, the black swellings, and a series of open, running sores.

"*Dio mi!*" cried Ermenegilda. "Why didn't you let us know?"

Piarina hung her head, and patted the cauldron, and pointed to Ermenegilda.

"You wanted to save me!" cried Ermenegilda. "I know! But what about yourself? Why would I want to live if it takes you, too?"

Piarina stirred no more, patted no more, pointed no more. Ermenegilda, wet with tears, put her great arms around her and whispered into her hair.

"If you won't be here, I'll want to be with him. If he won't be here, I won't want to be here, either."

Then she withdrew herself from the embrace and ran out of the hovel, leaving Piarina frozen before the fire.

A few moments passed. Silence filled the hovel. Then a voice from the shadows rose up in a raspy whisper.

"Piarina! I'm thirsty! Fetch me some water!"

Piarina was startled by the sound of her mother's voice; she'd almost forgotten she was there. But when she turned and saw her huddled by the wall, she suddenly realized what she would have to do. She only wondered, with their history behind them, if she could possibly find the forgiveness to do it.

[ornament]

WHEN THE SWELLING in her side had become the size of a melon and the greenish black blotches had begun to spread across her arms and throat, Miriam sent word, through Maria Luigi, for Piero and Gianluca to come visit her. She was aware that most of the island had contracted the pestilence by now, but still she did not want them to see that she was sick. So she wrapped herself in bolts and bolts of Maria Luigi's blue satin, then propped herself against a stack of cotton with Nicolo in her arms.

When Piero arrived at Maria Luigi's hovel, he was horrified to find the group of angry villagers gathered beneath Miriam's window. If anyone were to blame for this sickness, it was he; the thought that these people had chosen Miriam for their hatred made a wave of nausea pass through him. He tried to disband them; he pleaded with them to take their pain back to their beds. But they only ignored him and continued their tireless chanting.

Piero entered the hovel and made his way to the alcove. When he came upon the small space illuminated by the glowing candles, he almost forgot the horror that had taken over the island. Miriam and Nicolo looked so perfectly at peace, the candlelight on the blue satin was so gentle and soothing, he was able for a moment to free his mind from images of sickness and death. It was only when he actually saw Miriam's face — pale and shadowed and robbed of its delicate bloom — that he knew the horror was unavoidable.

"Thank you for coming," Miriam said as he entered. "Please — sit anywhere."

Piero crossed to the far wall and lowered himself to the straw. As he glanced around the room his eyes came to rest upon the statue of the Virgin, burnished yellow and gold from the light of the shimmering candles.

"This is very nice," he said.

"It's what sustains me," said Miriam.

Piero thought of his own statue of the Virgin — his statue of Miriam and Nicolo — and of the hope he'd had for the future of the island.

"Tell me how things are," said Miriam.

Piero tried to block out the cries outside the window. "It's all across the island," he said. "There's no one to help with those that are dying and no one to administer to the sick."

Miriam closed her eyes. "I hear they're calling it 'Beelzebub's dance,'" she said.

"There's a moment — a frenzy that comes — at the end."

"I know. I've seen it with Fausto. It's awful."

"Giuseppe Navo's been out to Burano, Pescatorno, Ponte di Schiavi. They have it, too. It's all across the lagoon. All over the mainland."

Piero and Miriam were silent for a moment, the cries outside the window like the patter of heavy rain. They tried to move beyond the violence in those cries, to concentrate on the candles, the satin, the energy between them. Then, suddenly, the sounds broke off in midcry — and the voice of Gianluca was heard.

"Get away from here!" he cried. "Go! *Now!*"

Piero and Miriam could hear no response — only the clanging of pots and the shuffling of feet as the ugly band dispersed. A moment later they heard the throwing open of the door to Maria Luigi's hovel and a faint cry from Maria Luigi at the hearth; then Gianluca appeared at the entrance to the alcove. He leaned against the wall — he was obviously in great pain — but his eyes were alive with their usual defiant luster.

"They won't bother you anymore," he said. "I'll kill them if they do."

"There's no point in killing them," said Miriam. "They'll die soon enough on their own."

"Perhaps it really is the end of the world," said Piero.

Miriam lifted Nicolo, who in his usual manner had remained perfectly quiet, up against her shoulder. "It isn't the end of the world," she said.

"How do you know?" said Gianluca.

She stroked the infant's curls in a slow, steady movement. "Because Nicolo is well," she said. "He hasn't been touched by the sickness."

"And what about you?" said Gianluca.

Miriam paused. "It started for me days ago. But Nicolo is well. And there are sure to be others like him."

Piero looked away as Miriam said this; he did not have the courage to admit that, like Nicolo, the pestilence had passed him by. Miriam, however, saw his reaction and instantly interpreted its meaning.

"Is it true?"

"I think so."

Miriam closed her eyes. "*Grazie, Dio,*" she said. "*Grazie.*"

"What are you talking about?" said Gianluca.

"Then that's been the answer all along," said Miriam. "I couldn't imagine how Nicolo would survive if no one else were to survive. But you'll take care of him. You'll take him away to where there is no sickness."

"I don't know that there is such a place," said Piero. "But I'll try."

"You bastard!" cried Gianluca.

"You must promise me that you will come for him as soon as I'm gone," said Miriam.

"Don't talk like this!" cried Gianluca. "You aren't going to die of this!"

"I am going to die of it, Gianluca," said Miriam. "Most of the island is going to die of it."

"No!"

"Listen to me," she said. "We have so little time." She leaned forward and drew one of the tapers toward her so that its light cast a plain glow over her face. "I asked you here because our lives have been bound up together since I first came to Riva di Pignoli. I didn't choose it — but you didn't choose it, either. I asked you both to be father to my baby. The truth is that neither of you is his father. Nicolo was inside me when I came to Riva di Pignoli." She paused for a moment as her words penetrated. "Now it looks as if only Piero will be able to raise my child. So I'm asking you to stay with me, Gianluca. Until one of us is seized by this terrible dance. Stay here, be here with me."

Gianluca looked at her, her beauty couched beneath a death mask, her body illuminated by the countless flames that scattered the tiny space. It was difficult for him to comprehend that all the jealousy he had felt toward Piero had been unfounded. That there was a nameless, unknown other who had fathered Miriam's child. He tried to consider what she was offering him: even a few hours beside her would be more ecstasy than he could hope for, and if those hours were followed by death, it would be a magnificent farewell. But the thought that she might die first — that he might have to watch her grow frail and feverish and hurl herself into that final convulsion — was too much for him.

"No," he said, in almost a whisper. "No." Then he turned and stumbled across the hovel and out into the night.

Miriam closed her eyes and tried to breathe through her pain. "Go after him," she said. "Please, Piero — see that he's all right."

Piero remained frozen for a moment, his eyes fixed upon Miriam; then he rose and followed after Gianluca. He'd broken into a run now — Piero could just see him at the edge of his vision, racing out across the fields beside the Vedova Scarpa's hovel. Piero chased after him, aware of his pain, aware that his suffering went beyond his understanding. And aware that no matter how fast they ran, nor how far they got, they could never outdistance this terror that was following so close behind them.

# *Chapter* 18

B Y THE END of the first week there was not a hovel on the island that had not been touched by the sickness. The villagers who were still in the early stages of it tried to take those who had died across the water to be buried in the cemetery. When that became too difficult they put them in their gardens and their fields. Finally they could do no more than throw a piece of muslin or an old cloak over their faces and leave them where the final pangs had taken them. The smell was awful; the people lit bonfires of juniper and ash along the Calle Alberi Grandi, but the thick sweet smoke only intensified the odor of death.

A few of the villagers tried to come up with their own cures in feeble imitation of Piarina. Paolo Guarnieri ran about his hovel in circles holding a sprig of blessed thistle over his head. Siora Bertinelli rubbed a mixture of bog-bean, spearmint leaf, and horseradish on her swellings, which made them burn so badly that she had to roll herself in a washtub lined with lard. Silvano Rizzardello — who had lost his wife and both his children in the very first days — crawled up on his roof and began covering himself with salt.

The Vedova Stampanini and Giuseppe Navo faced the specter of death with a feeling of familiarity. The Vedova had watched her ten children, her husband, and most of the people she had grown up with pass away; Giuseppe Navo had watched the Vedova as she had watched them. So now, as their own ends drew near, they decided to prepare a final meal — a last, lavish supper — before the ultimate throes of the sickness were upon them. Giuseppe ventured out into the lagoon and brought back a pair of gleaming *cefalo*. The Vedova worked for hours making pureed beans with bacon, almond milk pudding, *sopa di pollo*, dried peas with anise, breadcrumb compote, *zampone*, and clove-and-ginger tarts. They laid it all out on the small table where they had shared so many meals and ate, in silence, for seven hours. Then they wrapped themselves up in each other's arms, convulsed in the dance like a pair of teenage lovers, and died.

The Vedova Scarpa had stayed inside her hovel since the meeting at the new village center. As the sickness came over her, however, she gathered her belongings into a burlap sack, donned the pale green gown she'd worn when she'd first met Luigi Scarpa, and went out to the western docks where he'd disappeared on a fishing expedition so many years ago. For the next three days she stood there holding a small net bag, in the hope that when she evaporated into spirit he would spot her, and hand her his catch, and guide her into heaven.

In the Ca' Torta all was silence. The three Marias were sunk in the fever, and Orsina lay groaning in her bed as she awaited Enrico's return. She'd ordered whatever servants were still mobile to remove everything from the bedchambers, the *androne*, the dining chamber, the *salone*, and the main portico, place it all in a pile at the center of the rose garden, and set it on fire — banking on the theory that it was never too late to relinquish one's attachment to material posessions, and that the Holy Spirit might still be embraced upon one's deathbed. She knew Enrico would come; no matter how hard he'd tried to avoid her company throughout the years of their marriage, he would never desert her in death. And sure enough, on the night after she took to her bed, he arrived at the door of their chamber — barefoot, in a hair shirt, and covered with the ugly black sores — and together they prayed that God would forgive them for a little excess.

Only Beppe Guancio and Romilda Rosetta thought to go to the Chiesa di Maria del Mare. Beppe got there first; he dragged himself from his bed when Piero went to see Miriam and stumbled through the fields to the tiny chapel. When he went inside he did not have the strength to light even one taper — but he knew that God could see him whether it was light or it was dark, so he tiptoed down the aisle and knelt before the altar and begged to be delivered from his pain.

Romilda Rosetta found her pain invigorating. From the moment the soreness started in her side, she viewed it as her final, most challenging trial. She stayed at the Ca' Torta while the sickness spread throughout her system, following Orsina's orders in the absence of Ermenegilda's.

But when the pain became excruciating she went to the *chiesa*, crept unknowingly into the darkness behind the prostrate Beppe Guancio, and lay down in a gentle cross of supplication.

It was a gesture that nearly everyone on Riva di Pignoli, had they seen her perform it, would have understood. For when the flesh blackened, and opened, and oozed, there was no choice but to turn to the spirit. Romilda Rosetta had simply had a head start.

※

WHERE THE SICKNESS made the other villagers' bodies grow heavy, it made Piarina feel lighter than ever; she practically floated through the door as she went outside for the first time since she'd fallen during the storm. Piarina had tried to induce herself to save Valentina — but after an entire day of prayer before the lone candle in the corner of the hovel, she still couldn't bring herself to do it. For months and months her mind had been filled with thoughts of murder; it was not so easy to wipe such things away. So when Valentina fell asleep she took the candle in her hand, went out to the edge of the island, and vowed to follow the circuit she'd traveled on the night she brought the spring until she found the grace to let her mother live.

She journeyed through the night, around and around the island, searching for the softness, the forgotten moment of tenderness, the sudden insight into her mother's nature that would allow her to reach past a lifetime of jabs and whacks and hold her to her heart. The Vedova Scarpa, who stood waiting at the docks for Luigi, was convinced it was not Piarina she saw but her ghost: the young girl's feet barely touched the ground, and her stick-bone body glowed brighter than the candle that guided her. Siora Bertinelli, who had gone to the eastern shore to soak her sores in the lagoon, claimed she saw Piarina walk on water: there was a point in the shore where the land curved in, creating a shallow cove where one could wade — Siora Bertinelli swore that Piarina ignored the indentation and continued straight across the surface of the lagoon. But circle as she might, Piarina could find nothing to help her. When dawn came she searched the grass and the trees and the line of the horizon for a shred or a speck to give her understanding. But all she could think of was how much the pain from the sickness felt like the pain from being beaten, so she finally gave up and went home.

When she reentered the hovel Valentina was still asleep — though in a different spot, having obviously awakened in pain during the night. Piarina went to where she lay, her breathing heavy, her face sallow and drawn from the fever moving through her. She thought of all the times she'd sat at her knees, how hard she'd tried to please her, how much the beatings had hurt. And she knew that she still loved her; and she knew that she still hated her; and she knew that, try though she might, she could not forgive her. So she wiped away the bit of spittle that trickled from the corner of her mouth and crept to the hearth where her cure sat simmering.

She couldn't give it to Ermenegilda, and she wouldn't give it to Valentina. So the only thing to do was to spill it off into the fire. After lifting the cauldron from its hook, she lowered it to the floor; then she tilted it onto its side, and the hot, sticky liquid began slowly to drain away. No more than a few drops had poured off, however, when the door to the hovel flew open.

"Wait!"

The sound of Ermenegilda's voice arrested Piarina's movements. Without releasing the cauldron, she turned toward the door as her old friend moved swiftly to her side.

"You can't," said Ermenegilda. "It isn't right."

Piarina looked down at the cauldron, perched on its edge, its contents ready to run off into the flames. Then — her doe eyes sparkling with a last trace of hope — she looked back at Ermenegilda and, one last time, pointed her finger at her.

Ermenegilda closed her eyes. "That isn't what I mean."

Piarina turned back to the hearth and began to tilt the cauldron over again.

"All right," said Ermenegilda. "All right. Get it ready."

Piarina flushed with joy as she lowered the cauldron back to the ground. Then she scampered to the table, fetched a small clay bowl, returned with it to the fire, ladled the contents of the cauldron inside it, and presented it without ceremony to Ermenegilda.

Ermenegilda placed her hands over Piarina's as they grasped the bowl. A tremendous heat passed between them, a current of love kindled strong by sickness. But instead of drawing it into herself, Ermenegilda pushed the bowl toward Piarina.

"You take it," she said. "Please, Piarina."

Piarina quivered at Ermenegilda's suggestion. She dropped her head and shook it furiously; she tried to pull away. But Ermenegilda kept her hands tight over her hands and would not let her escape.

"This thing won't leave many behind," said Ermenegilda. "Who knows what an awful world it's going to be?

But whatever's left, whatever it comes to, they're going to need all the magic they can get. You made the cure, Piarina. You're the one who should take it."

Piarina looked into the bowl she clutched between her hands. She thought of how much concentration had gone into her struggle to find the ingredients, how much pain had been channeled into her efforts to produce the cure. And she saw that it had never once occurred to her to use that cure for herself. Her gifts, in all their magic, had always been for others; her spirit had grown so accustomed to bruising it did not recognize the chance to be healed.

"Take the life you offered me, Piarina," said Ermenegilda. "I don't want it. Take it for yourself."

Piarina felt the heat in her hands pass up through her arms and spread throughout her body. Ermenegilda released her grasp. Then the lucent child drew the bowl to her lips and drank the mixture off. When she'd finished the last of it, Ermenegilda lifted her up into her arms and carried her to the bed.

"Rest awhile," she said as she tucked her in. "I'll be back."

And she left the hovel.

Piarina lay with her eyes closed and listened to her mother's snoring. She felt the heat rise up to her head and spread down through her belly and into her legs. And gradually, as the heat intensified, she felt a light begin to radiate inside her. At first it was not much more than her usual glow, but it grew and grew until she shone so brightly that the hovel began to vibrate. Valentina groaned; she tried to cover her eyes; she complained that the glare was keeping her from sleeping. But Piarina couldn't hear her. She could only feel the light.

Growing brighter. And brighter. And brighter. And brighter.

And brighter.

❧

THERE WAS NO LIGHT to guide Gianluca on the night he fled from Miriam's alcove; his body raced forward without knowing where it was going while his mind stayed rooted upon a single, unbearable image: the look of death that had fallen over Miriam's face. He ran until he reached the village center, where his eyes fixed upon the statue of Miriam and her child. Unable to bear this any more than he had been able to bear the sight of the actual pair, he hastened to the entrance of the *campanil* and began climbing the makeshift stairs that led to the bells. When he reached the belfry he tore the central bell from its place and, holding tightly to the base of the stone archway opening out of the southern wall, began dashing to bits the wooden framework he'd just raced up. The power of his blows was so great that the entire stairway buckled and caved in within a matter of seconds. Gianluca hurled the bronze bell in after the wreckage; then he stood upon the ledge beneath the archway and began to howl.

It was not a howling like the howling of the night of the storm. Where that had been a catharsis, this was purely rage. He could not accept what was happening to his island, and he could not keep himself from venting his fury that it was happening.

By the time Piero reached the *campanil*, Gianluca had already begun his savage cries; he stood there, inches from the base of the tower, as the terrible sounds rang out over

the pestilent night. When he went to the entrance to try
to climb after him, however, he found that Gianluca had
destroyed the internal structure completely, making it impossible for him to follow behind him. So he closed his
eyes and hugged the stone walls — the great wails riding
over the *campo* expressing the rage that he himself could
not. He stayed that way until the moon rose. Then he left
the tower and returned to Beppe Guancio's hovel to sit
out his lonely vigil over the dying island.

MIRIAM SAT BEFORE the altar and watched the candles.
The pain was like a fire upon her now, but if she breathed
evenly and watched the candles, she could bear it. Nicolo
lay in her arms, looking up at her with wide eyes; Maria
Luigi lay moaning in the next room. And though Miriam
wished that she could go to her and comfort her in her
pain, she knew that if she tried to move, Beelzebub's dance
would come upon her instantaneously.

As she sat there, her eyes upon the flames, she thought
about her time on Riva di Pignoli. She thought about the
kindness of Fausto and Maria Luigi, the diligence of Siora
Scabbri's chickens, the despair of the villagers who had
gathered outside her window. And she thought about
Piero and Gianluca. How faithful they'd been, how generous and devoted, despite her unwillingness to choose between them. She realized that though her mind had been
fixed upon what she thought she could teach them, in
reality they had taught her more. About constancy. And
compassion. And the intricate threads that ran between
passion and piety.

As the pain grew stronger, Miriam thought about the longing that had followed her through her life. Not even Nicolo had been able to draw off its pressure, and she realized, as she sat there, that she had spent her entire life trying to absorb it, remove it, deny it. "Take it away," she'd cried to her mother and father. "Take it away," she'd begged the ass, the men, her child. But the longing had disappeared only for brief transcendent moments that made its return that much more unbearable.

She closed her eyes and felt the candlelight burn warm against her eyelids and felt the weight of Nicolo in her arms. She shifted him into her left arm and held him close to her body, while with her right hand she reached down to retrieve a small bundle that was lodged beneath one of the pillows that supported her. It was a scarf of white linen embossed with leaves that contained a small gold wedding band: the last of the objects contained in the parcel she had brought with her to the island. Her mother had given it to her just before she died, and though Miriam had carried it with her wherever she went, she'd never actually thought she would wear it.

She drew the bundle up to her breast and placed it upon Nicolo's swaddled legs; then she drew back the folds of fabric to reveal the ring. She took it between her thumb and forefinger and held it up before her — a perfect circle of bright metal that reflected the flickering light. It seemed as strange to her as if she'd never seen it before or had never understood its purpose. She knew that purpose now, however, and with a simple movement slipped it onto the third finger of her left hand.

Miriam felt, as she sat on the floor of the alcove with the pain coursing through her like hot wax, that it was finally time to give in to her longing. To let it expand into

a white-hot yearning, to let that yearning transform into
something with no name at all. She felt her chest begin to
pound. She felt the heat rise to her shoulders, her cheeks,
her ears. Her eyes, though already open, seemed to open
again — she saw the statue of the Virgin, the bowl of water,
the bolts and bolts of cloth, as if she were seeing them for
the very first time. And though their forms were precise —
almost rigid — they poured out of themselves with an amaz-
ing fullness. And Miriam knew that if she concentrated,
this moment would last forever.

Just as she was about to give over to her state, she felt
a tugging at the satin that wrapped about her shoulders.
She looked down, and through the sea of light that en-
shrouded her she saw the face of Nicolo, knotted in fear
and confusion. He seemed far, far away, an object of
another world. But she managed to bridge the distance
with the fingers of her right hand and smooth the lines of
worry from his brow.

"It's all right," she whispered. "I'll be waiting for you."

In that moment Miriam understood that the longing she
had felt throughout her life had been the longing to return
to God. And as her body began to spasm, and she entered
that final dance, she knew that it was safe to leave Nicolo
and follow the brilliant starburst to its source.

❧

AS THE LIGHT in Miriam's alcove expanded, so did the
light in Piarina's little body. One fed the other, until the
shabby hovel that housed the prescient child shone
brighter than a bonfire in autumn. Valentina stayed huddled in the corner, her arms pulled up tight over her head,

while Piarina slept and glowed and slept and glowed and slept. Eventually she was awakened by Ermenegilda, who returned to the hovel pushing a wheelbarrow and carrying a fine lace dress.

"I brought you this," she said to Piarina, covering her eyes slightly as she held up the dress. "I used to wear it when I was your age."

The dress, though made for a child, was easily four times Piarina's size — but she let Ermenegilda slip it over her head and spread it out around her until her tiny body was lost beneath its folds. Then Ermenegilda, who was so covered with sores that she could barely move without crying out, knelt down beside the bed, placed her head on Piarina's chest, and sang her a last lullaby before leaving. They formed a stark tableau — Ermenegilda and Piarina in each other's arms, Valentina alone in the corner — until the song was over and Ermenegilda rose to go.

"One last thing," she said as she steadied herself against the wall behind the bed. "I'd like to take back the boxes."

Piarina nodded, and Ermenegilda began gathering up the coffers and caddies that were scattered throughout the hovel and placing them in the wheelbarrow. When she'd gathered them all she turned back to Piarina.

"*Addio, cara mia,*" she whispered.

Piarina raised her hands to her cheeks and patted them in farewell. Then Ermenegilda turned and left.

The light inside Piarina continued to burn brighter. Valentina tried to hide from it, but when the radiance had risen to an almost blinding level, she forced herself up, splashed some water on her throat and forehead, and looked about the room. When she saw that the light was coming from Piarina, she covered her eyes and staggered to the bed.

"You're glowing," she said.

Piarina nodded.

"What does that mean?"

Piarina gestured toward the empty bowl beside the hearth.

"You mean you took it?"

Piarina nodded again and reached up to take Valentina's hand.

"Well, *sangue di Dio*," said Valentina. "You're not so stupid after all."

Piarina laid her head back, still holding her mother's hand; Valentina eased herself down to the floor and leaned against the bed frame. Piarina watched the light intensify, watched it fill in the cracks between the roof beams and glint around the edges of the straw; Valentina kept her eyes closed tight against the ever-increasing splendor.

They stayed that way for a long while. Then Piarina suddenly bolted forward as Valentina felt an explosion of heat surround her. And at precisely the same moment that Miriam felt her longing flood to light on the opposite side of the island, the tiny hovel that housed Piarina and Valentina trembled — like a splinter in an earthquake — and burst into flames.

❦

ALBERTINO WAS IN so much pain, he could not lie down. So he wrapped himself up in one of the Vedova Stampanini's blankets and scuttled about his room like a distracted pigeon. He tried not to think about Gianluca, whose howls from the height of the *campanil* threatened to shatter his heart. He tried not to think about Ermenegilda — he'd gone to the Ca' Torta, but no one would answer the door; he'd climbed to her third-floor window, but the room was empty. He didn't want to think about what that emptiness signified, but he feared in his heart he would never see her again.

He therefore thought it was the effects of the fever when he heard her voice cry "Albertino!" and he turned to the east wall to see her moving across the radicchio patch toward his room. She was pushing the wheelbarrow filled with his boxes, and there was a look of exaltation on her face that belied her ghostly pallor. When she reached the near edge of the radicchio patch, she let go of the wheelbarrow and ran toward Albertino, who dropped his blanket and raced to meet her at the wall. Their bodies were on fire with the pestilence, but they grasped at each other and pressed themselves together in an extravagant, hungry kiss.

"Come," said Ermenegilda as she drew herself away. Then she turned and ran off toward the graveyard. Albertino glanced over at the barrow full of boxes — the coffer of ivory, the caddy of quartz — but they seemed only an accumulation of handles and hinges, a mountain of metal and wood. So he leapt over the wall and followed hotly behind Ermenegilda.

They passed through the stone entrance with the rusted-open gate, they passed the parcel of rosebushes and the palm trees and the pines, they passed the florid marble of Silvana Zennaro and the fluted granite of Guido Bo, until they once again faced the simple grave of Cherubina Modesta Colomba Ernesta Franchin. Ermenegilda got there first; she stepped up onto the flat stone marker set snug into the earth and turned to watch as Albertino approached. When he reached the edge of the grave, however, she raised her hand to stop him before he could step forward to join her. Then slowly — ribbon by ribbon, clasp by clasp — she began to remove her clothes.

Albertino stood there trembling as she revealed her flesh: soft and abundant and covered with hideous sores. Her breasts were striated with hot pink welts, her belly was a *campo* of harsh black kisses, her arms and legs were covered with blisters and boils. For Ermenegilda the ritual was essential. She was offering Albertino her soul, but her price was that he take her in full awareness of the contagion that had ravaged her body. If he could see how she looked and not turn away, she might forget the anger that had enveloped her so completely when he'd abandoned her after their first encounter.

Albertino was horrified — but he was also aroused. And his greatest desire was to somehow ease her pain. So when she'd removed the last stocking he tore off his tunic, peeled down his tights, and pulled his muslin shirt over his head to stand equally naked before her. His body too was covered with death, but the signs of life that stirred beneath his belly made Ermenegilda shiver with desire. As Albertino stepped forward she lay back upon her gown and drew him down on top of her. The contact of their bodies only intensified their pain, but they bore down against it as Albertino moved inside her. It began as a slow movement — a delicate fugue — but it built and it built until it became a violent frenzy. They screamed as their bodies thrashed together; pain flooded into pleasure and poured back into pain.

Ermenegilda reached the end of it first. She dug her fingers into Albertino's back and then lurched into a fiery, sweet convulsion. Albertino responded instantly, meeting tremor for tremor as the savage wave passed through him.

When the final spasm came, it was impossible to tell whether it was the spasm of love or the spasm of death. But to Albertino and Ermenegilda it made little difference. They were now but a pair of bodies entwined upon a grave. A heap of rotten flesh gone slightly rosy with the last faint traces of ecstasy.

# *Chapter* 19

WHEN PIERO WOKE to silence — no cries, no moans, no whispered pleas to God — he knew that the horror had ended. The light that streamed in through the lone window in the hovel no longer trembled in its path. The smell that for days had grown sharper and fouler was suddenly tempered by the salt in the air. Only the faint gurgling of Nicolo, in the basket beside him, forced him out of his reverie and reminded him of what lay ahead.

On the morning after he'd left Miriam's alcove in pursuit of Gianluca and found him, howling, at the height of the *campanil*, Piero began making hourly visits to Maria Luigi's hovel. Around *mezzogiorno* he found Maria Luigi slumped beside the hearth. Shortly after dusk he found Miriam, prone before her altar, with Nicolo lying beside her in the straw, staring up at the glowing tapers. He laid Miriam out on the streak of blue satin and closed her eyes; then he picked up Nicolo, wrapped him in his seaweed blanket, placed him in the cod-barrel cart, blew out the tapers, and headed back to Beppe Guancio's hovel.

Piero had never handled an infant before. He was surprised at how tiny he was, and how flexible, and how light. He was not sure what to give him to replace Miriam's milk, but Nicolo was even-tempered and easy and responded well to small spoonfuls of the *brodo corto* Piero had been living off since the sickness had come. Now, as he gazed down at him lying peacefully in his basket, he tried not to think about the responsibility he represented and to simply try to gain the child's trust.

"*Bon dì,*" he said.

Nicolo flapped a bit and made a sound like a midge hen. Piero lifted himself up off the straw and went to the corner, where he splashed some water on his face, urinated, and put on a fresh shirt and tunic. Then he unswaddled, cleaned, and reswaddled Nicolo, placed him back in his blanket in his cod-barrel cart, and headed outside to examine the condition of the island.

As he crossed the field that lay between Beppe Guancio's hovel and the Calle Alberi Grandi, he became aware again of the quiet that had greeted him upon rising. It was not an absolute quiet — there was the sound of birds and the subtle breathing of the new spring landscape — but what struck Piero was the absence of conflict in the air. At first he thought it was merely the absence of the past week's painful struggle against death, but he soon realized that it was also the absence of the conflict of daily life upon the island: the effort to churn the butter; the argument over the weight of a fish; the struggle to see the day. It was a peaceful quiet, but it was also an empty quiet. There were no more villagers in the village of Riva di Pignoli.

When he reached the Calle Alberi Grandi, he discovered the body of Maria Patrizia Lunardi. She was lying face up in the mud with a look of astonishment on her face. A few paces farther he found Brunetto Fucci sprawled across the path, his body seeming to intend in two different directions at the same time. Yet it was not until he approached the new village center that he came upon the figure that truly startled him: there, in the patch of path that wound through the clutch of pine trees, was Piarina — her dress black with smoke, her cheeks singed, her hair fleeced and speckled with bits of wood and straw.

"Piarina!" he cried. "You're alive!"

Piarina froze at the sound of Piero's voice. Then slowly she turned and in a series of stumbling steps began to move toward him. When she reached the point where he stood she stopped and peered down into the cart that held Nicolo. Piero knelt beside her; then she turned, laid her forehead against his chest, and began to cry. It was a naked weeping, filled with more understanding than a child her age ought to know of. And though Piero placed his arms around her and held her tight, he did not join in. He knew that once he started he might not be able to stop.

When her gentle keening had run its course, Piarina untangled herself from Piero's arms, traced a pair of grimy streaks across her face with her fists, and stepped back to look into Piero's eyes.

"What do we do?" she asked.

Piero was amazed to hear her speak. "We go away," he said. "We try to find others."

He looked out past the pines toward the clearing in the

road; he could see another figure lying off in the grass, but he could not tell who it was. "But first I want to bury them," he said. "In the cemetery. It may take a while, but I want to bury them all."

Piarina picked a charred piece of pinecone from her hair. "What can I do?"

Piero thought for a moment. "I could use the baby's cart," he said. "It's small, but it's strong and easy to maneuver. We could take him to my hovel and you could stay with him until I've finished."

Piarina nodded and stepped in behind Nicolo's cod-barrel cart. Then Piero led the three of them down the Calle Alberi Grandi and across the fields until they reached Beppe Guancio's hovel. He did what he could to settle them in, making certain that Nicolo was reswaddled and that Piarina felt comfortable and safe. Then he traveled back out to the *campo* to find Gianluca.

His howling had lasted three days and three nights; it had echoed across the island with a blood-filled rage that spoke for the entire village. On the third night, however, with most of the villagers having succumbed to the sickness, he cried his last cry and fell in a heap against the window of the belfry. Now, as Piero gazed up at his lifeless form — much as he used to gaze up at Piarina — he decided that he would bury him first, and that he would bury Miriam beside him.

He fetched a ladder from the garden of the *chiesa* and propped it against the tower; then he climbed up to where Gianluca lay slumped in death. He was quite heavy — it took a great deal of effort to lift him up over the ledge of the belfry window and carry him down the ladder to the ground. As he descended, step by step, he was surprised at how good it felt to have Gianluca's weight against him.

The power of his flesh was still palpable; he understood what Miriam had felt.

When he finally managed to reach the ground, he lowered Gianluca into the cod-barrel cart — his arms and legs dangling over the sides — and then wheeled him out to the western docks and transported him across the water to the graveyard. At the edge of the docks he passed the Vedova Scarpa; in the heart of the cemetery he found Albertino and Ermenegilda. But he kept to his task until Gianluca was buried with Miriam fast at his side.

Next he buried Albertino and Ermenegilda, placing them in another joint plot directly opposite Gianluca and Miriam; then he returned to the main island and, one by one, gathered the other villagers. The Guarnieris, who lay huddled together in the corner of their smoke shed; the Tortas, who lay clasping their crosses in their stripped-down beds; Siora Bertinelli beside her pastry oven; Beppe Guancio and Romilda Rosetta in the aisle of the Chiesa di Maria del Mare; and all the other bodies lying festering in doorways, beside the hearth, clutching a pair of hair combs, a bright ribbon, mouths open, gestures arrested, life snuffed out. He carried each as carefully as the next, dug each grave as deeply, laid each body in as gently and respectfully as he could. He worked all through the day and all through the night and into the following afternoon. And when he'd buried the last one — Armida Barbon, in a plot between Gesmundo and a sturdy pine — he headed back across the water to the north rim of the island, dug up what was left of that first swollen corpse, and buried it, for the very last time, alongside the others. Then he headed back to Beppe Guancio's hovel, where Piarina waited with Nicolo.

As he approached the hovel he heard the faint rhythm

of a flutelike voice pouring out on the air; as he entered the door he heard the words beneath the rhythm.

"You've got to heat it long enough to let the sediment rise to the top — if you do it right, it's like a skin you can scrape off. With good wax it doesn't matter, but you won't get much good wax, so you might as well learn what to do with what you'll get."

Piarina was standing with her back to the door, melting a stack of tapers in a shallow pot hanging over the hearth. Nicolo was propped up beside her on a mound of straw on Beppe Guancio's cutting table, eyes fixed upon her as she spoke.

"You mustn't add the lye until it cools a bit. That's the tricky part. But you'll get it right, I know you will. You're a smart one."

Piero crossed to the hearth and placed his hand upon her shoulder. "I've finished," he said.

Piarina wiped her hands against her sooty dress and looked up at him.

"I'm awfully tired," he said. "Is there anything to eat?"

"There's some pease pudding," said Piarina. "Lie down. I'll bring it to you."

Piero lay down on his bed while Piarina lifted the pot of wax off the hearth and replaced it with another, which contained a watery pease pudding. When it had warmed through she brought him a large helping and a glass of ale. Piero ate it eagerly and then closed his eyes and slept. His dreams were deep and intense, a series of strung-together images of blackened bodies and faces stamped with horror. A silent figure kept appearing with a look of accusation on his face: Piero was required to explain why he had been spared the pestilence, but when he opened his mouth a flood of *sardine* rushed forth. When he woke, quite early the next morning, Piarina was standing in the doorway looking out across the dirt field.

"Is it a clear day?" he asked.

Piarina nodded.

"We should get an early start," said Piero. "We may be traveling for days."

Piarina turned to face him — her dress freshly laundered, her cheeks and hands now a raw, clean pink. "Where will we go?" she asked.

"I don't know. I suppose we'll find out when we get there."

Piarina gathered several handfuls of pignoli into a burlap sack and lifted Nicolo into the straw basket. Piero took his spare pair of boots; his copies of Dante, St. Augustine, and Marcus Aurelius; Beppe Guancio's lantern; and his sculpting chisel. Then they headed out across the island toward the western docks. The air was sweet and fragrant as they moved through the fields and gardens; Piero found it difficult to believe that the stench of death could have vanished so quickly.

When they reached the Chiesa di Maria del Mare, Piero turned to Piarina. "Would you like to go inside?"

Piarina nodded, and Piero led her, with Nicolo beside her in his basket, into the *chiesa*.

As they stepped across the threshold and the door closed behind them, Piero became aware once more of the unearthly quiet that seemed to characterize his last days on Riva di Pignoli. A warm light was beginning to filter in through the thick windows beside the Correlli Madonna and Child, but the chapel still shimmered with the dimness of dreams and sleep.

Piarina went immediately to the stand of tapers that stood in the corner by the entrance. There were only three left, and they had wasted down to less than half their height, but there was a match beside them, so she lit them. The light they cast was weak and frail — nothing like the magnificent blaze Piarina had lately burned with. But Piarina found them reassuring and instantly dubbed them Ermenegilda, Valentina, and herself. She knew that both her friend and her mother were gone from her. But as she stood before the tapers, she felt — for the first time in her life — that her little flame glowed independently, and that she could survive without either their affection or their abuse.

Piero moved down the aisle and saw how the light widened as he approached the altar. The *chiesa* seemed an entirely different place to him from the one he'd come to so often to pray: a large room with an elaborate dais and a few expensive lamps. Still, the thought of leaving it was unbearable. He felt for the piece of parchment inside his shirt, the blunt declaration he'd kept against his skin throughout the exhausting labor of the last two days. It had been soaked through with his sweat, it had stiffened at its folds, its edges had curled, its surface had stained and yellowed. But when he drew it into the light, and opened it, and read it, its words were as clear and strong as when he had written them.

He knelt down. He closed his eyes. To whom could he pray if those words were true? He opened his eyes and looked at the face of the Christ child. The Madonna. The fish. He looked up over his head at the polished beams in the roof, followed them across to the pale stone walls, down those to the darker-colored stones in the floor, and back over the pews to the straw-covered spot where he knelt.

The work of God.

The work of man.

Piero couldn't say. There in the hallowed half-light of the chapel the presence of God once more seemed undeniable, and little seemed left to him beyond silence and simple prayers. But he'd written the words, and they'd changed him. He would have to wait and see.

He rose and walked to the stand of tapers where Piarina stood and placed the piece of parchment in the flames. He watched as it crackled, and smoked, and finally caught fire. Then he lifted up the basket that held Nicolo, took Piarina by the hand, and together they left the chapel.

When they reached the docks Piero suggested they take Giuseppe Navo's smallest fishing vessel, as it was light and swift. Piarina stepped in first, and Piero handed down the items they'd brought to take with them. When he lifted the bag of *pignoli* Piarina had gathered, it felt cumbersome and inordinately heavy; when he opened it he found a pair of sleeping turtledoves and a fresh beef pie perched on a bed of coins. He looked at Piarina, who blushed. Then he closed up the bag and lowered it in.

When he'd handed down everything — including Nicolo — he stepped in himself and began loosening the ropes that held them to the shore. As he was about to release the final one, he heard a grunting sound and looked up to see the Guarnieris' sow staring hopefully down from the edge of the dock. Piero turned to Piarina; Piarina giggled; so he motioned to it to hop in and they set off.

The lagoon was as still as one of the graves Piero had just dug. The sun cast a white sheen over the surface, which was interrupted only by an occasional bird diving down for food and the ripples that spread from the wake of their boat as they moved out into the water. When they'd traveled beyond the familiar shape of the cemetery island — beyond the rusted gates and the sunken frame of Albertino's now abandoned room — Nicolo suddenly let out a great cry. It was his first cry since the hour of his birth, and it rang out over the water with an unfettered sorrow. Piarina shuddered at the sound of it — but she reached into the basket and lifted him into her arms and stroked him gently the way Ermenegilda had taught her.

If one of the old birds of the lagoon had swooped down over the island — one who'd lighted upon the fish stalls from time to time or pecked a bit of grain left out by the Vedova Stampanini — it would have seen nothing more than an empty expanse of land with a few hovels, a few wells — some gardens, some fields, some bridges — a *palazzo* — a *chiesa* — a *campanil*, a *campo*, and a monument. Only if it flew in very close would it have noticed the diaphanous shadows of a group of villagers dancing gaily in the center of the *campo*. Only if it soared up very high would it have noted that the entire island was nothing more than a wrinkle in the seascape: a scrap of seaweed, a strip of bark. And only if it followed away toward the south-southeast would it have spotted the tiny *barca da pesca* with the man, the child, the infant, and the pig, as it gathered speed, and struggled toward the horizon, and scratched its presence against the light of the still-rising sun.